A D

Culver h.... ....

the long porch, holding an old musket. "Boone," he said.

Dan'l nodded to him. "Silas Culver, ain't it?"

"That's right. I'm here about that Injun you got moved in with you."

"What's that to you, Culver?" Dan'l said evenly.

"What's it to me? We don't want no stinking, throat-cutting savage living here in this town. Even if you did start it up here, it ain't your town, Boone."

Culver hefted the musket and cocked it. "That Injun is leaving."

"That boy is staying here in town till he's healed, Culver," he said in a low voice. "Now get out of here before you make me all stiff-necked."

Culver stood a couple of inches taller than Dan'l, and was a bearn of man. He aimed the musket at Dan'l's chest and grinned. "Hell. You ain't even got a gun. You think I'm one of them lily-livers what quakes at the mention of your name, big hunter?"

"I won't tell you again," Dan'l said to Culver.

"I'm going to kill that damn Injun, and if I have to kill you first, that's fine with me!" Culver said loudly.

"Then you better make your try," Dan'l said, drawing his big knife from its sheath.

THE LOST WILDERNESS TALES

DAN'L BOONE

DODGE TYLER

ALGONQUIN MASSACRE

LEISURE BOOKS   NEW YORK CITY

A LEISURE BOOK®

June 1996

Published by

Dorchester Publishing Co., Inc.
276 Fifth Avenue
New York, NY 10001

Printed in the United States of America.

ALGONQUIN
MASSACRE

Prologue

The bearded frontiersman sat on the narrow stoop before his cabin and carefully cleaned the Kentucky rifle that lay across his knees. As he worked, he watched the approaching rider. Gradually the horseman loomed larger, coming through the corn, rocking in his saddle. Finally the rider stopped just a few yards away. He wore a bowler hat and wire spectacles; he gave the impression of being a preacher.

"They told me in town where to find you. Are you really the great Indian fighter and explorer Dan'l Boone?"

The old man set the rifle aside and squinted up at the mounted stranger through clear, penetrating eyes. Boone was bareheaded; his hair was thinning and almost white. He had a tooth missing at the corner of his mouth.

"What if I was?" he asked suspiciously.

The rider dismounted, retrieved a large notebook from a saddlebag, and came up onto the porch, where the old fellow sat on a willow chair. The musket leaned against the log wall of the cabin beside the frontiersman, but Boone saw no need for it.

"I'm Adam Hollis. I've come all the way from Boston to find you, Dan'l. I'm pleased and mighty proud to finally meet up with you."

"I don't talk to newspaper people." When Hollis smiled, Dan'l liked the eyes behind the glasses.

"I'm just a library clerk. Mind if I shake the riding cramps out on your porch?" Hollis asked.

When Dan'l motioned grudgingly to a second chair not far away, Hollis slumped onto it and stretched his legs. The aroma of cooking food came to him from inside. He looked out past the cornfield to the woods and admired the view.

"Thanks," he said wearily. "People have been coming to me for years, selling me bits and pieces of your life story because of my special interest."

Dan'l grunted. "Most of them is selling swamp fog."

Hollis grinned. "I figured as much. But all those stories got my curiosity up, sir, and I came to realize your own story could be one of the great untold legends of the frontier. So I spent my life savings to get out here, hoping you might talk to me some about yourself."

The old hunter regarded Hollis sidewise. "You want to write down all that stuff? Hell, ain't nobody'll want to read about them times. We're in a whole different century, by Jesus. Nobody gives a tinker's damn about that early stuff no more."

Hollis shook his head. "You'd be surprised, Dan'l. You're already something of a legend—even in Europe, I hear. But I think that's just the beginning. If you let me document your life while it's all still in your head, generations to come will know what wild adventures you had."

The great hunter rose from his chair. He no longer enjoyed the renowned robustness or grace of his youth, but he still looked as hard as sacked salt. Dan'l went to the far end of the porch and stared out into the green forest beyond the fields, the kind of country that had been his home for all of his life. He finally turned back to Hollis.

"What would you do with these stories once you got it all writ down on paper?"

Hollis shrugged. "Publish them, but only if you wanted me to. At least we'd have them all down. For safekeeping, you might say."

Dan'l shook his head. "I can't say I'd want them in no book. Not in my lifetime. Not the real stuff. Most of them are too damned private. There's too many people out there who might not want them told. Or they might be moved to correct them, so to speak. Come out with their own versions so they would look better."

A resolve settled over Hollis. "All right. It can all be hidden away till long after you're gone if that's what you'd like. Then if the stories don't get lost somewhere down the line, maybe they will all come out later, at a better time, and be given over to some book people. That's what I would hope for."

Dan'l thought for a long moment. "You'd promise that in writing?"

Hollis nodded. "I will."

A laugh rattled out of the old man's throat. "I guess you'd want even the bear mauling and the wolf eating and the nasty ways some redskins liked to treat a white man when they caught him?"

"Yes, everything," Hollis said.

"There's treks into the West, the far side of the Mississippi, that hardly a man alive now knows about," Dan'l said, reflecting. "And these eyes have seen things that nobody's going to believe."

Hollis was becoming excited. "I'd want it all."

Dan'l took a deep breath in and called, "Rebecca! You better put a big pot of coffee on! Looks like we got company for a spell!"

As Hollis relaxed and smiled, Dan'l heaved himself back onto the primitive chair and closed his eyes for a moment. Finally, he said, "I reckon we might as well get going on it then."

Hollis was caught off guard. He fumbled in a pocket for a quill pen and a small ink pot, then opened up the thick but empty notebook. Hollis dipped his pen into the ink and waited.

"Most of it happened in about thirty years," Dan'l said quietly. "The important stuff. The stuff most folks don't know nothing about. That's when I got this raw hunger for the wild places, the far-off country where no settlers had been.

"I was just a stripling when I first started hearing about the land west of the Alleghenies," Dan'l said, his gaze wandering off toward the woods.

Hollis did not hesitate or interrupt with any questions. As the old man talked, he just began writing steadily in the thick book with an urgency he had never before experienced. He had to get every sentence down exactly as Dan'l said it. He could not miss a single word.

Chapter One

Captain Jock McKenzie eased his right hand down to the oiled leather holster at his waist and closed it over the butt of the Annely flintlock revolver there. The deadly, eight-shot repeating weapon could blow the crown of a man's head off at close range or tear a bloody path through him from chest to backbone and leave a hole the size of a fist. McKenzie had used the weapon to kill, maul, and mutilate in the colonies for years, and he had come to enjoy the butchery. At that moment, he sat menacingly on his gray stallion and glared at the mounted Algonquin chief before him.

"So that's your last word on the matter then?" he said in a low, even voice. "You won't submit your people to the service of His Majesty King George?"

Chief Longhair held McKenzie's hard look with a steady one. Beside the Indian rode two of his best warriors, and a hundred yards behind him sat the decrepit stockade fort his clan had taken over recently with the assent of the local Carolina settlers. Out in front of the fort stood a loose line of braves armed with bows and outdated muskets and looking anxious and winch-wire tight. McKenzie was flanked by two mounted underlings, and behind him were several lines of redcoats of the Fifty-fourth Royal Foot Brigade, Brown Besses at ready.

"You wish to make war on your own people," Longhair finally said to the uniformed captain. "It comes to us on the drums. But these farmers are our friends. We will not fight in your war, as our fathers fought with the French. We do not want more fighting."

"These stupid farmers defy their own monarch!" McKenzie said loudly. "And you do the same! Give your braves over to us or we will destroy your village!"

Longhair tried not to let the emotion show in his handsome face. "There are many women and children here. There are two white traders. The great hunter Sheltowee has guaranteed our safety here."

"Who? Dan'l Boone?" the rather small, wiry leftenant beside McKenzie said. "He can't guarantee his own place at Boonesborough!"

13

Sergeant Suggs, on the other side of Mc-Kenzie, spat onto the ground and wiped a hand across his big, ugly face. "If that trapper was here, I'd piss in his damned Quaker hat!"

There was some soft laughter among the front line of troops behind them. Longhair's warriors looked over at the chieftain quizzically since they didn't understand English, and they were surprised to see the deep scowl edge onto Longhair's aquiline face.

"This talking is finished," Longhair said coldly. "You will now go and leave us in peace."

McKenzie, known in Boston as the Mad Scot by his superiors, because of his reckless unpredictability, shook his head slowly. "You ignorant savages!" he hissed. Then, just as Longhair was turning his mount to return to the fort, Mc-Kenzie drew the revolver from its holster in a swift, fluid motion, cocked it, and fired.

The gun roared loudly, making the warriors beside Longhair jump, and the hot lead blasted through Longhair's face and tore his right ear off.

In almost the same instant, Leftenant Quinn, beside McKenzie, pulled a Mortimer repeating pistol from his belt and fired at Longhair's nearest bodyguard warrior, hitting him in the low chest and knocking him off his pony. Longhair was falling slowly from his own horse, his jaw working and making ugly sounds. The second warrior raised a musket to kill McKenzie, but brawny Sergeant Suggs beat him. He fired off his heavy-looking Brown Bess, the weapon flashing brightly in the morning air, and the second warrior went flying off the rear of his horse.

In the next moments, all hell broke loose in that clearing before the fort. Indians were firing from outside the fort, and several redcoats went down. McKenzie was shrieking, over and over again, "Fire! Fire at will!" The Indians' mounts were running off in all directions, and the British officers' horses were rearing and bucking with the excitement of the explosive action.

Several Algonquins fell, injured or dead, at the fort, and then the rest retreated inside and closed a big, heavy gate behind them. But the firing did not stop. Now there were Indians atop the parapets on the walk of the stockade wall, returning fire sporadically at the British regulars, and the redcoats were firing furiously. Gunfire made ears ring, and thick, white gunsmoke filled the air with its acrid, pungent odor.

"Return fire! Kill the bloody savages!" McKenzie was yelling, getting his mount under control and waving a long saber.

Ian Quinn had been thrown from his horse in the first firing, and was now on foot, grabbing his horse's reins in one hand and waving his revolver in the other. "Close up ranks! Fire in sequence!"

The front rank of redcoats knelt and loaded, and the second row aimed and fired at the fort. The ranks behind them kept filling in where a man went down ahead of them. Sergeant Aubrey Suggs, a heavy-built, broad-coupled man with a raw-meat face, strode up and down behind them now, dismounted, yelling wildly.

"First rank, fire!" he called out. "Hurry up, you bleeding babies! Get them muskets loaded! Second rank, get ready! Now fire!"

Suddenly there was less fire coming from the fort, and McKenzie realized that the Algonquins were running out of ammunition. He raised his saber again. "Along the firing line! Cease firing!"

Quinn waved his revolver. "Cease firing!"

There were a few more scattered shots, then silence. A few shots came from the fort, but hit nothing. Suggs came up to McKenzie.

"They're done for, Captain. Let's rush the fort and take all the braves we want. Maybe let the men have some squaw fun before we leave." He laughed an ugly laugh in his throat; then his face changed. He saw the small trickle of blood on McKenzie's left hand, running down from his arm. McKenzie had a flesh wound.

"Are you hit then, Captain?"

Leftenant Quinn came up at that point and heard the question. He saw the different look in McKenzie's face, a look he had seen once when they were fighting the French and there had been unnecessary killing.

"It's nothing," McKenzie said. But his face revealed a different emotion, a wild, uncontrolled rage, the rage that had earned him his nickname. "But we're not going in. It's gone beyond that."

The two other men exchanged looks. Behind them, soldiers were reloading and tending to wounded.

16

"What do you mean, Captain?" the short, wiry Quinn said. "There must be thirty good braves left in there. We'll make good use of them."

McKenzie's face turned crimson and he looked fiercely at Quinn. He yelled loudly into his face, "It's too late for all that! We're burning the fort with them in it!"

Quinn glanced at Suggs. Behind them, several soldiers turned with curious looks.

"Bring those men forward who can fire the torch arrows," McKenzie said to Suggs. "I'm going to burn this place to the ground. I don't want any prisoners. If anybody tries to get out, shoot them down. I want to make an example of this place."

Suggs, who had been with McKenzie in those previous battles, got a big grin on his face. "Good decision, Captain. No prisoners!"

Quinn had no more conscience than McKenzie, but he also had no courage to match his cold-blooded nature. He was always worried about consequences more than McKenzie or Suggs.

"What if women try to run, Captain, or children?" Quinn asked. "What about the white men in there?"

McKenzie looked down with an expression that scared Quinn. "Are you deaf, Quinn? I said no prisoners!"

"Yes, sir, Captain," Quinn said quickly.

A number of private soldiers had heard the exchange, and now were mumbling to each other quietly, with dark looks. They watched as Suggs brought ten soldiers forward with a low wagon. The wagon was loaded with torch-tipped arrows, and the men had had training in firing them. They had learned the tactic from the Shawnee, in the war with the French, which had recently ended. The torches were soaked in flammable oil, as defenders watched anxiously atop the stockade wall at the fort. McKenzie ordered the ten soldiers forward thirty yards, and they took the bows and torch arrows with them.

"Don't quit until the whole place is aflame!" McKenzie told them. "The wood is old, it will go up like tinder. I want an inferno!"

A shot rang out from the fort and dug up dirt at the feet of the firing squad as they lined up out in front of the troops.

"You, Suggs! Take a platoon and flank the fort all around. I don't want anybody escaping!"

"Yes, sir!"

In the next few moments, Suggs deployed some men around the perimeter of the clearing, and the firing squad readied itself. Then Quinn was giving the orders to fire, with the bulk of the troops looking on.

"Fire!" Quinn yelled.

Ten flaming arrows hissed out over the no-man's-land, arched up over the fort wall, and disappeared inside. Then the men were busy setting fire to the next bunch of torches, and drawing their bows and firing again. A shot rang out, and one of them fell like a stone. Quinn ignored him, and the firing continued. After just three multiple firings, McKenzie could already see fire licking above the level of the stockade walls inside.

"Keep firing!" he yelled. "I want nothing left!"

In the fort, the Indians were in a panic. Most of their buildings and tipis were afire and blazing brightly, and the fort was so small and congested that it was impossible to get away from the flames. There was a lot of yelling and screaming, and both men and women were catching fire in the rising holocaust. The two white traders had kept out of the confrontation, but now they realized that their lives were in grave danger. One of them, a large, bearded fellow, climbed to the parapet atop the wall and cried out to the attackers.

"You damn fools! There's women and kids in here!" He was waving a white flag. "We surrender! Stop it!"

But Sergeant Suggs leveled his musket at him, fired, and knocked him off the wall, a ball through his heart.

His companion, down in the fiery furnace below, saw his friend fall at his feet, and fear clutched at his guts. "Wait till Boone hears about this," he murmured amidst the yelling and moaning.

Women were running from buildings now, clothing afire, burning like torches. Some carried babies. Men were rolling on the ground, trying to put out the flames that devoured them. But it was a firestorm inside the fort. A few wrenched the big gate open and tried to run to safety, but musket fire cut them down. A few climbed atop the wall and dropped to the ground outside and met the same fate. The second white trader was one of those.

When the torched arrows had stopped coming, the interior of the fort was a holocaust. Men, women, and children were burning alive, with no way to get away from the flames.

Out in the clearing, McKenzie sat aboard his gray stallion and watched and listened as the scene from hell unfolded before him. Not once had he considered relenting before the fort was a burning torch. Not once had he thought of capturing any escapees alive.

His troops stood and knelt behind him, stunned and quiet. Some had angry looks on their young faces. The squad that had fired the torches slowly returned to their company, some shaking their heads, others looking as if they might be sick. Sergeant Suggs had enjoyed it all and had fired on a couple of escapees himself. He liked hurting people, and this had unleashed some dark emotion inside him.

Ian Quinn stood watching the flames and smoke rise dramatically into the sunny morning sky, and tried to comprehend what they had done. There were no more terrified cries now, no more screams of ugly pain. McKenzie ordered the troops all back to a muster, and by the time that was done, the flames had died down inside the fort.

"Quinn. Suggs. Let's go have a look," McKenzie finally said.

The three leaders rode by themselves up to the fort and through the big gate that was still partially opened, although charred black.

"All right, let's see if we did it right," the Mad Scot said in a pleasant, level voice when they were there.

They rode in with McKenzie at their fore, holding their hands up against the smoldering heat. It was a black hell. Buildings, tipis, equipment, and people were all charred beyond recognition. Bodies were still smoking, not looking human. Well over two hundred inhabitants had been killed in a fiery hell.

Quinn coughed and gagged with the smells.

Suggs grinned wearily, cheeks flushed. It had been better than any woman he had ever had.

"My God," Quinn said in a low voice.

McKenzie's stallion guffered from the heat and the smell. McKenzie cast a hard look at Quinn. "What's the trouble, Leftenant? Bit of a weak stomach, is it?"

He and Suggs exchanged a throaty laugh.

"Maybe we better not let the troops see this, Captain," Quinn said softly.

McKenzie looked at Quinn as if his first officer had slapped him across the face. "Not see it! Are you daft, man? Of course they'll see it! I want them to know what they've accomplished! There won't be many Algonquin opposing recruitment after this! Yes, we'll bring them in. And you can

21

lead them, my boy! See to it."

Suggs watched Quinn's face, grinning.

"Yes, Captain," Quinn answered. He turned and rode out through the gate, toward the stony-faced soldiers who awaited him.

He had no idea how to prepare them for what they were about to see.

Less than thirty miles away, at a hunting camp in northwest Carolina, Dan'l Boone sat at a low campfire with Uriah Latham. A trapper from Salisbury who had gone on two exploration treks into Kentucky with Dan'l, Latham had settled in Boonesborough near Dan'l and his pregnant wife Rebecca. Latham often accompanied Dan'l on hunting trips like this one.

Dan'l poked the fire with a willow stick. "Well, we only got five white-tail between us. I reckon we ought to move on south and maybe pick us up a couple of shaggies before we head home."

His voice was deep and rich. In his late thirties and squarely built, he wore rawhides. His tanned face had the beginnings of lines in it from exposure to all kinds of weather, and he now wore a full beard. He still wore a black, broad-brimmed Quaker hat over thick, long hair.

Latham swigged some coffee from a tin cup and threw some dregs into the fire, and they sizzled briefly there. He was a tall, thin fellow, dressed like Dan'l, but wearing a coonskin cap. In his early forties, he had a narrow, bearded face with dark eyes that squinted at you when he talked.

"I ain't all that anxious to head back anyway," he said to Dan'l, "with all this hard recruiting by the militia back there. I spent too much time shooting at them Frenchies to be thinking about taking up the gun again, and against our own army."

Dan'l spat into the fire. "Hell, this will all cool down right soon now. That was just a bunch of drunks that throwed that tea into Boston harbor a year ago. In another year, there won't even be no Continental Congress or Committee of Public Safety. Most of us is loyal British subjects. You and me fought alongside them redcoats not so long ago."

"I don't know. The king declared the whole damn colony of Massachusetts in a state of rebellion, Dan'l. Now there's talk of forming a Continental Army. I don't like the sound of it."

Dan'l looked over at him. "I'm just expecting the best, Uriah. Anyway, you and me got more important things to think about than who's taxing the damn tea. Who drinks it anyway? We got land to explore and settle. I hope they just leave us alone to get that done. I suspect . . ."

Dan'l paused and listened. He always heard sounds before other men, even Indians, and saw things in the forest that others could not see. He was now peering into the leafy trees just beyond the campfire, where late morning sun fell on them and made them shimmer. He had heard a sound, and now he saw movement in the distance. His hand went to his Kentucky rifle, which always rested within reach, and he rose with it in his thick hands.

"What is it?" Latham asked curiously. He had heard and seen nothing. He rose too, and brought his rifled musket with him.

Dan'l squinted down, and made out the shape of a rider coming straight at their camp. He focused on the figure, and then his face changed. "It's all right. I know him."

Latham relaxed as he watched the rider approach. In moments a big, bulky man with gray in his hair and a white mustache was in the clearing. He rode a dark, sturdy gelding.

"Dan'l," he said simply, stopping at the edge of the clearing, only twenty feet away.

"Jake Medford." Dan'l grinned.

Medford climbed off his mount and came over to the fire. Dan'l put his weapon down, then embraced Medford like a brother. "Damn, Sergeant! It's right good to see you."

Medford released Dan'l and clapped him on the shoulder. He was burly and rough-looking, and there were lines of aging in his weathered face. "None of that sergeant tripe, my boy. Call me Jake."

Dan'l turned to Latham. "Uriah, this is the man who recruited me into the goddamn Carolina militia and almost got me killed at Duquesne!"

Latham grinned and shook Medford's hand.

"That don't hardly seem a reason to make a man your friend."

"Well, Dan'l forgave me for that after about a dozen years," Medford said. "I think he softened up some after he took that Rebecca gal to his bed."

"She's about to deliver him a son any day now," Latham said. "But she can't keep him home long enough to talk about it."

They both laughed and Dan'l gave them a sour look. "You know me, Jake. I get this itchy thing after I'm in town for a day or two. I get all cramped up with it."

"You won't never be no homebody," Medford said. "Mind if I join you boys for a cup of coffee?"

"It would be our pleasure, Jake," Dan'l said.

They all sat down around the fire, and Medford peeled off a light coat. Even though there was still some spring snow in patches on the ground, the day was going to warm up nicely. Dan'l poured Medford some coffee, and Medford sipped at it.

"We was just about to ride south a ways, to maybe pick up a couple of buffalo," Dan'l said. "But that can wait. What brings you up in this direction, old-timer?"

Medford's smile had vanished, and they both noticed it. He held his cup in both hands, and looked into the guttering-out fire. "I got a couple pieces of bad news, boys," he said quietly. "I come riding here to tell you about it."

Dan'l exchanged a look with Latham. "You

ain't been to Boonesborough?"

"Oh, no, Dan'l. It's nothing about Rebecca or your kin. First of all, Massachusetts militia fired on British regulars less than a week ago."

"What!" Dan'l said in disbelief.

"The army was on one of its routine searches for stockpiled ammunition by them minutemen. There was a firefight at some place called Lexington. Then the militia harassed the column all the way back to Boston. There was a lot of deaths."

"By Jesus," Latham said quietly, "I knew it."

"What the hell's the matter with them up-northers?" Dan'l said bitterly. "We don't need this. Damn it!"

"The word is that the Carolina militia will double its efforts to get more recruits in. This thing is going to spread, Dan'l."

Dan'l shook his head and ran a hand through the thick, dark beard. His handsome face showed deep concern. "I wouldn't a thought it. There ain't that much to fight over."

Medford grunted. "Some say a whole continent. Whether it belongs to us or to King George."

"Does that matter to us? Out here in the deep woods?" Dan'l said.

"It might, Dan'l, eventually," Medford replied.

They sat there in silence. Finally, Medford continued. "There's something else, Dan'l. Closer to home."

"Yeah?"

"It's about Fort Stuart, where you settled them Algonquin a few months ago. The place abandoned by them early settlers."

"What about it?" Dan'l asked, a bad feeling starting in his insides from what he saw in Medford's face.

Medford took a deep breath. "I just come past there a couple hours ago. It's burned to the ground."

Dan'l's jaw dropped. He had worked hard to get approval for settlement of the Indians so close to Carolina settlers. But Longhair had been friendly to colonials from the beginning. Unlike some of his tribe in Pennsylvania and New York, where he had migrated from.

"What about Longhair?" Dan'l asked.

"He's dead, Dan'l. Him and everybody at the fort. Burned alive, most of them. Some shot."

"Good God," Latham murmured. "You knowed some of them personal, didn't you, Dan'l?"

"Who done it?" Dan'l said hollowly. "Cherokee?"

Medford shook his head. "A trader I met on the way here said it was British regulars under a man named McKenzie."

"Redcoats?" Dan'l said in real surprise. "I can't believe that!"

"I can," Latham said.

"You probably know they're out recruiting redskins to use against colonial troops, if there's fighting," Medford said. "Well, I guess Longhair must have refused to give his braves over. This McKenzie is known for an Indian hater. He figured on teaching the rest of them a lesson, I reckon."

"When did this happen?" Dan'l asked.

"Earlier today, just after dawn, it appears. I heard you was down here on the creek, so I rode hard to tell you."

"Any survivors?"

"Not that I could see. There was a couple of white traders there too. Both killed. It's a real mess, Dan'l."

Dan'l rose, grabbing the rifle again. "I got to ride up there."

The others rose too. "I'll go with you," Medford said.

"Maybe I better ride to Boonesborough and let them know," Latham said.

Dan'l nodded, then went to saddle his mount. A few moments later, they were gone, and their fire guttered out in the new silence.

It was early afternoon when Dan'l and Jake Medford reached Fort Stuart. Dan'l reined in fifty yards away and saw the white wisps of smoke still rising from the ruins in places. Corpses outside the fort were lying in awkward positions of death. The bodies of Longhair and his bodyguard warriors were covered by big flies. Turkey vultures circled overhead.

"He was one of the good ones," Dan'l said heavily.

Medford pulled at his white mustache and

nodded. "It gets much worse inside the fort."

They rode on in, and Dan'l smelled the stench of burned flesh long before they passed through the gate. The two of them looked around inside, and Dan'l shook his head slowly at the carnage. Very few Indians were even recognizable as something that had ever been alive. It was grotesque.

"That son of a bitch," Dan'l said, holding his nervous roan stallion steady. "That inhuman bastard!"

"I've heard of him," Medford said, holding a hand to his nose. "Even his superiors don't like him. He's a hindrance to their cause."

"Did you look around the perimeter?" Dan'l asked.

"Not yet."

"Let's see if anybody is alive out there."

They left the fort and rode around the stockade wall. There were several bodies out back, shot down as they'd tried to escape the roaring inferno. Dan'l tried to imagine the horror they must have gone through.

"I guess they're all dead," he said somberly.

He turned. Medford had dismounted and was leaning over a body. It was an Algonquin brave. "Hey. I think I heard this one make a sound."

Dan'l quickly rode over and climbed off his horse. He leaned down with Medford and turned the Indian over. His dyed rawhide shirt and pants were scorched, the side of his face was burned badly, and he had been shot through the side. He looked barely alive.

"I know this one," Dan'l said. "He's called Billy Two Tongues, because he can talk good in English. He spent some time in a white settlement when he was little, but he was treated bad. He never really trusted me, and didn't want Longhair to settle here."

"He ain't going to make it," Medford guessed.

Dan'l took his canteen off his belt and poured some water down Billy's mouth. Billy choked some; then his eyelids fluttered open. As soon as he recognized Dan'l, anger flowed into his eyes. "Sheltowee," he muttered, croaking. "Damn you!"

Medford glanced at Dan'l.

"Don't talk," Dan'l said. "You're the only survivor. You must bear witness to this." All in Algonquin. Dan'l could not read or write, but he spoke six languages fluently.

"The shame is on you, Sheltowee!" Billy choked out. He was young, in his twenties, and had always been a hothead. He had opposed settling among whites, but even though he was the son of a medicine man, Longhair had ignored him. "You said we would be safe here!"

"These farmers did not do this, Billy," Dan'l told him. "You know it was a renegade British soldier."

"Leave me to die," Billy said weakly. "I want to die with my people."

"He looks real bad," Medford said.

Dan'l pulled some bandage roll from a belt wallet and began binding Billy's wound. It looked rather shallow to him. "Help me get him aboard my horse. "I'm taking him back to Boonesborough."

"That's almost a two days ride," Medford said. "He ain't going to make it, Dan'l."

"He'll make it," Dan'l said. "I'll see to it."

"Leave me . . . to join my ancestors," Billy said thickly.

"Not yet, Billy," Dan'l said. "You're the only living proof of what happened here."

"The whites . . . will not care," Billy whispered. Then he lapsed into unconsciousness.

Medford caught Dan'l's gaze. "He might be right," he said.

Dan'l looked down at Billy's burned face for a long moment. "Come on," he said at last. "Help me get him up."

They lifted Billy aboard the roan, and when Dan'l got aboard, they tied him in a sitting position behind Dan'l, so they were bound together.

"I'd like to make the trip with you," Medford suddenly said.

Dan'l looked down at him. "Are you sure, Sergeant?"

A grin inched onto the wrinkled, leathery face of his friend. They had gone to Fort Duquesne together twice, and lived through hell. There was a special bond between them. "How sure do I got to be?" Medford said.

Dan'l returned the grin with a weary one. "Maybe I can get Rebecca to make you some of her famous flapjacks," he said. "She's been saying she wanted some company."

"Now wouldn't that just beat all," Medford said.

They both tried not to look into the fort again on their way out of the clearing.

Chapter Two

Billy Two Tongues was mostly right about the reaction of local settlers toward the massacre at Fort Stuart. A few were outraged, and another small percentage felt that the British commander ought to be reprimanded. But the vast majority had not liked the Indians in their midst anyway, and felt more comfortable with them gone. A few said they could find nothing reprehensible in McKenzie's behavior at all, that the only good Indian was a dead Indian.

Most of the latter group, though, were careful not to say any of that within earshot of Dan'l Boone. Dan'l had worked hard to get the emigrated Algonquin settled peaceably in Carolina, dealing with local and colonial authorities, and it was well-known that it was unwise to make

Dan'l your personal enemy. Even in Salisbury, where he rarely appeared nowadays, men were circumspect in their judgment of the massacre and its culprits. In Boonesborough, out in the Kentucky territory where Dan'l had taken Billy to his own home to recover from that personal hell, nobody spoke of the incident at all except to denounce it in the strongest terms. Nobody except for one man. His name was Silas Culver, and he was a big, tough bully who had come to Boonesborough to sell farm implements to the locals. When he was a younger man, he had almost been killed by Shawnee, and he had an abiding distrust of all red men. When he heard that Dan'l had brought Billy to his own house to nurse him, he decided to pay Dan'l a visit. Two days after Dan'l's arrival with Medford, Culver showed up at Dan'l's cabin.

Just before that, though, Dan'l and Rebecca had their own discussion about Billy and why Dan'l had brought him there. They were in the spare bedroom, where Billy lay on a hard cot, covered with a blanket, looking awful. Medford and Rebecca's cousin Sarah, who was living with Rebecca through the delivery of their baby, were in the big kitchen, having coffee together.

Rebecca had taken a compress off Billy's face, and was placing a fresh one on it to help the burns heal. She had already changed the bandage on his rib cage. Billy's face looked bad on the left side, where the burns were deep. Scar tissue had closed that eye, and part of his ear was gone. Charred, black skin was getting ready to flake away. The bullet that had hit him in the right side had passed on through without breaking bone, and it was healing well. But Billy, when he was conscious, was in a lot of pain, and Dan'l kept him liquored up. At the moment Billy was conscious, but just barely.

"We're out of bullets," he murmured, rolling his head from side to side. "Get the fire under control."

"He doesn't know where he is," Rebecca said to Dan'l, rising up from over Billy. She was a pretty, young woman, with dark hair and blue eyes, and she was dressed in a long gingham dress with an apron over her large belly. Dan'l had moved her here from Salisbury a couple of years ago, and she was getting ready to deliver their first child. They both hoped it was a boy.

"Too bad I had to brung him so far," Dan'l told her. He stood on the opposite side of the bed from her, staring down at Billy glumly. "But he's going to make it."

Rebecca moved away, sat down on a straight chair in a corner, and sighed deeply. "We can't keep him here, Dan'l. I'm getting close. I'm going to have to think on having our child."

Dan'l leaned against a wall near the bed. Billy had fallen asleep, and it was quiet in the room. They could hear Medford and Sarah talking quietly in the far part of the house.

"I know all that, Rebecca," Dan'l told her. "I reckon Billy will be on his feet in a week. Then

35

I'll find another place for him. I got to go to Fort Duquesne."

Rebecca looked startled. "When?"

"Right soon. They got to hear what really happened at Fort Stuart. That McKenzie maybe didn't tell it the way it was. He's got to answer for this."

Rebecca looked into his bearded face. "You can't leave me now! I need you here. You're never at home, Dan'l. Damn it, it's your child we're having!"

Dan'l went over and knelt at her side, and there was pain etched into his broad face. He ran a thick hand through his long hair, then placed it on her belly.

"You think I want this? You think I don't want to be here when my son is born?"

She looked at him accusingly. Her eyes were moist.

"You have to try to understand what happened at Stuart. Women and children burned alive. A whole village destroyed. By one crazy Scot who's out of control. I wish that bastard was in hell with his back broke!"

She touched his bearded face.

"I owe them, Rebecca. I put them there. I got to make sure McKenzie's superiors know exactly what he done. He's got to be stripped of command, and give a just punishment."

"They won't listen to you. You were in the Carolina militia. You're on their enemy list, I reckon."

36

"I fought alongside them against the French."

"So did Washington, and now there's talk of making him commander of a Continental Army."

Dan'l shook his head. "If it goes that far, we're all in trouble. I hope he thinks on that a long while." He rose. "I can't wait. This is important to us. Next, McKenzie might be burning settlers' villages. I'll try to get back before the baby comes."

Rebecca sighed again. "I reckon I should've knowed this when I hitched up with you."

Just then Jake Medford appeared in the doorway.

"Dan'l, there's a fellow outside to see you. Appears to be in a huff."

Dan'l nodded and touched Rebecca on the cheek, and she gave him a weak smile. Then he turned and left the room. Medford went outside with him, and young Sarah, blondish and slim, stood in the doorway and watched.

Culver had arrived. He stood stiff-backed a few feet off the long porch, holding an old musket. "Boone," he said.

Dan'l nodded to him. "Silas Culver, ain't it?"

"That's right. I'm here about that Injun you got moved in with you."

Medford and Dan'l traded a dark look. "What's that to you, Culver?" Dan'l said evenly.

"What's it to me? We don't want no stinking, throat-cutting savage living here in this town. Even if you did start it up here, it ain't your town, Boone."

"Maybe it's yours," Dan'l said deliberately.

Culver hefted the musket and cocked it. "It don't matter none. That Injun is leaving. We don't want him here."

"We?" Dan'l said. "I don't see nobody with you."

"There's more of us. They just ain't got the guts to come here. Now, get out of the way and I'll go in and drag that redskin out."

Medford took a step forward. "You out of your mind, man? Don't you know who you're talking to?"

"Boone's reputation don't scare me atall," Culver said loudly. He spat on the ground to show his contempt and raised the musket. "Get out of the way, old man, or I'll use this on you."

Medford's face showed quick anger, but Dan'l touched his shoulder and edged past him. He had no weapon except for the hunting knife on his belt, but that was within easy reach of his right hand. Rebecca appeared at the doorway, looking scared, beside Sarah, and Medford went and closed the door on them. Dan'l stepped down onto the dirt yard, just a few feet from Culver.

"That boy is staying here in town till he's healed, Culver," he said in a low voice. "Now get out of here before you make me all stiff-necked."

Culver stood a couple of inches taller than Dan'l, and was a bear of a man. He aimed the musket at Dan'l's chest and grinned. "Hell. You ain't even got a gun. You think I'm one of them lily-livers what quakes at the mention of your name, big hunter?"

"Look out, Dan'l." Medford's voice came to him, with fear in it now.

"I won't tell you again," Dan'l said to Culver.

"I'm going in to kill that goddamn Injun, and if I have to kill you first, that's fine with me!" Culver said loudly.

"Then you better make your try," Dan'l said, drawing the big knife from its sheath.

Culver saw the move, laughed arrogantly, and squeezed the trigger of the long gun.

Dan'l saw his thick finger whiten over the trigger, and leapt forward like a wild animal, growling in his throat. He shoved upward on the wicked-looking gun just as it exploded in fire, and the shot missed his head by an inch, then grazed Medford's shoulder, up on the porch. Dan'l held the gun's hot barrel with his left hand, with Culver glaring ferociously in his face.

"I'll kill you, you bastard! Now or later!" the bully yelled at Dan'l.

Dan'l thought of Billy Two Tongues inside, and his pregnant wife, and her cousin, and knew he was not the only one in danger from this man. He pulled Culver up against him, using the musket as a lever, then slid the long knife past the heavy gun and into Culver's stomach.

As Culver's hard eyes widened in surprise, Dan'l jammed the blade home into the heart cavity, up under the breastbone, lifting the whole weight of the other man onto his toes.

There were some gurgling sounds from Culver's throat, and then Dan'l let him slip to the ground. His right leg kicked at Dan'l's boot once, and he was dead.

"He was trouble," Dan'l said quietly, standing over the big man. "And I don't need any more right now."

Medford came down to look. "He bought it, all right."

"Go get Latham, and get him buried. Tell the militia captain what happened. But drag him out of here before the women get a close look."

Medford nodded his gray head. "It's done." He used to give Dan'l orders when Dan'l was a kid driving an ammo wagon under Colonel George Washington. Now Dan'l was giving them to him, and he didn't mind at all. Dan'l had grown into a leader, guiding several groups of settlers into Kentucky, and even taking on the job of sheriff in Salisbury for a brief time. Men had begun listening when he talked. Medford, his old sergeant, was no exception.

"I got to get inside and try to quiet the women down," Dan'l said heavily. "I'm leaving for Fort Duquesne later today, Jake. The sooner the better. In a couple of days, move Billy into Latham's place till he's up and around. Billy ought to stay here in Boonesborough till we find out if he's needed at Duquesne. Tell him that."

Medford nodded. "I'll talk to you before you leave."

The settlement was buzzing about the deadly

40

fight between Culver and Dan'l that afternoon, but Culver had been alone and had had no friends, and almost everybody was pleased to hear of his early demise. He had harassed and beaten people almost since his first arrival. The local militia commander ruled the death was in self-defense, and that was the end of it.

Dan'l left for Duquesne, the scene of earlier death and destruction in the war against the French, in late afternoon.

At Fort Duquesne, which was now occupied by the Fifty-fourth Royal Foot Brigade, Colonel Nigel Hopkins was in the midst of a rather serious meeting in his large whitewashed office that afternoon. He paced up and down behind his long mahogany desk, an antique brought over from London. Before the desk, at attention, stood McKenzie, Quinn, and Suggs, watching his every movement. All four men were in their red dress uniforms, and the threesome who had taken part in the massacre held tri-cornered hats under their arms. Quinn, looking rather small and pale, seemed scared. But McKenzie and Suggs regarded their commander with arrogance.

"When this gets back to Boston, there will be bloody outrage," Hopkins said as he paced, not looking at them. "I mean, bloody outrage. We're trying to befriend the bloody redskins, you damn fools!"

McKenzie scowled. "You can't make friends with these savages, Colonel. You must show them strength, make them fear you. They do now."

Hopkins whirled on his captain. "Damn you, McKenzie! They warned me about you when you transferred out here. You're insubordinate, unprincipled, and out of control. I've had seven requests for transfer out of your company since the massacre. You've made more trouble for me than you can ever imagine. Even the bloody Loyalists are complaining about Fort Stuart."

"What do we care what the goddamn colonials think?" McKenzie said fiercely. "We'll be killing them in another few weeks. We're at war, for God's sake!"

Hopkins could barely repress his anger. "You're not competent to lead our troops into any kind of fighting," he said bitterly to McKenzie. "I'm getting rid of you, Captain. You have a choice. You can either resign, you and your two stupid subordinates, or I'll court-martial all of you for slaughtering innocent women and children at Stuart."

McKenzie could not believe it. "You'd court-martial us for killing bloody savages?"

"I would, and I will, McKenzie. Now. Which will it be? A trial in a military court, or save the crown the expense?"

McKenzie suddenly ripped his red tunic off, with buttons flying in all directions, and threw it onto the floor. Suggs watched, grinning, but Quinn was stunned by all of this.

"There, you can keep your damned uniform,

and your commission," McKenzie said hotly. "I'm finished with this weak-kneed, bleeding-heart outfit."

"And I too." Suggs said.

Quinn hesitated, then nodded. "Yes. I'll leave with them."

Hopkins glared at McKenzie. "Damn good riddance, I'd say. I'll have your papers ready tomorrow morning early. I want you all out of here before noon."

"It will be a pleasure, Colonel," McKenzie said in his Scottish accent. "A damnable pleasure."

The following morning, McKenzie, Quinn, and Suggs all left the fort together. Wearing plain civilian clothing purchased from a local trader, and riding horses bought from surplus at the fort, they headed south and west, toward the mountains. McKenzie had convinced his two ex-comrades-in-arms that they could make a small fortune trapping beaver and ermine, especially if they poached from the Indians and colonials. Their plan was to work their way through the Alleghenies into the Cumberland Valley.

In the east, General Gage was in charge of all British forces. He had orders from London to put down any demonstrations by the Sons of Liberty and other such organizations, and make sure colonial militias were not stockpiling weapons and ammunition. The informal collection of activists calling themselves the Continental Congress was talking about a shooting war, and was trying to convince veteran George Washington to gather a colonial army that would fight for all Americans, not just individual colonies. In fact, since Lexington and Concord, some British leaders felt they were already in a war, and there was talk of forcibly disbanding all colonial militias.

McKenzie cared for none of that. He was just another colonial now, and he was not even sure he was a Loyalist. He felt betrayed by his own people, and figured he owed nothing to anybody. He would make money any way he could, without regard to morals or principles.

Of course, the Mad Scot had never had any principles. Before requesting duty in America, he had beaten a soldier to death in Birmingham, and then forced two others to lie for him to his superiors, to avoid prosecution. When he arrived in Boston, he came with the preconceived notion that all American colonials were backward, weak-minded sots who would have had to beg for a living in London, and that Indians were sub-human, to be treated like cattle or vermin. A wild-eyed lunatic with no feeling for others at all, McKenzie was known for his crazy behavior, and he looked the part, with his square, hard face, cold blue eyes, and the pink saber slash that ran across his left cheek.

Quinn and Suggs were perfect for him and his plans. Quinn was a follower and would do whatever McKenzie asked, without question. He had no reluctance about stealing or even killing, except to worry over consequences. Suggs was so ugly that men crossed the street to avoid him, and he enjoyed killing. He had murdered a fellow soldier in Boston because the fellow had embarrassed him, and had never been apprehended for it. Suggs was glad to be shed of the British uniform; now he had more freedom to do just as he wished.

A couple of days after their discharge, the three entered the mountains and began setting beaver traps along a wide creek. After they were all set, McKenzie took them trekking along a second, nearby stream, pulling the traps of settlers and Indians and poaching the beaver from them.

In hardship camp after a full day of that, Jock McKenzie was already enjoying this new life on the frontier.

"Hell, we should have done this long ago," he said happily to his partners. "This beats soldiering by a country mile."

Suggs grinned at him. "We're going to be rich, by God!"

Quinn giggled, looking small next to Suggs. "We don't even have to set our own traps." Now that they were out of uniform, Quinn's officer rank was forgotten, and he deferred to the bigger, more aggressive Suggs. Suggs grabbed a stick Quinn was holding, with a chunk of rabbit meat on it.

"Here, for krikey's sake! Let me show you how to do that. You've got no bleeding brains at all, Quinn!" He held the meat over the hotter part of their fire.

It was night, and rather balmy for mid-spring.

McKenzie sat on a log across from them, holding his own chunk of meat over the fire. "I tell you, boys. In six months we'll be able to return to Boston with money bags full of cash. We'll stay in the finest inn and dine on real beef. Maybe I'll even sail to London. Visit Edinburgh again. Aye, what a vision it is!"

"I'm going to buy me a fat whore and keep her for a week," Suggs said. "She'll never walk again when I finish with her." He laughed a throaty laugh.

Quinn just listened. He looked over at the stack of drying beaver skins that they had worked on all afternoon and wondered what the skins would bring at Fort Cumberland. He thought of Dan'l Boone, and how that hunter had set the Algonquin up at Fort Stuart, and he worried. "I just want to get clear of this wilderness as soon as possible," he said quietly. After several years on this side of the Atlantic, both he and Suggs spoke more like colonials than Brits.

"I never saw more of a worrier, and it's the truth," Suggs said to him caustically. "I guess you need a ramrod up your back, lad."

"Having a wee bit of a second thought about all this, are you, then?" McKenzie grinned. His facial scar shone brightly in the firelight. "Not the least happy about the past and auld lang syne? Buck up, old chappie. All that will be forgotten in a week. We've got a new life ahead of us for a while here. Content yourself. We've got the best of it now. With setting our own traps and poaching, we can clean out an area like this in a month, then move on into the Cumberland. We'll blame what we do on the colonials when we talk to regulars, and on the regulars when we see colonials. We'll get that war started well before King George could."

"We'll have them shooting at each other in no time, out here on the bloody frontier!" Suggs offered. He tried to talk like McKenzie, and be like McKenzie, but he never uttered a thought that had not come from McKenzie's mouth.

Quinn forced a smile. "That should keep them off us, then," he managed.

"Of course it will, my lad!" McKenzie said. He turned at a sound from the trees and rose from the fire.

Suggs rose too. "What is it?"

"I believe we have company," McKenzie said.

In the next moment, there was a rustling and a rider came into view. In another moment, he was in the small clearing.

McKenzie rested his hand on the revolver at his side, and squinted down on the rider. The mule tethered to his mount was loaded with pelts—beaver and ermine. The rider was dressed in cotton clothing, with a loose, long shirt caught at his waist with a wide belt and shoepacks on his feet. His hair was plaited at the back, tied in a leather thong, and his head was covered with a coonskin cap.

"Evening, gentlemen," he said to them. He was

a slim, rather young fellow with an open, friendly face.

McKenzie nodded soberly to him. "Boy."

"I'm looking for a campsite along the creek here. Mind if I join you to warm my hands?"

McKenzie hesitated, eyeing the long rifled musket in the man's saddle scabbard and the other equipment on his mount. But mostly he was studying the stack of hides on the mule's back.

"Why, we'd be honored, laddy!" McKenzie said quickly. "Tether your animals beside ours, over at those hemlocks over there."

"Much obliged," the young man said.

While he was at the trees, McKenzie turned to Suggs surreptitiously, and raised his eyebrows as he gestured toward the pile of hides.

The young man came over to the fire. "My name is Briggs, boys. I'm a corporal in the Carolina militia. Taking some hides and things to headquarters in Salisbury."

"Ah," McKenzie said to the fellow, "a military man. My name is McKenzie. This here is Suggs and Quinn. We're trapping along here for the Fifty-fourth Royal Foot."

Quinn gave McKenzie a surprised look. He could not imagine why McKenzie would give their real names, with their load of poached skins lying on the ground not far away.

"Pleasured," Suggs said with little enthusiasm.

The fellow called Briggs looked curious.

"You're with the regulars? How come you ain't wearing the uniform?"

McKenzie smiled winningly. "Oh, they let us dress like this when we're out on the fringe trapping. Right informal. Like you militia types, if you please."

Briggs looked uncertain. "I just never seen no Brits that waren't in uniform."

"Well, there's a first time for about everything, bucko," Suggs said in too tough a voice.

Briggs regarded him sidewise. "So you're out here trapping?" He eyed the pile of staked-out skins on the ground.

"That's right," McKenzie said. "We had us a good day pulling traps."

Briggs went over and looked at the skins. "Nice beaver."

"Bonnie good skins," McKenzie offered, casting a quick look toward Suggs.

Quinn had risen now too, and looked very uncomfortable. "We never seen a stream like this," he said nervously.

Briggs turned and studied his face, and McKenzie hurled a secret, fierce look at him.

"McKenzie," Briggs said.

He was just saying the name, not catching McKenzie's attention.

"Yes?" McKenzie said nicely.

"Oh. The name seems to ring a bell in the back of my head," Briggs said musingly. "I just can't remember why."

Quinn turned a scared look at McKenzie.

"Maybe you just imagined it," Suggs said with a thick voice.

"Maybe."

"It's a common enough name," McKenzie offered. "Shall I tell you how many there are in Edinburgh?"

Briggs tried a slow smile. "I reckon a lot."

"Exactly," McKenzie said smoothly.

Briggs went over and held his hands above the fire. "I really stopped to ask about poachers," he said suddenly.

Quinn's heart fluttered in his chest, and he slipped his hand down beside his Mortimer repeating pistol. His mouth suddenly tasted like old paper.

"Poachers?" McKenzie asked.

"Yes, there's been some along this stream in the last couple of days, according to some trappers I met. I just wondered if you seen anybody hauling other people's traps."

McKenzie came up close to him. "Now why would we see anything like that?"

Briggs shrugged. "Just a thought. You been in the area."

"We ain't seen nothing, laddy," Suggs said.

Briggs looked over at him.

"You think we've been poaching this stream, don't you, Corporal Briggs?" McKenzie said abruptly.

"I didn't say that."

"But you've been thinking on it right hard, isn't that true?"

50

Briggs hesitated. "It crossed my mind." He glanced toward his mount, twenty yards away, where his musket rested.

"That's a goddamn lie!" Suggs said loudly.

"We wouldn't do that," Quinn protested in a hesitant voice.

"Shut up, Quinn," McKenzie said.

Briggs swallowed hard. "I'm not making accusations," he said. "I'm not a constable. I'll just get my things and go find myself a campsite, and not bother you no more."

McKenzie nodded and smiled. "It's been interesting indeed," he said pleasantly. "And may you go in peace."

Briggs walked past McKenzie, toward his animals, and McKenzie drew the Annely revolver at his hip. When Briggs was past him, he swung it down over the crown of the younger man's head.

There was a dull outcry, and Briggs slumped to the ground, almost unconscious. He lay there moaning, on his side.

"What the hell!" Quinn said incredulously. "Why didn't you let him leave?"

"Oh, for God's sake!" Suggs said.

"He was trouble," McKenzie said easily. "And besides, look at the pelts the man has. You want pelts, don't you, Quinn?"

"Why, yes, but—"

"Then we should take them when they're available, shouldn't we, perhaps?"

Suggs drew his long musket from a groundsheet, and loaded and primed it. He came over, aimed it at Briggs's head, and cocked it.

But McKenzie shoved the gun aside. "No, you fool!"

"What?" Suggs said. "Let's be done with him."

"There might be other trappers in this area. You want them to hear the booming of that cannon, then?"

"Oh, shit," Quinn said. "We don't need this."

"Yes, we do," McKenzie said, as if explaining to a child. "What he has is bloody exactly what we need! Look, he's coming around. Suggs, pull the poor bastard to his feet."

Suggs followed orders, and soon Briggs was standing with his help, looking dazed, blood running from the back of his head and into his braided hair. His hat lay on the ground.

"Please," Briggs said thickly.

"Do you have a shovel on your irons, man?" McKenzie asked him.

Briggs hesitated. "Yes."

"Go retrieve it, Quinn."

Quinn looked at his ex-captain, then went to Briggs's horse. In a moment he was back with the narrow-bladed shovel. McKenzie handed it to Briggs.

"Now, laddy. Take it over there away from the fire, and dig a nice hole. Long enough and deep enough to lie in."

Briggs looked into his evil eyes. "No. Don't do it."

McKenzie stuck the revolver into his face. "Did you want to argue, then?"

Quinn was shaking his head. Suggs began grinning. He loved this kind of thing. "Better get your ass over there, bucko," Suggs said.

Briggs walked over to a wide place in the clearing. He put the shovel to the ground, then looked at McKenzie. "I know you're the poachers. But I won't report it. I swear it. Just take my stuff and let me go."

McKenzie smiled. "Dig," he said.

Briggs began digging, his mind racing now. He saw no way to do anything but obey. Maybe if he just kept talking to them, they would spare his life.

"You watch over him, Suggs," McKenzie said.

Somewhere out in the mountains, a bear roared. Suggs went and stood near Briggs, holding the musket at ready. McKenzie went and sat by the fire again. "Quinn, go count the skins on that mule."

Quinn looked at the digging man for a moment, then nodded. "Right, Captain."

"And don't call me captain," McKenzie said.

Quinn busied himself over by the animals.

"I'm a non-commissioned officer in the Carolina militia," Briggs said as he dug. "They won't like this. Why don't you just let me leave? You got a real haul with them skins. I won't even take my mount."

The hole was taking shape. "Dig deeper," McKenzie said. He swigged a cup of coffee, unconcerned about Briggs. He had no feelings for the corporal. Or for anybody.

"There's almost thirty pelts over here," Quinn said. His voice now held greed in it. "And half of them are ermine."

"Now, I'll bet that made you come all over queer." McKenzie grinned at Quinn, hearing the excitement in his voice. "It's right bracing, isn't it, lad?"

Quinn gave him a sheepish look, then cast a quick glance at the digging man.

"Quinn will spend the gold right along with the rest of us," Suggs said. "He just doesn't like dirtying his bloody hands to get it."

The hole was getting deeper. Briggs slowed down, hoping Suggs did not notice. "There's a platoon of militia in this area," he offered in desperation. "They'll know where I am. I met up with them yesterday."

McKenzie rose and walked over to the hole. Briggs was sweating from the work, and from raw fear. Pain rocketed through his head from time to time, and blood was drying on his neck.

"Get some out of that corner there," McKenzie said.

Briggs turned wearily and dug some more.

"A man has to have a proper burial," McKenzie said. "Otherwise, the bloody vultures will bring unwanted visitors tomorrow, isn't it so, lad?"

"Mr. McKenzie, I don't want to die. I have a family back in Salisbury. You must have a family of your own back in England."

Suggs gave a low laugh.

"England, is it?" McKenzie said. "No, you're

bloody wrong again, old chap. It's a bloody Scot you're dealing with here. And I've got no one. Isn't that pleasant?"

"I appeal to your sense of humanity."

McKenzie looked into the hole. "Lie down."

Briggs gaped at him pitifully.

"I said, lie down." His revolver pointed at Briggs's face.

Briggs got into the hole, and lay down in the length of it, a small whimper sounding in his throat.

"There. Just fits. You've done a bloody good job, Corporal. Bloody good." He sighed. "Now cross your bloody hands on your chest. Like a nice fellow."

"Oh, God," Briggs muttered. "Oh, holy Jesus."

"Quinn, bring your side arm over here," McKenzie said.

Quinn swallowed hard. He came over and drew his Mortimer. He looked at McKenzie.

"You do it. Place it up against his chest, so the sound doesn't carry. That's a good lad."

"I thought you or Suggs . . ."

McKenzie shook his shaggy head, and Quinn thought the scar was particularly livid. "No, no. It's you, lad. To show that you're with us."

Suggs chuckled behind Quinn.

Quinn had no problem with killing. He had done plenty of it. But he disliked the idea of having to worry over it. And this worried him.

"All right."

He stepped down into the hole, straddling

Briggs's supine figure. Briggs closed his eyes and began mumbling.

"Praise be to God, for anyone who calls upon the name of Jehovah will be saved."

Quinn aimed the gun at Briggs, then pressed it close to his chest.

"He said, I am the First and the Last, the Resurrection and the Life. He that comes to me, even though he die, will come to life."

McKenzie turned to Quinn. "Shoot that bleeding son of a bitch!"

Quinn squeezed the trigger. There was a dull explosion, and Brigg's body jumped in the hole. The hot slug had pierced his heart, and burst it like paper.

A tic jumped in McKenzie's scarred cheek.

"He's dead," Quinn reported.

"Then bury him," McKenzie said without looking into the shallow grave. "Both of you. Then make sure his animals are secure for the night."

Suggs looked over at him. "What are you going to do?"

McKenzie's glare made Suggs hold his breath for a moment. "What am I going to do? I'm going to sit here and plan your bloody future, you thick-headed sot."

Suggs looked chagrined. "Hell, I was just asking," he said in a low voice.

That was all he ventured to add. He had learned long ago that you did not cross McKenzie when he was like this.

It wasn't safe.

Chapter Three

Dan'l Boone stood before the adjutant's desk, in the outer reception area at Fort Duquesne headquarters, and watched while the young officer there read his identification papers.

He looked up at Dan'l suddenly with widened eyes.

"You're Dan'l Boone?"

Dan'l regarded him curiously. He looked a little like a bear, standing there with his beard and long hair. He carried the Kentucky rifle under his arm, the one his comrades had begun to call "Ticklicker" because Dan'l could reputedly kill a tick on a bear's nose at five hundred yards with it.

"The one from the French War?"

Dan'l was getting impatient. "Is the colonel in?"

The youngster rose, neat and prim in his red tunic with its polished brass buttons. "Oh, I'm sorry, Mr. Boone. Or is it sergeant?"

"What's the matter with you, boy?" Dan'l asked easily.

"I apologize. It's just that I've been hearing about you for such a long time. About how you fought alongside us at Duquesne, and practically told General Forbes how to do the fighting on that return trip."

Dan'l finally grinned. "Nobody told Forbes much of anything," he said. "He was a good general. Beat that Braddock all to hell."

The adjutant grinned, then quickly looked over his shoulder. "Yes, sir. It's just a surprise to see you in front of me. I thought you'd look . . . older."

"Older! Why, hell, boy, I ain't forty yet! Give me a couple more years, will you?"

"I'm sorry, Mr. Boone. The colonel is ready to see you. Just knock and go on in."

Dan'l grinned again and slapped the young officer on the shoulder as he passed. A moment later, he was inside Colonel Hopkins's private office.

"Well, Boone!" Hopkins greeted him, shaking Dan'l's hand. "How good to see you again! How have you been? How is everything in Boonesborough?"

Dan'l set his rifle up against the end of Hopkins's desk, and took a deep breath. "It's kind of hectic, Colonel. The missus is going to give me a baby pretty soon now, and I got to try to work around that. How are things with the Fifty-fourth Royal Foot?"

The colonel shook his head. "How can it be, when we're worried about this uprising, Boone? Are you still in the Carolina Militia?"

"No, I been up to other things. Settling land, mostly. But I still do some trapping too."

Hopkins offered him a chair, and in another moment they were both seated.

"I hope you aren't allowing those dreadful hotheads in Salisbury to get your back up, Boone," Hopkins said to him quietly. "We don't have any differences, we and the colonials, that should start us shooting at one another. Hell, we're all Englishmen, after all."

"Tell that to Colonel Gage." Dan'l smiled. "He's the one racing up and down the woods with armed men, looking for trouble."

"He's following orders, of course. I'm a bit afraid, frankly, of what this summer will bring."

"Well, I just hope if there's fighting, it stays away from the frontier," Dan'l said. "I had enough of war."

"Hear, hear," Hopkins said.

Dan'l had taken his dark hat off, and was now fingering it on his knee. "Colonel, I guess you know about Fort Stuart."

Hopkins shook his head. He was rather tall and athletic-looking, and had a long face. "I thought you might mention that. McKenzie has already been cashiered. He was an embarrassment to us."

"Is that what you call a weasel nowadays?" Dan'l said evenly. "An embarrassment? He murdered over two hundred friendly Indians, counting women and children. He burned them, Colonel."

"I know. It's a damn shame. Ruddy bad show."

Dan'l fixed him with a hard look. "McKenzie's a goddamn snake, Colonel. Ain't you got no plans to punish him?"

The colonel averted his gaze. "We would have tried him, of course. But we gave him the option of resigning. To be rid of him immediately."

Dan'l was furious. "That ain't good enough, by Jesus! All you done is turn him loose on the frontier, Colonel. To lie, cheat, and kill. That's the kind of skunk he is, from what I hear."

Hopkins blew out a long sigh and accepted the criticism. Dan'l's judgment was as well respected among the British Army as it was in the backwoods.

"I can't argue with that. And maybe we did act hastily. I guess I hoped he and his officer and sergeant would head back to Boston and maybe take a ship home."

"My sources say he went south and west," Dan'l said. "Right where he's going to cause us more trouble."

"Boone. I wish there were something I could do. But we gave him his choice, and he took it.

If he breaks any laws, your militia or sheriffs can pick him up. But my hands are tied at this point, don't you see?"

Dan'l's face was glum. "I see, Colonel, the same old buffalo-chip palaver when it comes to making a Brit pay for wronging a settler or a red man. I never liked it when we was fighting with you, and I ain't liking it any more now."

"I really am sorry, Boone."

Dan'l rose from his chair, and Hopkins rose too.

"Well, I want you to be the first to know, Colonel," Dan'l said slowly, "if I ever get that murderer of babies in my gunsights, he's going to be one sorry-looking son of a bitch when I get through shooting."

Hopkins nodded gravely. "I don't think anybody here would shed any tears," he said.

"I'll see you sometime, Colonel," Dan'l said without smiling.

Hopkins came around the desk. "Boone, this might not be the time to ask this, but we could swear you in as a regular. It's been done before. You've good judgment and fine leadership qualities. Maybe you could help keep some of our own hotheads in line in the coming months. And help head off another shooting war."

Dan'l just stared at him for a long moment, then shook his head slowly. "You're right, Colonel. It's the wrong time to ask."

He turned and left the office.

When he left the fort, Dan'l stopped at the

small settlement that had grown up outside the palisade walls to buy some black powder and lead at a tent store. Figuring his ride back home to be a peaceful one, he was deep inside himself as he packed the supplies aboard his stallion, hitched at a post in front of the big tent.

He was just getting ready to mount and ride off when three British redcoats came and stood around him.

"I say, hunter. What you got in all the pouches? Squirrel meat?" the biggest of them asked, and then they were all laughing.

Dan'l turned to them soberly. "You boys got business with me?"

"Yeah, so we have," a smaller one piped up. "We want to see what you got in them stinking bags."

Dan'l just looked at him. When he started to put his foot in a stirrup, the third fellow grabbed at his arm. "Hey, what's your bleeding hurry, mate?"

Dan'l turned back to them again, and something went hard inside him. They wanted to harass him, have a little fun at his expense. Or worse.

"So you want to play," he said.

"Now you got my drift, hunter!" the big, ruddy-faced fellow said cheerily. "We want to bloody play. Now, why don't you just empty them bags? You could've stole something from the fort, right?"

More laughter.

Dan'l regarded him evenly. "You think maybe you're going to open them bags, frog shit?"

The big man's face reddened. "Yeah, I think so, you son of a bitch!" He motioned to the small one, who held a Brown Bess with a bayonet. The fellow released the bayonet and handed it to the big fellow, grinning now.

Dan'l's skinning knife was in a saddlebag on the far side of his horse, so he just reached into the nearby saddlebag and withdrew a tent spike. It was iron, sharp, and almost as long as the bayonet. "I reckon this will do," he growled, facing the big man.

The small man laughed, but as he assayed the spike, the smile left his lips. He and the third fellow glanced quickly at their bigger companion to see his reaction. He backed up a step and put on a deep scowl. "All right, matey," the big man said. "If that's the way you want it, I'll cut your bleeding liver out!"

But at that moment, a sentry at the fort's gate, just fifty yards away, called out to Dan'l, "Mr. Boone! Is everything all right over there?"

Dan'l glanced toward him. "Everything is just dandy."

The small soldier's eyes widened somewhat, and he re-focused on Dan'l. "You ain't . . . *Dan'l* Boone?"

Dan'l squared off, facing the big man, who looked like he was ready to attack. "The same," he said. "But don't let that make no mind to you. I reckon this ought to be right enjoyable."

The companions of the big soldier both looked toward him. The smaller one said, "Henry. This here is Dan'l Boone."

But the big fellow was just over from Britain, and had never heard of Dan'l. "So?" he growled.

The third soldier licked suddenly dry lips. "Boone here is the trapper, Henry. The one that fought at Fort Duquesne. Here."

"Fought here? Have you gone round the bend? Get out of my way."

The small fellow quickly moved up to his hostile comrade, and began whispering into his ear. Dan'l relaxed and let the spike drop to his side. As the small man whispered, a different look came onto the big fellow's face, but he kept looking at Dan'l warily.

Dan'l looked exasperated. "You want them bags or not?"

The whispering had finished, and now the big man swallowed hard and dropped the bayonet to his side. "Uh. Sorry, governor. It was all in fun, like you said. No harm done, right?"

Dan'l stepped close to the big fellow and suddenly threw his left fist into his belly.

The soldier bent double, then fell onto his back, gasping for air. The other two backed away with looks of abject fear on their faces. Dan'l stepped over the big man, waited for him to focus on Dan'l, then raised the sharp stake high above his head, and brought it down with such force that the soldier clenched his eyes in terror. The stake impaled itself into the ground just beside the soldier's left ear.

The redcoat uttered a sharp cry, then realized he was all right. He was still gasping for air. "Bloody Jesus!" he said raggedly.

Leaving the stake in the ground, Dan'l straightened and looked down at the big man. "This is your lucky day, soldier. Mark it on the calendar."

Then, with the three of them looking on wide-eyed, along with several other civilians and soldiers, Dan'l mounted his horse and rode off casually, as if nothing had happened.

He had re-established his reputation at Duquesne.

Later that same day, almost a hundred miles south and west, at a remote settlement in the mountains called Blakey's Camp, it was raining.

Jock McKenzie had ridden into the place earlier that morning with his cohorts and decided to hole up there until the weather cleared, and then had decided to sell off some of the beaver pelts they had stolen and poached. The trading had finished, and the three had gone to the public house for ale to warm their insides and take the chill off.

After they had buried Briggs out at their camp, McKenzie had purposely dropped a British powder horn at the site, and the next traveler to come along had spread the word that a British unit had killed and robbed a Carolina militia courier. Area settlers were angry, and McKenzie was very pleased with himself. McKenzie enjoyed the prospect of helping start a shooting war between the colonists he regarded as idiots, and his old employers, who had humiliated him by forcing him out of the army. Also, a war between Britain and her colonies would create chaos along the frontier that would benefit his illegal activities. Militia and lawmen would be otherwise occupied, maybe for years to come.

Blakey's Camp was a thrown-together place, with a makeshift palisade that was falling down in places, and a loose collection of log buildings and tents inside the fence. There was a small store, a livery stable, and the pub, which also let rooms for the night. A self-appointed magistrate also served as law officer, but he was seldom called upon to serve in that capacity.

The Blakey Public House usually did a brisk business in the evenings, but it was only early afternoon on that rainy, overcast day, so there were just a few customers, and by the time McKenzie's party had had a couple of rounds, the only other patrons were a couple of ugly-looking trappers sitting at the rear of the place. A barkeep busied himself behind a short counter while his clerk peeled potatoes over a big pot at the far end of the counter, preparing for an evening meal that was generally served at dusk.

The Blakey was very primitive, unlike the fine public houses in Boston and Charleston. It was the best building at the settlement, but it still had hand-rived rafters and rough-plank floors. The front door closed on leather hinges, there were no glazed windows, a smelly fireplace heated the room, and there was a pickle barrel on one wall. Hanging crooked on the wall behind the counter was a dusty engraving of King George.

McKenzie and his men were discussing yesterday's poaching activities, and McKenzie was enjoying their success.

"Do you see how easy it all is, lads?" he asked as he swigged the dark ale. "Give us six months and we can return to Boston in style."

"I'll buy meself some fancy shirts," Suggs said in a gravelly voice.

Quinn laughed softly. "And in the meantime, we'll keep the fires of hatred kindled out here, by krikey. Did you hear that local earlier? Salisbury is in a bloody uproar about their Corporal Briggs, and they think the blinking Brits done it. You were right, Jock. This is right bracing!"

"I see you're in the spirit of it now, Quinn. That's bonnie good. We'll take this poaching thing right to the end."

"And then some," Suggs added.

The barkeep was not paying any attention to the conversation, but the two men at the corner table in the rear stopped talking when they heard the part about poaching.

McKenzie held up his empty ale mug. "I say, barkeep! Keep the bloody grog coming, will you?"

The barkeep nodded, and then brought a large pitcher of ale to their table and set it there.

"There. That ought to keep you boys quiet for a while." He was a balding man with a small pot-belly and wire spectacles. He had meant no offense by the remark, but McKenzie was now looking at him with a frown.

When the fellow started to turn to leave, McKenzie stopped him. "Just a minute, barkeep."

The fellow turned back to him, a little impatiently. "Yes?"

"What's your name?"

"Why, it's Smyth. With a Y."

"Ah. Smyth with a Y. Well, Smyth with a Y, are you bloody telling us we're making too much noise?"

Smyth looked from one face to the other, and did not like what he saw. "Of course not. I just meant . . . the ale should last you for a bit."

McKenzie reached to his side and laid the big Annely revolver on the table very conspicuously. "I hope to heaven you weren't ragging us, Smyth."

Big Suggs turned his red-meat face up to Smyth. "Yeah, we hope that ain't what you was doing, you damn water-fly."

A hard silence settled over the room as the two men at the rear table, and the potato-peeling clerk, stopped what they were doing to listen.

The barkeep was scared now. Quinn reached to his waist and laid his Mortimer on the table, not far from the Annely. They only needed to be cocked and fired.

Quinn said nothing. But he was enjoying this new power, and his old fear of consequences was buried in this new kind of fun. He watched Smyth's face turn ashen on seeing the second gun, and a little thrill passed through him.

"No, sir," Smyth replied for the second time. "It wasn't nothing like that. Not at all."

"You have any women here?" Suggs said. "I mean, for sale?"

Quinn laughed.

"Oh, no. We don't cater like that," Smyth said quickly.

"How about little boys?" Suggs said loudly, and burst out in guttural laughter.

Smyth did not see the humor. "Well, I'll just get back to work, boys. If you need me for—"

"Why don't *you* entertain us?" McKenzie said.

One of the men at the far table chuckled quietly, and McKenzie glanced that way.

"I . . . don't know what you mean," Smyth said nervously.

"I mean, sing or dance for us," McKenzie said. "I'll make it worth your time. A few coppers, perhaps."

Smyth smiled weakly. "No, no, gentlemen. I'm afraid I have no voice for singing."

The clerk at the rear rose slowly and disappeared through the door to the back room. He had decided to go tell the local lawman what was happening. McKenzie saw him leave, but paid no attention.

"Then dance for us," McKenzie went on, swigging more ale. "You know how to dance, surely. Come along, Smyth, the haggis is in the fire, lad!" He picked the gun up and let it dangle loosely in his hand, menacingly.

Quinn and Suggs exchanged pleased looks, while Smyth just stood there, not knowing what to do. Suddenly McKenzie turned the muzzle of the gun to the floor and fired it.

It roared loudly, making the curtains jump at the boarded windows, and causing the ears of those present to ring. The bullet chipped wood in the planking just in front of Smyth, and then bounced up and burned a shallow scratch into his calf.

He yelled and grabbed at his leg.

"Move, laddy, move!" McKenzie called out.

Smyth hesitated, then began limping about, in a hopping, jumping movement. Both men at the far table were laughing, and Suggs laughed the loudest. Quinn had a big grin on his narrow face and had grabbed his Mortimer. He looked over at McKenzie. "Shall I give him some of the hair of the dog, then?"

McKenzie made a sour face, watching the pitiful attempt by Smyth. "Hell, no. He makes me want to bloody puke. Get back to your bloody bottles, you sot."

Smyth did not wait for a second invitation. He turned and limped away behind the counter. McKenzie, Suggs, and Quinn were laughing again. When they looked up, suddenly the two men from the other table were there.

"We like your style," one of them said to McKenzie. He was McKenzie's height, and burly, wearing a hair shirt and boots that came to his knees. He had a bearskin cap on his head and an earring in his right ear. His nose was broken in two places. A militia cavalry pistol hung at his hip.

"Yeah, you're real entertaining," the second man told them. His voice was thick, not unlike that of Suggs, and he was slim and wiry like Quinn, but taller. He wore dark clothing and an eastern, bowler-type hat.

"Who the bloody hell are you?" McKenzie said without a trace of friendliness.

The twosome did not take offense. The first of them said, "I'm Jed Spencer, and this here's my partner, Amos Weeks. We do trapping for a living."

"We didn't steal from your bloody traps," McKenzie said levelly. "Go look to your own kind."

Weeks spoke up now in a high, reedy voice. "We ain't here to make no accusations, boys. We just want to talk."

"Mind if we join you?" Spencer said.

McKenzie looked them over warily. "Hell. Why not?"

The two newcomers pulled up chairs. They had brought their own glasses, and McKenzie poured them some ale.

"I'll bet it was you boys what pulled them traps

71

down on the Little Muddy," Spencer said with a grin.

McKenzie eyed him soberly, but said nothing.

"You're English, ain't you?" Spencer went on.

"What if we was?" Suggs said.

"We got it figured you're McKenzie," Weeks said to him. "That burned that Algonquin bunch out."

"Too much figuring can be bloody deadly," McKenzie said.

"Bloody deadly," Quinn echoed, looking a little nervous.

"We done some trap pulling ourselves," Spencer added. "We was born and raised in these parts, and know every river and stream for fifty miles around. Know where all the trappers place their equipment. We could work together."

"If you know all of that, mate, why do you need us?" Suggs asked him, wiping a sleeve across his crooked mouth.

Spencer leaned forward. "We like the way you use your guns. Some of these trappers go around in bunches. Three or four. Two of us run into trouble, we can't handle it. With five, none of them could stop us. We could poach every stream from here to Kentucky. There ain't hardly no law out here. Incidentally, you done us all a favor with that burning of Fort Stuart. Them Indians didn't belong there, living close to white folk. That was the doing of that Boone fellow. He's a goddamn Indian-lover all of his goddamn life."

"That bloke doesn't have the brains he was born with," Quinn remarked. "He can't write his own name."

This was the second time McKenzie had heard Dan'l Boone's name recently. "This Boone, he's a trapper himself?"

Spencer nodded. "He fought beside the likes of you when he was just a kid. Does a lot of guiding for trekkers now. They say he's the best shot on the frontier. I wouldn't ever pull his traps. It ain't worth it."

McKenzie's interest was piqued. He considered himself a sharpshooter and a skilled hunter. "We Highlanders are the best bloody marksmen in the world," he announced to Spencer. "We can handle the likes of your Boone, never fear. You show me one of his bloody traps, and I'll pull it myself."

Spencer smiled. "I'm sure you would, McKenzie. What do you say, then? Should we join forces?"

McKenzie was still cautious. "That depends, if you want to go all the way with us."

"All the way?" Spencer said.

"This poaching will run out after a bit," McKenzie said. "The boys and I've been talking. The real money is in robbing men's purses. Not their beaver traps."

Spencer and Weeks exchanged a look. "Well. To be honest, we've done some of that too."

McKenzie grinned. "Ruddy good show! I've in mind laying along the main trails and post roads.

Maybe even taking down a coach now and then. It could be bloody lucrative."

Spencer and Weeks were grinning too. "Sounds like our kind of thing, McKenzie."

"We'll try to put it all off on others," McKenzie went on. "Stop a military transport and blame it on the colonials. Drop a word here and there, or a clue. Steal from a traveling drummer and say it was renegade royals. They're ready to believe any wrong against each other, anyway."

"We'll start a bleeding frontier war," Suggs said loudly.

Spencer laughed a deep laugh. "Then we're in?"

McKenzie eyed him carefully. "So long as you understand, my bucko, who's running the bloody show."

Spencer hesitated. "Sure. You're calling the shots, McKenzie."

McKenzie started to reply again, when the door to the outside opened, blowing a sharp gust of wet wind in, and a middle-aged man entered. He was wearing an oilcloth coat and an eastern-style hat, and sported a gray mustache. He stopped and looked at McKenzie's group, then at the frightened barkeep behind the counter, who now just huddled there trying not to hear too much of the conversation.

"Smyth," the newcomer said. His coat was slick with rain.

"Mr. Doyle," Smyth managed.

Doyle walked over to the table where the five

men sat, and all eyes were suddenly on him. He opened his coat and showed an old one-shot pistol displayed prominently across his stomach.

"Evening, boys," he said. "My name is Doyle. I'm the law here in Blakey's Camp."

They all looked him over with disdain. Suggs allowed a low chuckle to escape. Doyle gave him a hard look.

"Are you a constable, then?" McKenzie asked.

"Something like that," Doyle said, eyeing the Mad Scot somberly. "I hear you been having yourselves some fun in here, boys. Shooting off your guns and hoorawing the management."

"Now who would say a thing like that?" Spencer said with a slow grin.

"We weren't doing anything marvelous bad, Doyle," McKenzie told him. "You may content yourself on that point. It's just that your barkeep here is such bloody good sport."

"He shot at me, Doyle!" Smyth yelled out angrily. "You have to lock them up!"

McKenzie frowned. "You really ought to do something about this chap, Doyle. He can be a bit of a nuisance."

Doyle made a face. "We don't allow any shooting in Blakey's Camp," he said. "There's a sign out there that says so. It's the law here."

Suggs looked up at him. "Is that the law of the crown, governor, or just some local pissy-ass law?"

Doyle's face colored, and McKenzie saw him start for the pistol at his waist, but then hesitate.

"I see a couple of you are carrying side arms. I'll just have to take them along with me. You can get them back when you leave town."

"That ain't good enough, Doyle!" Smyth called out. "They ought to be locked up."

Nobody paid any attention to him.

"You have the infamous notion," McKenzie said incredulously, "that we'll give our guns over to you? Are you just a wee bit daft, man?"

Doyle exhaled in frustration, then drew the old pistol from his belt. "Don't make me use this, boys."

Weeks barked out a quick laugh. Quinn just watched McKenzie's face and that of Aubrey Suggs. Suggs suddenly looked a little wild.

"Do you have that weapon primed, mate?" McKenzie said in a soft, cooing whisper.

Doyle looked down at his gun and realized McKenzie was right. He had yet to prime the gun. He looked back up at McKenzie with uncertainty in his face. "Don't worry about my gun. Just give yours over and there'll be no trouble."

McKenzie had not re-primed his own weapon after playing with Smyth. He shrugged inside himself and merely nodded to Suggs, almost unnoticeably.

Suggs drew a knife from his belt, a narrow, long one he had stolen from a dead Algonquin at Fort Stuart. It was a war dagger, very wicked-looking, and Suggs was good with knives. He had learned to throw them as a young man in Bristol. He did not carry a side arm ordinarily. He hurled the blade at Doyle without warning.

The knife turned over once, hissing through the air, and buried itself to the hilt in Doyle's chest.

Doyle was taken completely by surprise. He looked down at the handle of the weapon as if he did not quite understand what had happened. Then he looked up at Suggs as if Suggs might be a lunatic just escaped from an asylum. A moment later, he fell forward onto his face.

"Oh, my God!" Smyth yelled out from behind the counter.

"Well?" McKenzie said to Spencer. "Will you do the honors?" He nodded toward Smyth.

Spencer studied McKenzie's face and understood. McKenzie was testing him. He drew the cavalry pistol on his belt and readied it while the others watched. Smyth was hysterical. He came out from behind the counter.

"Please, no more shooting!" he pleaded, his voice shaking. "The whole town is yours now!"

"Oh, we know that." McKenzie grinned.

Spencer aimed at Smyth, and Smyth suddenly turned and ran toward the back door. Spencer fired and hit him in the center of his back, and Smyth kept running until he crashed into the rear wall with his face. When he slid to the floor slowly, he left a smattering of blood on the whitewashed wall.

Spencer turned to McKenzie. "Anything else?"

McKenzie made a sound in his throat. "That will do for now, lad." He rose to his feet and the others followed. "Let's just get clear of here. The rain's stopped."

They all headed out through the still-open doorway, and they found the clerk out on a narrow porch, the one who had gone for Doyle. He looked very scared.

"So there the little bastard is," Suggs said. He started for the clerk, but McKenzie stopped him.

"What's your name, lad?"

The young man stood there looking from one face to the other. "Johnny."

"Well, Johnny boy. This is your lucky day. You go tell it around that there's some royals out of uniform here, from the king's Fifty-fourth Foot, and we've just disciplined a couple of bloody colonials for insulting the crown. Can you do that then?"

The clerk nodded. "Yes."

With a wave of McKenzie's hand, the fellow was gone.

"They might come after us," Quinn suggested.

McKenzie smirked. "If you were them, bucko, would you?"

Quinn gave a wry grin, but did not reply.

The question was apparently a rhetorical one.

Chapter Four

Back at Boonesborough, Dan'l Boone reported his failure with Hopkins to Jake Medford and Rebecca. Medford had been staying in Dan'l's House until his return, and was angry about Hopkins and his treatment of the situation. Rebecca, though, said she had expected the outcome.

"They have no feeling for these people," she told Dan'l, holding her belly in the kitchen. "Remember, it was the French who befriended them, Dan'l. The Indians have never liked the British, nor the other way around."

After supper that evening, when Dan'l and Medford were sitting in the parlor sucking on corncob pipes, and the sisters were cleaning up at the other end of the house, Dan'l had a visitor.

Medford answered the door, and brought two uniformed men back into the room with him.

Dan'l rose to greet them. "Oh, Captain Emery," he said to the shorter of his visitors. He extended his hand in a firm clasp. "I don't believe I know your companion."

"This is Colonel Frank Davison, Dan'l. From your old neck of the woods, Salisbury."

Dan'l raised his brows and shook Davison's hand. "Well. This must be right serious stuff." He grinned. "Glad to meet you, Colonel."

"The same here, Dan'l," Davison said. He was a bit taller than Dan'l, quite thin, and wore a goatee. He was the commander of the sizeable Carolina Militia garrison at Salisbury, back east.

"I served under the colonel for a while," Medford explained to Dan'l. "At Fort Cumberland."

"And we were glad to have the sergeant here with us," Davison said. He sounded very educated, and that always intimidated Dan'l a little.

"Can I offer you some coffee?" Dan'l said. "The wife always got some brewing."

"No, I just want to talk with you in private for a brief time," Davison said. "I mean, just the four of us."

Dan'l nodded. "Sit down, Colonel. Jake, will you close that parlor door?"

Medford went and closed the door, and a moment later they were all sitting around Dan'l's fireplace, facing each other and a low, crackling fire.

"I understand you just got back from Fort Duquesne," Davison said. "To ask that something be done about McKenzie."

Dan'l nodded. He had tapped his pipe out, and now sat empty-handed, one leg crossed over the other. He had removed his rawhide shirt, and from the waist up wore only yellowed long underwear. He felt no embarrassment. Dan'l had never observed protocol or formalities. He ran a hand slowly through his thick, dark beard. "They already got rid of him. Without any other punishment."

"We know that now," Emery said. "He's down in the mountains, raising hell south of here. Poaching, we think. Killed a militia courier and stole our pelts. Tried to make it look like the regulars did it, but some hunter saw him in the area. We think he has his officer and sergeant with him, the ones that were kicked out with him. They were at Stuart."

Dan'l shook his head. "That son of a bitch."

Emery cast a quick look at Davison to see how he reacted to the profanity. Medford smiled slightly.

"We know how you feel about these murderers, Dan'l," Davison said soberly. "We know it was you that put the Algonquin in at Stuart. You thought they were safe from trouble there. Neither they nor you could have anticipated the kind of thing that overtook them. McKenzie, of course, acted entirely on his own. I know Colonel Hopkins, and he would never order such an atrocity."

"No, he wouldn't," Dan'l said.

"Incidentally, I understand you saved one of them."

"Oh. Billy Two Tongues," Dan'l said. "He's over at Uriah Latham's cabin. Jake here tells me he done real well while I was gone. He'll be scarred up some, but he'll be all right." He grinned behind the beard. "He still ain't talking to me. Says I spoiled his grand exit. Wanted to join his ancestors, I guess."

"I'll be damned," Emery said.

"He'll be gone in a few days," Medford told them. "Latham says he'll be glad to be rid of him. Says he's an ornery bastard to live with, and to make things worse, talks better English than Latham."

They all laughed lightly. Then Davison turned to Dan'l. "I wonder if he'd testify against McKenzie, if we ever bring him to justice."

"The law is going after him?" Dan'l asked.

Davison shook his head, and drew his mouth down. "There's not much law out there in the woods, Dan'l, you know that. But he killed a Carolina militiaman. That gives me jurisdiction."

Dan'l nodded. "So that's why you're here."

The fire crackled quietly in the fireplace, and made shifting patterns on their faces.

"We want him, Dan'l. For Corporal Briggs, and for all of those Algonquins he burned alive. He's a soulless man, and God only knows how much havoc he can wreak out there on the frontier. We want him. Dead or alive."

Dan'l sighed deeply.

"I reckon you got cause," he said. "I reckon we all got cause."

"Since you have a special interest in the Algonquin, Dan'l, we thought you might want to help us on this," Emery said.

Dan'l looked over at him. "You got the whole damn militia. Ain't that enough?"

Now it was Davison who spoke. "This job doesn't require a squad of soldiers. It needs somebody who knows the woods. Knows this country. That's you. I'd give you all of the riflemen you can use. You'd carry an officer's rank, and get paid for the work."

Dan'l shook his head slowly. "Rebecca is expecting in less than two weeks. Hell, she needs me here. She'd raise Cain if I left again."

"Well, she does have her sister, Dan'l," Medford said, leaning forward on his chair. "And with me riding with you, we could get it done and over before she's due, and get you back here."

"You with me?" Dan'l grinned slightly.

Medford nodded. The wrinkles in his face showed clearly in the firelight, and Dan'l thought he looked old for the first time. "You think I want to stay here with a couple of skittery women while you was out there doing what we both do best?" Medford said.

Davison watched Dan'l's uncertain face. "I knew about the baby coming, Dan'l," Davison said. "I wouldn't have come, but I think you're the best man to get this particular job done. You could wait till the missus delivers, but can you imagine what this black-hearted scoundrel can do in the next two or three weeks?"

"There's another couple of villages of Algonquin east of here, as you know," Emery added. "They're related to Chief Longhair's people. They're up in arms about the massacre, and talking about making war on all whites—English *and* colonists alike. Maybe if McKenzie is brought to justice, all of that will cool down."

"I *might* be able to get back here in time for Rebecca," Dan'l acknowledged, thinking it over.

"We'll give you a platoon of militia if you think they'll help," Davison said. "We'll take them from Emery's garrison here. They might be men you already know."

"No," Dan'l said. "If I go, I'll just take Jake here. But I'd want him on the payroll too."

"That would be no problem," Davison told him.

Dan'l rose from his overstuffed chair, and the others followed suit. "Let me think on it," he said quietly. "Let me talk with Rebecca. I'll let you know tomorrow."

Davison nodded. "I'll appreciate it, Dan'l. We'll wait to hear from you." He adjusted his blue tunic. "Incidentally, General Gage has demanded that all colonial militia be disbanded within sixty days."

Dan'l frowned. "Did that come from London?"

"We don't know. Several governors have already told him to go to hell, in so many words. I expect Virginia and Carolina will do the same."

"And if they wasn't to defy Gage?" Dan'l said.

"Then we would be out of business, and you might have trouble getting paid. I have to be honest with you."

Dan'l grinned. "You don't leave a man much, Colonel."

Davison nodded ruefully. "I know, Dan'l. I know."

Dan'l had a long talk with Rebecca that night in bed, with her full belly against him and the luxurious warmth of her beside him. Surprisingly, she understood the importance of his proposed mission completely, and with heavy reluctance gave her blessing to the project. She urged him fiercely, though, to take great care, and to try to be back before his child was born to them.

The next morning, he and ex-Sergeant Medford rode down to Uriah Latham's place, where Billy Two Tongues was up and hobbling about and getting on Latham's nerves. Billy had announced his intention to leave in the next couple of days, and his plan was to go into the mountains and do some trapping on his own. He had heavy scarring on the left side of his face, partially closing that eye, and he was ashamed of the way he looked. He just wanted to hide out in the woods and have as little contact with other people as possible.

Dan'l advised Latham what he and Medford

were doing, and asked Latham to look in on Rebecca once in a while, and Latham was pleased to do so. Dan'l wished Billy good luck, but Billy would hardly acknowledge Dan'l's remarks. When Dan'l left, he understood why Latham wanted to be rid of the Indian. He seemed the most ungrateful Indian Dan'l had ever run across, and the most contrary.

Dan'l and Medford reported in to the local garrison, where a combined Virginia and Carolina force had been placed to protect the settlement from hostiles, especially Shawnee. Davison was very pleased that his recruitment of Dan'l had been successful, and supplied Dan'l and Medford with lead ammo, black powder, and primers. They were also given saddle packs and enough provisions to last two weeks. By mid-morning, they were gone, heading out into the foothills to the south, in the direction where McKenzie had been last sighted.

That afternoon, not far to the south, Jock McKenzie reached into a saddle wallet, took out a telescoping field glass that he had stolen from the Fifty-fourth Foot, and held it up to his eye. Yes, there it was. A hide wagon with two hunters aboard, crossing the narrow stream before him. His gray stallion guffered softly under him as he put the glass away. He turned to his four underlings, who sat mounted behind him.

"They're heading right at us. Disperse into the trees."

The four horsemen split into two pairs and went behind the cover of hickory and elm on either side of the trail. McKenzie rode on up to the stream as the wagon came out of the water and halted in an algae-encrusted backwater, its horse's legs submerged almost to the knees. There were two grubby-looking buffalo hunters on the buckboard looking warily at McKenzie. Their hide wagon was stacked with dark brown, robe-quality buffalo hides, folded neatly and stiff as boards.

"Best of the day to you, gentlemen!" McKenzie said to them from twenty yards away.

The two dirty-looking men just looked at him. They wore soiled cloth pants and shirts, with a lot of straps and equipment hanging from their shoulders, and black hats. One had a mustache, the other a full beard. The bearded one had the reins.

"I was wondering, is this the way to Fort Cumberland?"

McKenzie's horse was very nervous under him, and the driver of the wagon noticed that. He looked around in the trees, but did not see the ambushers. His companion carried a pellet musket across his knees, and was gripping it firmly with both hands.

"You're nowhere near Fort Cumberland," the driver said, curtly. "This trail don't go to Fort Cumberland."

McKenzie walked his mount forward a few paces. The wagon still stood in the backwater of the stream. "Are you sure, then? I was told back at Blakey's Camp that this was the way."

The two hunters relaxed some. The one with the gun spat tobacco juice onto the ground. "You one of them Englishmen, are you?"

"Well, fairly close, I suppose. I'm a Scot, you see. Over here to make my living trading in furs and such."

"Shit," the driver drawled. "Ain't no goddamn English or whatnot going to make it in these here woods, mister," he said with a sly sneer, while his partner grunted out a laugh.

"You is lost, boy!" the partner offered.

"Yeah, you can't get to Cumberland from here," the driver added, having fun with it now.

"I see," McKenzie said, his face somber. He was going to enjoy this more than he had thought.

"Now you just get on out of our way, English," the driver told him. "We got man's business to tend to."

McKenzie smiled nicely, and the driver thought he saw something he did not like in the smile. "No, no, boys," McKenzie said. "It's not me that's making way. It's you, you see."

Scowls grew quickly on the hunters' faces. The man with the gun raised it threateningly. "We'll just see about that."

McKenzie raised his arm high above his head. "All right, lads! Now!"

The hunters began looking about them again, and in the next moment the woods were filled with the raucous noise of exploding guns. Quinn and Suggs fired from McKenzie's left, and Spencer and Weeks let loose from the right. In the first blast of fire, the driver was hit in the low chest, his partner in the belly, and the horse in the left eye.

The hunter with the gun raised it to fire at McKenzie, but McKenzie beat him with his Annely. He hit the fellow in the high chest, and knocked him off the buckboard and into the shallow water. The struck horse then kicked him in the hip and fractured it.

Now McKenzie's four gunmen rode in, repriming their weapons as they came. As the driver tried to pull a side arm from his belt, Suggs shot him with his Brown Bess, blowing a neat hole through him from side to side. Spencer fired at the man in the water, splintering his skull and making gray matter fly everywhere. Weeks missed the driver as he fell from the wagon, and hit the horse a second time, in its chest. It sat cockeyed in the water, kicking its last, while the driver moaned and slipped under the surface of the mucky pool.

The riders all sat around on their mounts as the gunsmoke cleared, looking down into the backwater pool. The horse and both men were dead and bleeding so heavily that the backwater was crimson with the thick blood. Some of it was flowing pink into the stream itself.

"Look at the water," Quinn said, fascinated. "It's red."

McKenzie walked his stallion into the reddish water to get a better look at the hides aboard the wagon. He did not even bother to glance at the two dead men.

"Looks bloody good, lads. There must be a hundred hides here. Good ones. From clear across the Alleghenies. They'll bring us hard cash when we run onto a trading camp. Cut that dead animal loose and get the wagon out of there. We'll hitch the packhorse to it."

"Right, Jock!" Quinn said excitedly.

"And go through their clothing and belongings. They might have gold or silver on them. Look in their bloody mouths. Take any gold fillings you find."

Spencer looked over at McKenzie. "Fillings?"

McKenzie gave him an even look. "Any problem with that, Spencer? Afraid to get your hands dirty, man?"

"Hell, no," Spencer replied. "It's just that . . . well, the dead deserve *some* respect, don't they?"

McKenzie shook his shaggy head. His hair was growing longer, and he had a stubble of beard too. "Isn't that just marvelous sweet now?" he said sourly. "Respect for the dead, is it? Shall I tell you what I think of the dead, my lad? I think they don't bloody exist, you see. These chaps are turning to muck before our very eyes. In a day, they'll smell worse than horse dung. Get the bleeding gold out before it smells too. That's what I think of the bleeding dead."

Spencer took a deep breath. "Whatever you

say, McKenzie. You're running the show."

"Now that's a good lad," McKenzie purred.

Spencer dismounted like the rest of them and waded into the crimson-stained water.

Later, just as dusk was falling, Dan'l Boone and Medford rode along that same trail, and found the three corpses in the muddy backwater—two men and their horse.

They had been riding hard for many hours, and both were exhausted. Dan'l felt a special urgency about this mission because of Rebecca, so he had pushed himself and Medford harder than he ordinarily would have.

There was still some light in the sky when they found the bodies, and flies were already buzzing on the parts of them that stuck out of the water. The pool still had a distinct pink coloration.

"I'll be damned," Medford said through his white mustache. "What a mess."

"They were buffalo hunters," Dan'l said, wading into the water. "There's a hide over there in the muck. And this horse has got harness on. It was pulling a hide wagon."

"Who would have did something like this?" Medford said.

"Jock McKenzie," Dan'l said with finality. "It waren't nobody else, Jake. Look over here, at them hoofprints. McKenzie bought some mounts from the royals when he was let go. These is Brit-shod mounts. At least, three of them are. Looks like McKenzie picked up a couple friends."

Medford shook his head. "You don't have no trouble guessing how he expects to make a living, I reckon."

"That demon from hell," Dan'l said to himself. "Look at the blood still in that river pool. He ain't got no heart inside of him, Jake. He ain't really human."

"Well, he left a clear trail," Medford said, pointing to where the tracks headed off into the woods, toward the mountains. "I guess we ought to find out where it leads."

Dan'l looked up toward the sky. "It's almost dark. Better off to wait till dawn probably."

"The sooner we come on them, the fewer people might get their heads shot off," Medford said. "Anyway, you got time agin you, Dan'l. We ought to track as long as we can pick up spoor."

Dan'l sighed slightly. Medford was right. "Oh, hell. Let's follow it a ways. We might come in sight of their camp."

They headed off on the trail immediately. They had no time to bury the dead in that mushy pool. It was all beyond burial and niceties like that.

Medford deferred to Dan'l when it came to tracking, letting him ride out front. Dan'l tracked better than most Indians, and he was particularly good when the stakes were high. They rode into hilly country, through stands of white oak, then pine. The trail led through gullies where ruffled grouse flew up in front of them, and wild turkeys

skittered away into the underbrush. But Dan'l ignored them, not knowing whether they might be
within earshot of their quarry. They got into
rocky country after dark, and Dan'l kept having
to dismount to refind the trail. Over one hard-
rock ledge, Medford figured there was no way to
keep from losing the way. But Dan'l could have
tracked across a sheet of glass. He circled and
spiraled on foot, weaving and retracing his own
way, and finally he found a scratched rock and a
busted twig of a dead shrub.

"Here," he said to Medford. "Several animals
passed here within hours. Heading due west over
this rock face. It's our bunch, all right."

Medford was awed.

It got dark faster than Dan'l had expected, and
he found himself tracking by the light of a half-
moon, which he did not like to do. He finally
turned back to Medford, reining his horse in.

"Well, we got a start on it. Let's find a flat place
to put our bedding down and spend the night.
We won't build a fire. We might be too close."

"Sounds good, Dan'l."

Dan'l moved his roan stallion into some thick
juniper, watching for a good place to encamp. As
he moved along, though, he began to feel uneasy
about progressing farther. He could not identify
a reason, but he always trusted his instincts. He
slowed way down, making Medford curious. He
stopped and listened. He heard an almost inau-
dible snapping of a small twig somewhere in the
dark. He held his hand up for Medford to see.

"What is it?" Medford whispered.

Dan'l put his finger to his lips. Slowly, with great deliberation, he slid Ticklicker out of its saddle holster. It was already loaded, with the ramrod in place in the barrel. He removed the rod and primed the gun and cocked it. Medford, seeing all that, pulled an old cavalry revolver out of its belt holster and began loading. Halfway through, there was a sound in the trees, and then a shot.

Medford felt the fireball enter his skull at the right front, and tear through his head like a bolt of lightning, causing wild, colored lights inside him, and then he was toppling off his mount. He was dead when he hit the ground.

"Jake!" Dan'l cried out.

Another shot rang out from a closer position, and tugged at Dan'l's rawhide shirt. He saw the flash of the gun in the dark, and returned fire with the Kentucky rifle. There was an outcry from the trees, and then two more shots. The first one hit Dan'l's stallion in the brain, and the next one punched him off the animal before it could fall under him.

They went down separately. Luckily, the horse fell away from Dan'l, not on him. Dan'l lay on the ground in an awkward position, feeling blood running down his side, raw pain ripping through his rib cage. Medford's horse was rearing and plunging, and finally ran off.

Dan'l had lost the rifle, and could not find it in the dark. He looked over at Medford, and groaned with the realization that his old sergeant was dead.

Damn, Jake! I knowed we come too far!

A horseman came out of the trees. And another. Dan'l watched them come, and knew who they were. The wild-looking one with the facial scar had to be McKenzie. The slight one was Quinn, and the big one was McKenzie's old sergeant, Suggs. The fourth one had to be one of the newcomers to the group.

McKenzie looked down on Dan'l for a moment, holding his Annely revolver trained on his head. "I told you we were being followed," he said to the others. He had left Spencer to watch over their camp, a half-mile farther up in the hills. Weeks, the man Dan'l could not identify, dismounted and stood over Dan'l.

"This one's still alive."

The others dismounted too. Quinn went to make sure of Medford, and was pleased to see the side of his head blown off. "This one's dead."

Suggs aimed his Brown Bess at Dan'l's chest. He had already reloaded. "This one soon will be." He squinted one eye down to fire.

"Just a minute," McKenzie said, walking over and looking at Dan'l. "There's a look about this one. Who are you, old sport?"

Dan'l glared up at him, holding a hand over the wound in his side. "They call me Boone."

Suggs's eyes grew large, and he and Quinn exchanged a quick glance. "Dan'l Boone!" Suggs said in a half-whisper. "I shot Dan'l Boone!"

Quinn came over to look too. Weeks was holding his left arm now, where Dan'l's only shot had
creased his flesh. "The son of a bitch hit me."

"If I seen you, you'd be dead," Dan'l grated out.

McKenzie laughed at the remark. "I like him."

Quinn caught McKenzie's eye. "Kill him.
Now," he said nervously.

Suggs nodded and aimed at Dan'l's head.
"Yeah. Now is good."

Dan'l propped himself up on an elbow. "Only
a goddamn Brit would have to shoot a man twice
to kill him."

Suggs's ugly face creased in frustration, and
his finger whitened over the trigger of his musket
for the second time.

"Goddamn it, I said to wait!" McKenzie roared
out.

All of the others looked at him. Dan'l was hot-
angry at himself for trying to go too far in the
dark and getting Medford and himself killed for
the trouble. He thought of Rebecca, and the unborn son he would never see.

"Tie him up," McKenzie said, glaring at Suggs.
"I want to take him back to camp."

Quinn regarded him sidewise. "What the hell
for?"

"Because it bloody well pleases me," McKenzie
said harshly. "We've captured the infamous
Boone, the hunter everyone keeps telling me
about." His voice lowered. "The fellow that put
the redskins in at Fort Stuart, right? And I'll wager he came after old Jock to arrest him. Eh?

Don't you see the pure pleasure of it, then? You want this to be over in a flash? No, bring him back, I say. I'm going to bloody enjoy this."

Weeks came over to him. "McKenzie. Spencer and me been out here a mite longer than you and your boys. We know a little about this fellow. Suggs is right, kill him now. You don't take a wounded grizzly into your tent, by Jesus. This is the same."

McKenzie's eyes narrowed. "You're actually frightened of a side-shot, unarmed man! I jolly well can't believe my ears. What the hell is the matter with you flaming girlies? You're going to enjoy this, I promise you!"

Suggs sighed, reluctantly stepped over Dan'l, and took a short length of rope from his belt. He leaned over Dan'l as if about to handle a cougar, and began tying his hands as Dan'l's eyes burned into his head.

"All right," Suggs muttered to himself as he worked. "He goes with us."

Jock McKenzie grinned widely. "Of course he does." he said.

Chapter Five

A half hour later they were back in McKenzie's camp. It was mid-evening, the moon had risen higher, and there was plenty of light from their bright campfire. They were cooking up some stew in the pot that hung on a spit over the fire.

They had not buried Medford. They had not even looked at the corpse again. Dan'l had barely managed one last glimpse at it as they led him away. He could not remember feeling lower in his life. Medford had recruited him in Salisbury, those many years ago, when Dan'l was just a kid, and they had fought twice at Fort Duquesne together. The only one outside his family who had meant as much to him was John Findley, who had fired his imagination about exploring Kentucky.

McKenzie, Quinn, and Spencer now sat around the fire on stools they had found aboard the hide wagon. Suggs was tending to the animals, and Weeks, his wound now bandaged, was over at the wagon, tying the hides down better.

Dan'l lay on the ground near the fire, tied hand and foot. His shallow wound had just grazed his floating ribs, and had already stopped bleeding. But it ached like a bad toothache, and his right shoulder had been wrenched in the fall from his dead mount.

They had made no effort to go after Medford's horse. They had gathered up Medford's musket and Dan'l's rifle and brought them into camp, and Dan'l had seen them dump them aboard the hide wagon. They had also found Dan'l's skinning knife and confiscated that too.

Dan'l lay there waiting. He knew that if he could not escape, certain death lay ahead for him. Either slow or fast. It looked like it would be slow.

"What do you think, Boone?" McKenzie said as Dan'l lay thinking about the stupidity that had put him there. He had listened to Medford when he'd suggested forging ahead, when all his instincts had told him otherwise. He had listened because he wanted to get this behind him and return to Rebecca. Now he would never see her again.

Dan'l looked over at McKenzie and said nothing.

"Doesn't that stew smell bonnie good, heh?

Makes your mouth water a wee bit? Of course, prisoners don't get the stew. They don't get anything, my lad. Maybe a bit of water from time to time. If they behave."

"Go roast in hell," Dan'l said.

McKenzie did not like that. The tic in his cheek jerked once as he rose and walked over to Dan'l. All four of his men stopped what they were doing to watch him. He stood over Dan'l, and a hard grin had taken hold of his square face. The scar glowed brightly in the firelight.

"What did you say?" he said softly.

Dan'l looked up at him, and growled through the thick beard. "I said, misfits like you was usually took from their mama's milk too soon. You ain't never growed into a real man."

Suggs's jaw dropped open. Quinn looked quickly at McKenzie and rubbed a hand across his mouth. Spencer and Weeks gaped at each other with saucered eyes; then Spencer swallowed hard.

McKenzie just stood there for a moment, not reacting visibly. Quinn thought briefly that he might do nothing. But then the wild look came into McKenzie's soulless eyes.

"Mother's milk, you say?" His voice was soft. "Misfit, is it?"

Suddenly, and with savage ferocity, he kicked into Dan'l's side, the one with the wound. There was a loud thumping sound, and a low outcry from Dan'l, and then he was hissing in renewed pain, and gasping for breath.

Quinn had begun holding his breath.

"Haven't grown up, then?" McKenzie said. "But it takes a grown man to do this fancy step, nay?"

He whirled in a pirouette; then the heavy boot came again, this time thudding against Dan'l's back. Another stifled outcry from Dan'l, and through his teeth he gritted, "You damn slime!"

"Ah! And still there's fire inside!"

McKenzie did another turnaround, in a fancy dance step, arms flying, and kicked Dan'l directly in the face.

Bone snapped in Dan'l's nose, and he grunted in shock, then fell into a daze.

Spencer moved over to Weeks and the wagon.

McKenzie circled Dan'l's head, tripping lightly, humming a little tune to himself, relaxed now, the anger simmering away. The boot came again, up against the side of Dan'l's head, and put him out cold, a blackness moving mercifully in on him.

McKenzie danced around some more, like a Highland kilt dancer, and Quinn could almost hear bagpipes in the background. Another savage kick to the chest, and he was still not finished. A fierce one to the thigh.

Finally he quit, out of breath. He looked down dizzily at Dan'l, like a drunk. "Yes. Very nice."

Dan'l lay like a lump of tendered-up beef. He looked dead.

Quinn started breathing again.

"Good God," Weeks said quietly so McKenzie could not hear it.

"Now," McKenzie said, turning to the others. "You see how much *fun* this can be?"

"*Now* kill him," Suggs said, not looking at Dan'l.

McKenzie shook his head. "My good fellow! This isn't the end of it. Not a bit of it, lads. Throw some water on him, Quinn. Then two of you get him onto his feet."

Quinn eyed him sidewise. "He won't be able to bloody stand."

McKenzie just gave him a look. Quinn took a pot of cold water from beside the fire, and threw it in Dan'l's face.

Dan'l sputtered and came awake. His nose was swelling, his left eye was closing, blood caked his lower face, and dark bruises were appearing. He coughed and grunted in pain. He felt as if he had been run over by a herd of buffalo. Twice.

"See, he's all bloody right," McKenzie said, grinning. "Now, Suggs. Spencer. Stand the bloke on his feet."

Suggs gave McKenzie a look, but obeyed. Spencer and Weeks came over from the wagon, and Spencer helped Suggs raise Dan'l up. He was like a limp rag in their arms. He hardly knew that he was off the ground.

"Hold him up, Suggs," McKenzie ordered. "Weeks, go get that length of rope from the rear of the wagon. Quinn, there's a bramble bush over at the edge of the clearing there. Cut some long branches from it, and wind that rope around them. Get some nice long thorns, if you will. You and Spencer can wind that all around our prisoner. Then get that big sack under the buckboard."

They followed orders, not speaking. In just a few minutes, they had braided the thornbush into the rope, and were winding it around Dan'l's shoulders, arms, chest, and stomach while he kept going in and out of consciousness. The thorns embedded themselves through his clothing, into his flesh, but he took no notice.

"Now dump him into that bag," McKenzie told them. "And hang him on the back of the wagon, so he's off the ground."

Spencer turned to McKenzie. "What's the point? Ain't he had enough? Shoot him in the goddamn head."

"We don't need him, Jock," Quinn agreed. "He's only trouble."

McKenzie looked Spencer in the eye. "Who did you say is the brains of this bunch, laddy?"

Spencer hesitated. "You."

"Well, there you are, then." He glanced over at Quinn. "Don't ever question the wishes of your captain, Leftenant."

Quinn just stared at him.

"You'll all see how much pleasure can be had. He'll travel in the bag, with the thorns a-rubbing and chafing and gouging." A grin. "Then, when we make our camps, we'll take him out and ask him to entertain us. When his mind goes, he'll be more apt to follow orders."

Spencer gaped at him as if he had gone mad.

"Any questions then?" McKenzie said.

There were none. Three of them got Dan'l into the sack, then dragged him to the wagon and hung him on a hook at the back of it, off the ground. He swung gently there. Damn, Weeks said to himself.

Inside the sack, Dan'l came to again, and could not figure out for a minute where he was, or what had happened to him. Then he remembered the kicking, and he got a flash of himself being stuffed into the sack. He felt the thorns sticking into him like small knives, and he knew what they had done. His face throbbed, his body ached in various places, and he thought for a moment he might throw up, but he did not.

"You son of a bitch," he mumbled through a bloody mouth. "You better kill me."

Then he passed out again.

The next day was sheer horror.

The gang moved on, working its way north and west, toward a small settlement where they could sell the buffalo hides. Hanging from the rear of the wagon, Dan'l bounced about, and his injuries throbbed and ached and the thorns sliced into his flesh.

At one point, he almost wished they would shoot him.

Almost.

At noonday, when they stopped for a brief

meal, they still did not feed him. He was becoming dehydrated too, and realized his weakness would increase as he was deprived of water. He hung in the bag, and hated McKenzie.

McKenzie came to him before they moved on again, and asked through the sack if he wanted water. Dan'l grunted yes, and McKenzie poured a basinful of dirty water over him, through the cloth. Dan'l muttered an obscenity, and McKenzie laughed loudly. Just before they started off, though, and under McKenzie's orders, Quinn cut a small hole in the sack and poured some fresh water into Dan'l's mouth. He sucked it in eagerly, taking any advantage they would give him.

"We don't want him to die on us," McKenzie said.

In early afternoon, the group pulled traps they found along a blue creek, and Dan'l could hear them talking about the quality of the skins. Poaching was a serious offense on the frontier. A man could go out of business or even starve if his traps were poached, and it was considered worse than horse theft. But McKenzie did not care about any of that. There was no law to deal with, only the trappers themselves, and he welcomed confrontation.

By late afternoon, they had run onto a stage trail, and followed it for miles up into hilly country again. When they had been on it for almost two hours, a horse and buggy came along.

The gang waved the driver down. McKenzie

and Spencer were riding up in front of their hide wagon, with Quinn driving it, and Suggs and Weeks were bringing up the rear. They all reined up in place, and McKenzie and Spencer walked their mounts on up to the buggy.

"Top of the day to you," McKenzie greeted the older man.

Dan'l could hear it all from where he was, in the sack on the back of the wagon. But he was only half-conscious.

"Afternoon," the buggy driver said warily.

"We're running a bit short on provisions," McKenzie said. "Would you perchance have any flour or coffee aboard that you could easily spare?"

The potbellied older man shook his head, looking the group over. "No, nothing like that. Just on an overnight visit to my sister. Lives in the valley over there. Sorry I can't help you."

McKenzie did not move from his path. "Well. What about money, then, governor?"

"Money?" the other man said, his face going straight-lined.

"Yes, Father. Money. Do you have any on you, then?"

The driver hesitated. "No. No money. We mostly barter out here, you know."

McKenzie leaned forward in his saddle, and it squeaked under his weight. "What's that I see under your buckboard? Is it not a compartment with a lock on it?"

Dan'l was fully conscious now, and his pains

were only bearable if he did not think about them. As he listened to the conversation he realized the buggy driver had seen his last sunset. He would never arrive at his sister's house. "Son of a bitch," he muttered thickly, his voice not audible through the bag.

"Yes, it's a compartment," was the reply. "But there isn't anything in there. Now, if you'll just let me pass, I'll be on my way."

Spencer drew his cavalry pistol and primed it while the other man looked on. Then he cocked it, and aimed it at the driver's chest. "Sure you won't give that some thought?" he said in a hard voice.

Inside the bag, Dan'l struggled weakly with the bonds on his wrists, which were tied in front of him. He only succeeded in making the rope cut into his flesh, and the thorns jab into him around his chest and side.

"You bastards!" he said, panting with the effort.

"Why don't you just open that box up?" McKenzie said nicely. "And let us have a wee look inside?"

The driver paused and looked at the gun, and then at the other gunmen. He got a key from his pocket and unlocked the box, and the lid fell forward. Inside was a money bag.

"Ah, what have we here?" McKenzie said lightly.

He moved up and reached into the box, coming out with the small bag. He opened it by pulling a drawstring. There were gold coins inside. British sovereigns.

"Well, well," Spencer said.

"What is it?" Suggs called out from behind the wagon. He had heard Dan'l's last muttering, but ignored it.

"It's gold, lads," McKenzie announced. "Imagine, and this fellow was sure there was nothing inside. What a surprise it must be!"

"I . . . forgot it was there," the driver said quietly. "Please. Take it and let me be on my way."

McKenzie fondled the buggy horse's nose. "A piece of good horseflesh, as well. I suppose we could get a few shillings for him in the settlements." He turned back to the others. "Come on up then, lads."

Suggs and Weeks spurred their mounts forward and joined McKenzie. Quinn held the reins of the hide wagon and watched. McKenzie threw the bag of coins over to Suggs, who looked inside it and grinned.

"I think we'll camp here," McKenzie said. "It's getting late in the day, and we've had a touch of good luck. This is as good a place as any."

"What about him?" Spencer said, waving the gun at the buggy driver.

McKenzie turned toward the wagon and remembered Dan'l. He turned back to the frightened driver with a grin. "Stake his rig out with ours, and tie him up."

Spencer raised his eyebrows questioningly, but McKenzie just said two words. "Do it."

It took a half hour to make camp and get a fire going. They were in a rocky clearing, rather high in a range of hills. There were splotches of spring snow left in the deep underbrush, but the air was warm. They tied the prisoner's hands, then bound him to a sapling just at the edge of camp. Every few minutes he would plead for his life, but nobody listened. They heated the stew again, and the five of them ate, then sipped coffee around the fire. When dusk came, McKenzie went to the rear of the hide wagon.

Hanging in the sack back there, Dan'l heard McKenzie coming. Then he saw his dark form come between him and the light from the fire. A moment later, McKenzie cut the rope that held Dan'l off the ground.

When Dan'l hit hard, several thorns bit deep into him, and he cried out a muffled cry. He heard McKenzie laugh quietly. Then McKenzie opened the sack and bent down to look in at Dan'l.

"Oh, dear! You look fearful bad, laddy! Come on out of there, there's a good chap."

Dan'l peered out of the wide opening, and could see McKenzie standing there. He lay there and hated McKenzie more than he had ever hated before.

"Ah, you need your bonds cut. How thoughtless of me." He reached in and untied Dan'l's hands.

Dan'l felt circulation flow back into them, but that only made them hurt worse. He moved his stiff arms slowly. His side wound throbbed, but seemed to be healing. He had thought McKenzie had busted a rib in the kicking, but now he figured it was just badly bruised. He could survive, if they let him.

He crawled out of the sack while McKenzie watched, and saw that Quinn had come up behind McKenzie to see what was going on. It took Dan'l several minutes, but finally he was free of the big bag.

"There, now isn't that better?" McKenzie said.

"Now what?" Quinn said.

McKenzie moved over to Dan'l's feet, and cut those bonds too. He ignored Quinn. Over at the fire, the others had turned to watch.

When Dan'l straightened his legs, they gave him fits of pain, but McKenzie just grinned broadly. "I say, isn't this smashing, Quinn?" He unwound the brambles from around Dan'l.

Quinn regarded Dan'l darkly.

"Bring him over to the fire," McKenzie said.

Quinn looked at him. "Me?"

A slow glance by McKenzie was enough of a reply for Quinn. Handling him like a poisonous snake, he helped Dan'l to his feet and toward the fire. Halfway there, Dan'l threw his arm off, and limped the rest of the way on his own. McKenzie and Suggs laughed loudly.

Dan'l looked around like a shot bear and saw their new prisoner, tied to the tree, terrified.

"Good Jesus!" Weeks said, taking a step back, away from Dan'l. Of the five, he was the one who knew the stories about Dan'l and his exploits, and he did not like it that Dan'l was still alive.

McKenzie joined Suggs and Spencer, seated at the fire, and gestured toward an empty stool. "Sit down, hunter, before you fall," he said with a grin.

They all watched Dan'l. He stood there for a moment, looking at their faces, so he would remember them. Then he half-collapsed onto the stool. McKenzie motioned to Quinn, who brought a cup of water to Dan'l. Dan'l knew they were just keeping him alive to make the fun last. He took the cup in both hands and drank, spilling some of it into his beard. It felt good, and gave him strength. Suggs was laughing quietly, but holding his musket lightly across his knees.

"What do you want . . . from me?" Dan'l finally said in a guttural voice. "Why don't you . . . kill me?"

McKenzie leaned toward him. He was just a few feet away. If Dan'l could get to Suggs's musket and wrestle it away from him, he would turn it on McKenzie and blow the Scotsman's face off. But Dan'l did not have the strength to clean the blood from his beard.

"Now let's not talk of killing, my boy. Not now. Weeks here has been telling me all about you. He makes you into some kind of legend, bucko. Do you feel like a legend now?"

Dan'l glared at him.

"I hear you kill bears with your bare hands, and eat wolves for breakfast. Is that right?"

No response.

"Weeks says you practically took Fort Duquesne by yourself. You must be almost bloody invincible, old sport. You'd agree with that, I'll wager?"

"I reckon you could talk a man to death," Dan'l said, "if you didn't have a mind to shoot him."

Spencer laughed at that, until McKenzie scowled at him. Then his face went sober. McKenzie looked back over at Dan'l. "Are you saying I talk too much, then?" McKenzie said nicely.

Dan'l regarded him balefully. His eye was still partially swollen shut. A few brambles were still wound around him, freed from the rope, and his rawhides were decorated with dark patches of blood. His beard was caked with dried blood, and his long hair was thick and wild.

"I'm saying you're . . . so damn low, McKenzie, you'd have to stand on a ladder to kiss a snake."

The tic in McKenzie's cheek jumped so sharply that Weeks saw it fifteen feet away. Suddenly McKenzie was breathing shallowly, and he wore a taut, crazed expression on his scarred face.

"Did you hear that, boys? The great Dan'l Boone has a low opinion of me. Goodness, I'd better mend my ways."

"Let me blow his goddamn head off!" Suggs said fiercely. "And get it over with."

McKenzie was under control again. "No, I'm going to give the hunter a chance to redeem himself, lads."

112

Dan'l looked up at him.

McKenzie drew a knife from his belt, and Dan'l noticed it was his. McKenzie stuck it into the ground at Dan'l's feet. "You see that bleeding wayfarer tied to that tree over there, Boone, my lad? Well, we have to dispose of him, you see."

"Oh, Jesus," the buggy driver mumbled, hearing everything.

Dan'l looked over at the man, and felt sorry for him. There would be a lot of this, if McKenzie were allowed to run free on the frontier.

"You take this knife, your knife, and end his miserable life with it, you see. And I'll release you."

The other prisoner whimpered. Suggs got a big smirk on his evil face. "You're so bloody clever, Captain."

Quinn's face lighted with interest, as did Spencer's, but Weeks stared at McKenzie as if he had lost his senses.

McKenzie looked seriously at Dan'l. "I mean it. When we break camp tomorrow morning, I'll leave you here. If you can survive out here in your condition, why, you're free, man. It's a bloody good deal. A woodsman of your caliber, a legend in his own time," he said with a hard grin. "You'll surely make it."

Dan'l regarded him bleakly.

"All you have to do is take your own knife, and stick it in that fellow's chest."

Weeks shook his head and walked over to the hide wagon. Quinn ran a hand across his mouth, watching. Dan'l took a deep breath. "You back-water scum," he said.

McKenzie's pleasure overcame his momentary anger. He smiled tautly. "Is that a yes?" he said. "It's a damn fine deal."

"You make me want to puke," Dan'l grated out.

McKenzie shook his shaggy head. "You disappoint me," he said quietly. "Really, you do." He grabbed the knife, wiped it clean on his trousers, and walked over to the tied man.

"It's right simple," he said, and he spun and drove the knife into the prisoner to its handle.

The fellow's eyes widened, and he made a few gurgling noises, then fell dead against the ropes. McKenzie turned to Dan'l. "There, you see? You could be a free man now. I'm a man of my word, you know."

Weeks was shaking his head again. He was not at all certain they should have thrown in with this man he now considered slightly insane. Spencer was sober-faced too. Suggs was nodding his thick head in affirmation of McKenzie's black deed, and Quinn was breathing unevenly.

Dan'l rose unsteadily from his seat. "You black-hearted son of a bitch!" he gritted out. He took three steps toward McKenzie, and fell flat onto his face.

He lay there, breathing hard, listening to McKenzie and Suggs laughing at him.

"What a pitiful, lackluster legend," McKenzie said in disdain. "Tie him up again, Suggs. I'll sleep on his fate tonight. Under the stars. Ah, what a life this is, lads!"

Dan'l rolled over onto his back, groaning.

If there was a hell, this must be what it was like.

Chapter Six

Less than a mile away, Billy Two Tongues had just stopped to make camp for the night when he spotted the flickering light in the trees from McKenzie's fire.

Billy had left Boonesborough the morning after Dan'l's departure with Medford, without having any idea where Dan'l was headed. Billy had traveled generally south, with the idea of doing some trapping in the mountains, in the area of the burned-out Fort Stuart. He had no way of knowing it, but his path had taken him more directly toward the outlaws than Dan'l's had, and now he had come to a place where their paths almost intersected.

Billy started to make camp despite knowing that others were encamped nearby. But then he remembered that there could be hostile white hunters out here, or even Shawnee, his mortal enemies, so he decided to go take a look.

He left his dark brown stallion staked out in a small stand of hemlock and went toward the other camp on foot. He was still sore from the gunshot wound, and the sun made his face burn where the scar tissue bunched up on it. His eye was not quite closed on that left side, so he still had good vision. His hair was long and wild-looking, with a beaded band around it. He wore rawhide clothing, but brightly beaded, unlike Dan'l's. His only weapon was a long, thin war knife, similar to the one Suggs carried. His mount's irons did not even have a saddle holster for a long gun.

If Billy's dislike of most white men had been pronounced before Fort Stuart, it amounted to something like hatred now. He had not liked being nursed to health in Boonesborough, and had not even tried to get along with Uriah Latham. He had left Latham's cabin before he was really healed, because he could not stand being tended by a paleface. He had been fluent in English ever since his early, abused years in a frontier settlement, but he refused to speak it to Latham, except when absolutely necessary.

Billy remembered his early childhood, before his parents were killed by Pennsylvania settlers, with a kind of reverence. It seemed to him like a shining past he could not return to, when he played in his village on a stick horse, shook rattles made of dried buffalo scrotums, and watched the shaman pull the guts out of a dead badger to read the reflections in its blood. And listened in fear to a storm while his mother explained to him about the great Thunder Spirit and how it must be appeased.

He could never get that back, he knew, any more than he could make Fort Stuart rise from its ashes and command all those friends and kin to laugh and live again and make his life worth living. They had gone to the Nether World, to join the Old Ones, and Billy knew he should be there with them. If the hunter Boone had not interfered, Billy would be. When Billy came to within a hundred yards of the camp, he could get glimpses of it through the trees. He saw two vehicles, and a string of animals staked out. He got down on all fours, and crawled closer, hugging the ground as a wolf would.

Fifty yards away. Thirty.

He was at the perimeter of the camp, and could hear men talking and moving about. He edged even closer.

Suggs was standing beside the fire, kicking the coals up. Quinn was sitting on a stool across from him, staring into the flames. Spencer was almost asleep on a groundsheet, and Weeks was sitting against the base of a wagon wheel.

Billy's eyes widened slightly when he saw Dan'l, tied to a sapling in a sitting position, looking half-dead. Then he saw the other prisoner, still tied to the other tree, with the knife sticking out of his chest.

Boone, Billy said in his head. He hunkered down, blending with the deep shadows.

"How long is he going to keep this up?" Quinn said to Suggs, referring to McKenzie, who was nowhere in sight.

Suggs hunched his thick shoulders. "It's getting to be a bloody bother. I don't see much point now."

"Maybe he'll die in the night."

"Not if McKenzie keeps watering him like a goddamn rosebush."

"Where did you say he went?"

"He said he was going out to pick up some firewood. I said we'd go, but he bloody *likes* to collect firewood. Used to do it in Scotland as a kid."

"Maybe we could help Boone along," Quinn said with a sly smile. "Take that knife and stick it in him while McKenzie's gone. Say he just died over there." He sneaked a look at Dan'l.

Dan'l was awake and heard everything they were saying. He kept his head down.

"You know what, that's a ruddy good idea, my boy. I'll do it me bloody self. That'll put an end to putting him in that bloody sack and taking him back out and listening to his bleeding insults."

At that moment, out on the perimeter, Billy heard footsteps just behind him in the night. He flattened himself to the ground, freezing like a rabbit, and suddenly a dark figure walked right past him, carrying a load of wood, almost stepping on his left arm. It was McKenzie, and he stopped at the very edge of the clearing when he heard Suggs talking.

Suggs had walked over to the dead prisoner, and was now pulling Dan'l's skinning knife from the man's chest. He turned to Quinn. "I'll just jab it in where it won't show." He grinned, like a truant schoolboy. "Then I'll stick it back in this bloke's chest, where it come from."

McKenzie strode into the clearing and hurled the firewood down. Suggs whirled, a defensive look on his face. Quinn swallowed back sudden fear in his throat.

"What the bloody hell do you think you're about?" McKenzie said in a low, hard voice.

That woke Spencer up, and Weeks was looking over at them now. Dan'l raised his head just slightly. It appeared that McKenzie had arrived back just in time.

"Why . . . we was just going to have some fun with your other prisoner," Suggs said weakly, trying a smile. "Isn't that right, Quinn?"

Quinn turned from McKenzie to Suggs. "Uh. Yeah, that's right."

"You blinking fools!" McKenzie growled at them. "I bloody well heard what you were up to." He walked up to Suggs and grabbed the knife away from him, then caught Suggs's face in his other hand and shoved the tip of the blade up under Suggs's chin.

"Hey, what the hell—"

120

"Did you get the notion that you're suddenly running the show here?"

"Jesus, no!" Suggs sputtered.

Quinn backed up a couple of steps, and Spencer rose to his elbows, over on the other side of the camp. Weeks sat up straighter at the wagon.

Out at the perimeter, in the deep shadows, Billy focused on the man who had almost walked over him a moment ago. *"McKenzie!"* he whispered under his breath, spitting the word out. He had gotten a good look at the British commander before he had been shot at Fort Stuart.

McKenzie broke the skin on Suggs, and a drop of blood wormed its way down his throat. "God-*damn!*" Suggs blurted out.

"Boone is *my* plaything," McKenzie said in an intense, low voice. "Do you quite understand?"

"Yes, for God's sake!" Suggs gasped raggedly.

Quinn was impressed. Suggs was a bigger man than McKenzie, and a tough one. But he was no match for their ex-captain, and Suggs knew it.

McKenzie released him and turned to Quinn, who cowered before him. "I expected better of you, Quinn."

"I suppose we . . . got bored."

McKenzie gave him a sour look. He threw Dan'l's knife into the ground, where it stuck, hilt up. "Tomorrow morning, at *my* pleasure, I'll take care of our hunter. In my way. And I assure you, it will be entertaining."

That was the end of the talking. McKenzie threw some more wood on the fire, and they all settled down for the night. Dan'l watched glumly from the tree they had tied him to, and wondered what McKenzie had in store for him when this night was over. They had bound him so tightly that there was no way he could loosen the bonds and escape in the night. In fact, he was losing feeling in his hands, and they were turning blue. Even if he had been uninjured, he would have had great difficulty trying an escape. But at that moment, he was as weak as a cougar kitten, and in constant pain.

Out in the tree line, Billy lay on his belly and allowed a hatred to build inside him for Jock McKenzie. He had had no plans to go after the men who had burned his people out, but now here he was, unexpectedly confronting them. And they were about to kill the man who had been sent to bring them to justice. A man who inspired dislike in Billy, even though Dan'l had helped give his people a new home, but nevertheless a man who had saved Billy's life.

Billy lay there in the blackness. They were all down now, including McKenzie, except for Weeks, who had fallen asleep sitting up against the wagon wheel. McKenzie had not put anybody on sentry duty, or to guard Dan'l. He was a very confident killer.

Billy took a deep breath, and made a big decision. His heart was not in trapping at this time, anyway. He would devote some time to McKenzie.

McKenzie was snoring lightly. Billy could

sneak into their camp and just slit his throat. But there would be noise, and he would probably be caught and killed, along with Dan'l Boone. Or he could do the smart thing. With Dan'l on the perimeter of their camp, it would be less dangerous to go cut him loose and take him away while they slept. Then, maybe later, they could work together to get them all. It was a distasteful thought to consider riding with the hunter, but he had obviously lost the sergeant Medford, and it would require at least two to bring this bunch down.

Suggs was snoring too now, and everybody seemed to be asleep. The fire had almost guttered out, and the horses were quiet on the far side of camp.

Billy began a slow, inch-by-inch crawl around the perimeter of the clearing, until he reached a point close behind Dan'l's tree. Dan'l appeared to be asleep too. The hide wagon was just a few feet away, and he saw Dan'l's and Medford's guns hanging on the back of it, in a sling. He reached forward and touched Dan'l's shoulder.

Dan'l jumped slightly and grunted. "It is me. Billy Two Tongues."

Dan'l could not turn far enough to see him. He lct that information sink in. "What?" he mumbled. He was half-conscious.

"Shhh! Do not speak!" Billy said in a fierce whisper.

Billy saw McKenzie roll over onto his side. He waited for several minutes. Not far away, Weeks was slumped heavily against the wagon wheel. Billy worked on the knot that held Dan'l to the trunk until it finally came loose. Then he unwound the binding.

Dan'l leaned forward, and watched Billy come around to face him. Billy touched his finger to his lips, and the scarred side of his face glowed ugly in the low firelight. He slowly inched the knot loose at Dan'l's wrists. Dan'l rubbed the circulation back and winced in renewed pain. Then he helped Billy untie his ankles.

When Dan'l was completely free, Billy looked across the camp. Spencer was snoring quietly, and Quinn mumbled something and went back to breathing hard.

Billy crawled to the wagon, took the two guns out of their cradle, and crawled back to Dan'l. Motioning with his head, he assisted Dan'l up with his free hand, and helped him stumble away with him into the trees.

Ten yards, then thirty. Dan'l tripped and collapsed. Billy pulled him up and threw Dan'l's arm around his shoulder, still keeping the guns in his left hand.

One of the camp horses neighed softly, but nobody woke. Billy could still see Weeks as he adjusted his position on the wagon and slept on.

Billy continued dragging Dan'l through the woods until they were well out of sight of the camp.

Chapter Seven

"Now your medicine and mine are the same," Billy said.

Dan'l was slumped behind Billy on his stallion, hanging onto his waist. They had ridden all night, off and on, into the mountains, stopping only to give Dan'l brief rests. Now they were high in the rocky area of the Appalachians, and new light was burgeoning in the east, giving the sky a dull, rosy hue.

"I have prevented your journeying to your ancestors, as you earlier deprived me. You may curse me now, as I curse you."

Dan'l was in no shape to argue. He grunted softly.

"Now we must both do some very courageous thing, in order to die with honor. It is so written."

"I have to . . . go back and kill McKenzie," Dan'l mumbled.

Billy sighed. "You will go where I take you. You nursed me back to health after Fort Stuart. Now I must heal you. We ride to a small village of Algonquin, up high in the mountains. They are hostile toward all whites, after Fort Stuart. But I think they will receive us. They will make you well."

"I . . . don't have time for that," Dan'l said, wincing when he moved.

Billy scowled. "Be silent, or I will feed you to the turkey vultures!" He kicked his mount in the ribs, and rode off into higher terrain, toward the small village he knew was up there, hidden away from the white man's eyes. He could see this hunter was going to be difficult. Perhaps even more difficult than he himself had been at Boonesborough. But it was imperative now to Billy that he make Dan'l well.

Dan'l had no strength to protest further. They rode all that morning, through pines and cedar and patches of snow, with Dan'l falling asleep regularly and almost falling off the horse.

In late morning, they arrived at the tiny village.

A couple of fur-clad children ran out to meet them first as they entered the village with its tipis and wickiups. Soon dogs came barking, and women stared openly. Finally the men emerged from the dwellings, and eyed Billy with hostility. None carried weapons.

Dan'l was conscious. He looked around

numbly, and saw the decorated tipis. The people wore soft buckskin clothing, and some heavy cloth. There was a small corral at the rear, with a few scrawny horses in it. Older boys carried half-size spears, with quivers of arrows on their backs. Women sat out in the open, by low fires, sewing or kneading dough. The fires were fueled with buffalo dung and kindling. One woman was combing her black hair with a porcupine-tail hairbrush. She stopped brushing and spat toward Billy and Dan'l.

Billy rode right up to the large, communal tipi, with several young men following alongside his mount, eyeing warily the long guns Billy had tied at the back of his saddle.

When they stopped in front of the big tent, a young man went inside to announce their arrival, and in a moment a large, well-built warrior came out, looking very fierce and somber. Behind him emerged an older fellow, wearing a chest shield of hide and beads and a headdress of osprey feathers that he had obviously just donned for this meeting. Beside him came a middle-aged fellow wearing deer horns and a brightly colored cloth skirt-blanket around his hips. Billy figured these last two to be the shaman and the chief.

Billy raised his hand in greeting and spoke in Algonquin. "Peace, brothers. I come to you for help."

The young man who had announced their arrival frowned. "Help! You bring a white face here and ask for help?"

The big warrior concurred. "We do not allow these palefaces in our midst. You insult us with his presence."

"Wait," the chief said quietly. "This white man looks familiar."

"He is the great hunter Boone," Billy told them. "He brought our people to Fort Stuart."

"Ah," the chief said. "Yes."

"Then he got them killed," the warrior said evenly.

Billy nodded. "Yes, but it was not his fault. A renegade English massacred our people at Stuart. I was there. I am Billy Two Tongues."

The warrior grunted. "The half-white. He speaks with the snake's tongue of the white face."

Billy cast a somber look at him. "I am true Algonquin and no friend of the white man. But this man saved my life at Stuart, and he hunts the evil English."

Dan'l, coming around from half-consciousness, heard the last exchanges. "Get me out of here," he said weakly to Billy in English.

The chief came and looked Dan'l over.

"The English did this to him," Billy said.

The chief nodded. "I am Gray Fox. Welcome to our village." The big warrior gave the chief a hard look, which he ignored. "Take him to this tipi over here."

Billy rode over to the rather small tipi the chief had pointed to, dismounted, and took Dan'l off the horse.

"They don't . . . want us," Dan'l was mumbling.

128

"Silence!" Billy told him, exasperated. He dragged Dan'l into the tent, and laid him down on a soft pallet, then covered him with a blanket.

Chief Gray Fox looked in. "We will tend him," he said. Soon Billy was settled into another tipi, and women came to bathe Dan'l's wounds and force some watery soup down him. Slowly, hour by hour, he got better. The swelling started going out of his nose and face, and the bruises in his back and chest did not hurt so much. The gunshot wound received a poultice.

They were amazed at his recovery. By supper time he was eating solid food, and in early evening he was sitting up and demanding they send Billy to him. Billy came, but only briefly.

"We are safe here, and you will be aided in your healing," he told Dan'l. "Then we will move on."

"We?"

"We will talk on it later."

Dan'l got a long, restful sleep that night, and the next morning he was ravenous. They could not bring him enough food. He had two bowls of a corn mush, and they fed him several pounds of venison when he requested it. He washed it all down with some hard liquor the women sneaked in to him. They liked him immediately because he could speak to them in their own language, and they tried to fulfill his every wish.

On the afternoon of that first full day, Dan'l and Billy were invited to a palaver in the communal tipi.

Dan'l could walk, but still limped on a badly

bruised thigh where McKenzie had kicked him so hard he had almost broken bone. He and Billy were received by Chief Gray Fox, the shaman—whose name was Running Wolf, and the warrior who had been so hostile to them, who was a son of Gray Fox and whose name in English was Big Cedar. They all sat around a small groundsheet of bear fur, where the shaman had cast small bones and pebbles before their arrival, to learn more about the strangers. The material was still lying there, as an open reminder that they *were* strangers. The shaman looked hostile.

Neither Dan'l nor Billy spoke. In a palaver with a chief, it was impolite for a guest to speak first. The shaman was without a headdress this time, but had painted his face in bright stripes of red and yellow, and had draped a wolfskin over his narrow shoulders. He lighted a long warrior's pipe that he had just tamped with a quilled stick. The pipe was red-dyed walnut, with a carved wolf effigy for a bowl and two eagle feathers dangling from its stem. He sucked on the pipe and got it going while everybody sat and waited. Finally, he handed it to Gray Fox, who smoked it briefly, then handed it to his son. He did likewise, and only then was it passed to Billy.

Billy nodded and took a couple puffs on the pipe, then handed it to Dan'l. Dan'l was accustomed to all this because he had palavered with Cherokee, Shawnee, and Algonquin on previous occasions. He took a long drag on the pipe and handed it back to Gray Fox, which was considered proper protocol.

Also on the bearskin was a cooking paunch made from a buffalo stomach, which contained goat's testicles, cooked brown. Gray Fox took one and offered the paunch to his guests. Billy and Dan'l each took one, and ate them slowly, then made a show of enjoyment, even though Dan'l had no taste for them whatever.

Finally, Gray Fox spoke.

"You were at Fort Stuart?" he asked Billy in Algonquin.

"Yes. I was the only survivor."

Dan'l let his glance drift around the interior of the tipi. There were bench-type shelves on the ground around the perimeter. On them sat a highly decorated ceremonial drum with deer painted on its sides, a finely woven water bottle dyed several bright colors . . . and three human skulls that looked a thousand years old. Dan'l remembered that the Algonquin were one of the "barbarous" tribes that used to kill all captured enemies and eat them. Only three tribes of Indians had ever been known to practice cannibalism.

Gray Fox and Billy were talking about the horror at Fort Stuart. Billy had just told Gray Fox how McKenzie had shot anyone trying to escape the holocaust. Even women and children.

Gray Fox looked very sad. "We had heard this, but did not want to believe it was that bad."

"May I speak, Great Chief?" Dan'l finally asked.

Gray Fox nodded. "Of course."

"The man who did these things has lost his command and is dishonored in the eyes of his people, and also we who live among you. He will be punished. It is just a matter of time."

"You go to kill him?" Gray Fox asked.

Because his Algonquin speech was not as fluent as his Cherokee or Shawnee, Dan'l used his hands freely to supplement the spoken word with the universal sign language.

"My charge is to bring him to the white man's court, where he will be tried and hanged," Dan'l said. "But I suspect it will come to killing."

Gray Fox nodded. "Since Billy Two Tongues now has no clan of his own, we have made him one of us."

Dan'l looked over at Billy, who smiled slightly.

"Billy wishes to accompany you on your mission," Gray Fox went on. "And we concur in that wish. There are five of them. For one man it is too dangerous. You have lost a partner. Billy can replace him."

Dan'l gave Billy another hard look. "Billy has cast an evil eye on me," Dan'l said, touching his face under his right eye. "Because I prevented his honorable death."

"That medicine has been cast out of him," Gray Fox explained, "in his bringing you here. We ask you, in the name of friendship, to take Billy with you in your long hunt for these evil persons."

Billy turned to Dan'l. In English he said, "Also,

I ask you. It would do me honor, Sheltowee, to ride with you."

Dan'l thought for a long moment, then nodded. "I have never ridden with a red face. But I have fought beside them and against them in the war with the French. The ones I knew always fought bravely and well. I will take Billy, and we will be partners."

Gray Fox smiled. "The Great Spirit will be pleased."

He took up the pipe again and puffed on it once more, signaling that the meeting was over.

Dan'l tried to stay off his back for most of that day, and his incredible healing powers were making him well fast. But in late afternoon he received unexpected help.

The shaman, Running Wolf, was a hater of all white men, and Dan'l had sensed that in the palaver with Gray Fox. But Gray Fox had ordered him to work some magic on Dan'l, and in late afternoon Running Wolf came in to follow those orders, if reluctantly. Scowling all the while, he did a dance over Dan'l, shaking rattles and rubbing a healing stone over his wounds and bruises, the latter in the shape of a shoveler duck. There was a lot of high-pitched chanting, and the waving around of bangles and fetishes.

Dan'l wondered if the belligerent shaman had not thrown in a couple of curses, to balance out any good accomplished by the ritual. But at any rate, the next morning he was greatly improved.

The day after that, he surprised everybody by

announcing that he wanted to leave. He was still hurting in places, and he did not really have his strength back, but he was eager to head out and look for McKenzie's trail before it got cold.

"You are not healed," Billy told him. "Gray Fox will be disappointed if you leave like this."

"I'll heal on the trail," Dan'l said to him. "You fix it with Gray Fox. If you're coming, be ready after breakfast."

They left just a half hour after the morning meal. The chief gave Dan'l a roan mare, and also two saddle boots for the long guns Billy had retrieved, so Dan'l rode out with his favorite rifle on his mount's irons.

Late in the day, after hard riding that weakened Dan'l some, they found the camp where Billy had come upon McKenzie and Dan'l. They spent almost an hour looking things over, examining the ashes from the fire, inspecting bits of dropped food, measuring the freshness of the animal tracks. They concluded that the gang had left there only that morning, after making thorough reconnaissance forays out from camp to try to locate the escapees. They had changed direction and were headed north now, apparently concerned about running into trouble if they went west after Dan'l and his rescuer. McKenzie knew that he had to avoid Algonquin villages because of what he had done at Fort Stuart.

It was just like before for Dan'l, following McKenzie's trail again, getting off his mount and circling for spoor, just as he and Medford had done. As dusk fell, Billy suggested the same thing Medford had.

"We can go on for a while, if you are strong enough. They have eight hours start on us," he said in English.

"No, the light's almost gone," Dan'l told him. "I ain't going to get bushwhacked twice by that same son of a bitch. We'll take it up again tomorrow at dawn."

"Just as you say, Sheltowee."

The fact was, there was not an Indian on the frontier who would question Dan'l in matters of hunting and tracking. He was the acknowledged expert's expert, and that was why he harbored such guilt about Medford. It was not up to Medford to know when to quit. The responsibility had been Dan'l's, and he had allowed thoughts of home to mar his judgment.

Even though Billy was fluent in Dan'l's native tongue, he was not a talker. He sat across the fire from Dan'l that evening, ate his dried beef, and said little. Also, he was still diffident toward Dan'l. He treated him more like a business partner than a friend, a man to get a job done with, and nothing more.

Dan'l did not mind. He was comfortable with Billy. He liked men of few words, and he liked Billy's contrariness. It was unusual for an Indian to act that way with a white man, and Dan'l valued it for its rarity. They had sat silent most of the evening before Dan'l finally spoke to the Algonquin.

"Why'd you save my life?" he said. "If Mc-Kenzie'd caught you, he'd've skun you alive."

Billy held his peace for a long moment. "Maybe I wished to do what you had done to me," he said soberly. "Because of you, I walk around in this world where I should not be, with this face people do not want to look upon."

"Hell, that?" Dan'l said. "Damn, even now you're prettier than most white men I know."

Billy hesitated, then let a brief smile move his mouth.

"The stories I heard are true. You are a strange person, Boone."

Dan'l grinned through the dark beard and adjusted the wide-brimmed, Quaker hat on his head. "Most of what you hear about me is horse pucky. The good and the bad. I never wrestled no bear to death, and I didn't kill no two dozen Shawnee with a rifle butt. That's all swamp fog."

Billy snorted. "I was hoping the one about the Shawnee was true," he said. The Shawnee had been deadly enemies of the Algonquin since the Algonquin had moved south and west.

Dan'l nodded. "Oh, I killed my share, all right. There wasn't many left at Fort Duquesne that second time there. But I never enjoyed it, like some fellows. White or red, I'd a lot rather talk it over than spill some blood."

Billy studied Dan'l's rugged, square face. "You are a hard man to know, Boone."

"Most of us is, ain't we?" Dan'l said.

Billy picked up a stick and poked at their low fire.

"What about McKenzie? Would you rather talk with him?"

Dan'l's face grew somber. "Oh, I told him. He knows there won't be no more talking. Not now. He had his time for talking. I reckon it'll be him or me, if we face down again."

"I can't wait," Billy said grimly.

The next morning they picked up McKenzie's trail with relative ease, and followed it all through the early part of the day. The trail led through rolling hills, up toward Kentucky, and now Dan'l was closer to home than when he had been captured by McKenzie. They found themselves on the Boone Trail, named after Dan'l and his brother Squire for treks they had made leading settlers into the Shawnee territory. But then the McKenzie gang's trail headed west, through a low pass in the mountains. By early afternoon, Dan'l and Billy were west of the high country, and coming out into undulating hills and more open country.

The trail disappeared for a while through rocks, but they picked it up again on a grassy plateau. Like Medford before him, Billy marveled at Dan'l's uncanny ability to follow a trail where there was no evidence of its existence, at least none an ordinary man could see.

They had run low on the food sent with them by Gray Fox, and Dan'l knew they would have to shoot some game soon. With that in mind, Dan'l was glad when they came upon a small herd of buffalo.

Even though there were only a couple dozen animals in the herd, they were big, healthy bison, and Dan'l decided they should shoot a couple for their meat.

Billy had no experience at all with buffalo, but had heard that the Shawnee hunted them on horseback, riding in among the animals and shooting them at close range, on the run. He was surprised, therefore, to see Dan'l dismount a hundred yards from the herd, downwind.

"Get your musket," Dan'l told him as he staked his mare to the hard ground. "We'll take them from that dead log up here."

"You will not ride in on them?"

Dan'l shook his shaggy head. "No, this way works best with a good gun. Just do what I do."

Billy nodded and followed Dan'l to the log. They went on their hands and knees, so as not to spook the animals. Dan'l noticed that the spring grass had not come up yet, and they were crawling over dead, dry fall grass which was what the buffalo were grazing on.

A sharp, dry wind had risen, and was blowing right toward them, over the backs of the buffalo. A big bull turned and looked directly at them, but did not seem to see them. Dan'l could see moisture glistening on his nostrils, and spring flies buzzing on his coat.

"I'll take that big bull closest to us," he told

Billy. "See if you can bring down that cow beside him. When you hear my gun go off, fire as quick as you can."

Billy acknowledged, and Dan'l aimed. He saw something in the trees beyond the meadow that looked like a small dark cloud approaching. He focused his attention on the bull buffalo, and squeezed the trigger of his Ticklicker.

There was a loud explosion, and the buffalo fell like a stone, hit through the heart. Billy fired too, and the cow yelled and went down beside the bull, kicked for a moment, and was dead.

"Nice shooting," Dan'l said. "Now let's—"

But the small herd, which had only looked on nervously when the two kills were made, were suddenly snorting and pawing, and as Dan'l rose to his feet to have a better look, they began running toward the two men, who were now in the path of a stampede.

"Down!" Dan'l yelled. "Get down!"

They both lay flat against the big log, and in seconds the buffalo were all around them, thundering past, jumping the log and running around it, hooves kicking, eyes fixed in panic. Billy felt unreasoning fear climb into his chest, and he started to get up to run. Dan'l turned.

"Stay down!" He threw himself on top of Billy, knocking him to the ground just as a big bull jumped the log and missed them both by inches, one of its hooves thumping Dan'l in the leg as it passed. It was a wild, tumultuous melee, dust rising around them, hooves flailing, the smell of the pelts in their noses.

Just as suddenly the buffalo were gone.

The ground still shook under the two men, but the buffalo were already on their way out of sight. Dan'l looked, and saw that their mounts had pulled up stakes and were gone too. Then he turned back toward where they had run from.

"Oh, hell," he said bleakly.

Billy looked, and his face grew ashen. The black cloud was bigger now, and Dan'l could see the tips of the flames licking at the trees as the whole thing moved into the dry-grass clearing.

It was a wildfire. Unusual in the spring, but very deadly.

"We must run!" Billy said loudly, remembering the awful fire at Fort Stuart, when he had thought he would be consumed by the raging flames.

"No, we can't outrun it." Dan'l said. "Come on! The buffalo! They're our only chance."

"What?"

"Follow me!"

Dan'l scraped some dirt out from under the log and jammed his rifle into the pocket there. Then he yanked Billy's musket from him and did the same with it. In the next moment, he was running right at the fire.

Billy stood there, thinking the great hunter had gone crazy. But then he reluctantly ran out onto the meadow after him.

"What are you doing?" he yelled.

They could hear the crackling roar of the big fire as it rolled toward them three hundred yards away. The smoke from it was already in their eyes and nostrils.

Dan'l ran to his dead bull. Both shot animals were on their sides, legs sticking straight out. Dan'l grabbed a long knife from a belt sheath, one of two that had been given to them by Gray Fox, shoved it into the chest of the bull, and ripped it open from breastbone to testicles, along its belly.

"Open yours up too! Empty it out and get in!"

Billy watched for just a moment, as Dan'l reached into the insides of the buffalo and began yanking intestines out. Billy slit his animal open too, and followed suit.

Dan'l worked feverishly, pulling entrails out, his hands and arms bloody and sticky to the elbow, crimson smeared on his clothing. The fire was a hundred yards away now, and moving swiftly. He choked in the smoke of it, gasping for breath, and could hear Billy coughing, near him.

The fire was fifty yards away.

"Get inside! Bury yourself in it!" he cried out, hardly able to see Billy through the smoke.

He pried the big ribs apart, and thrust himself headlong into the chest cavity. Billy was doing the same thing fifteen feet away. Dan'l brought his legs in behind him, and let the opening close up. Then the fire was there, roaring over them.

It was awful. The flames licked at the two animals, burning their coats off and cooking their meat. Inside the bull, Dan'l felt as if he were inside a furnace. His face and hands burned as if the fire were inside the cavity, and his clothing smoldered as the moisture of the buffalo was sucked away, along with all breathable air. Finally there was no oxygen at all inside the animal, and Dan'l just lay there holding his breath, cramped and singed.

After five minutes of that, everything changed. The fire had passed over, burning the grass off the meadow, and now it was continuing into the trees, taking everything in its path.

Dan'l gasped and coughed raggedly. He had to breathe. He pried open the rib cage of the animal, stuck his head out, and sucked in great lungfuls of smoky air, coughing and choking. A moment later he saw Billy doing the same thing.

Dan'l pushed himself out of the cavity, and rolled onto the charred ground. He was covered with blood and slime from head to foot, and the hair on his left arm was singed, along with his trousers. His face felt sunburned, and he saw that his hands had turned a reddish color.

But he was alive.

He looked over toward Billy, who looked very much like him. "Are you—all right?" he croaked out hoarsely.

Billy sat up, coughing. "Yes."

Dan'l looked around them. All was burned and charred for as far as the eye could see. Trees, grass, shrubs. To the east, the fire was still sending black smoke skyward, as it burned itself out.

Billy struggled to his feet, and looked himself over. He was a bloody, sticky mess. Dan'l sat up, looked at him, and laughed out loud. "I never rode with nobody that looked like that."

Billy glowered. "Nor I." Then he laughed softly too.

Dan'l stood up and looked down at his clothing as Billy came over to him and said, "Now I believe all the stories."

Dan'l looked at him, and tried a weak smile.

"I would be honored," Billy said solemnly, "if you would be my friend, Sheltowee."

Dan'l grunted. "Hell," he said.

"I know now it was not my time at Fort Stuart. It was not my time today. Men like Sheltowee make time bend to their wishes. It has always been so."

Dan'l smiled and clapped Billy on the shoulder. "Come on, my friend. We got some cleaning up to do."

Chapter Eight

Billy Two Tongues was like a different person after the wildfire. He talked to Dan'l without letup, was open in his behavior, and treated Dan'l like a long-lost brother.

Dan'l was shocked by the change, but rather liked it. Billy had become a very likeable partner.

Billy talked all the way to the creek where they washed their bodies and clothing that warm spring day of the fire, telling Dan'l in great detail how he had almost suffocated in the bowels of the cow buffalo, asking Dan'l what it had been like for him, and praising Dan'l for knowing just what to do to survive.

They had to strip down naked to let their clothes partially dry before putting them back on, and Billy finally fell silent, embarrassed by his own nudity. But he could not help stealing looks at Dan'l's powerful frame as Dan'l sat on a rock and combed out his hair and beard. Billy had never seen a white man unclothed, even when living with whites as a boy, and he found he was fascinated by all that pale skin.

Next the guns had to be cleaned too, and Dan'l realized how lucky they had been that their black powder had not ignited when the fire passed over them. After they were dressed again and ready to take up the hunt, their next job was to track the horses down. That took most of the rest of the day. The animals had stayed together, and had run a big circle around the end of the fire, and then headed back the same way they had come. After walking for most of ten miles, Dan'l and Billy found them grazing quietly together at the edge of the plateau, where the fire had not reached. The animals shied away from them at first, but then came to them.

"We lost a half day on McKenzie," Dan'l complained when they were moving again. "It would be real nice if something went right one of these days." He was frustrated, pulled in two directions inside, because of Rebecca's pregnancy. But he knew now that he could not give up on McKenzie until they had caught him. No matter how long that took.

In late afternoon, at the crest of a grassy hill, Dan'l reined up and made a gesture to Billy to stop. Then he pointed down into the valley some distance ahead, where vultures circled over some black objects.

"What is it?" Billy wondered.

"Looks like a military bivouac," Dan'l said, shielding his eyes from the warm sun. "But something's awful wrong. Let's get a closer look."

They rode on down into the lush valley. They were on the southern fringe of the Kentucky territory of Virginia, and Dan'l's home now lay almost directly north of them. They were getting into Shawnee country, but Dan'l knew there was one more large settlement of displaced Algonquin a half day's ride to the west, Indians who had moved out of Pennsylvania and New York, like their Fort Stuart cousins, because of the encroachment of the white settler into their territory. A chief named Rain Cloud had led them there.

As Dan'l descended into the valley, he wondered if those Indians, or their Shawnee counterparts, had caused this trouble that he now saw before him. There were two burned wagons and several shot horses, and now they could clearly see dead men lying all over the area.

"Oh, hell," Dan'l said as they rode closer.

There were thirty men on the ground, all looking very dead, all in blue uniforms. A regimental flag lay torn on the ground, a flag Dan'l had never seen before. Wispy, white smoke still rose from the wagons. Several of the dead men had arrows sticking out of them, and a war lance was stuck into the ground in the middle of it all.

Three vultures flapped away at their approach.

"This looks bad, Sheltowee," Billy said. "The lance is Algonquin."

They dismounted, looking around at the high ground on the hills, making sure the Indians were gone. Dan'l walked through the fallen figures slowly. There was a lot of blood.

"Damn!" he muttered as he walked.

Billy went to examine one of the turned-over wagons. It was just charred remains, and again he was reminded of the holocaust at Stuart. His hand went unconsciously to his scarred face.

He heard a moaning sound from the other side of the wagon.

He quickly walked around it, and saw a man lying there. He had captain's insignia on his uniform. He was sooty and dirty, and had been shot in the chest and the head. His eyelids fluttered open and he saw Billy.

"No!" he cried.

Billy turned toward Dan'l. "Here! Over here!"

Dan'l hurried over, and saw that the captain was alive and eyeing Billy warily. He knelt over the officer.

"It's all right. He's my friend. What happened here?"

The captain licked dry lips. Blood was caked on the side of his head, and on his blue uniform. "The Algonquins. Chief Rain Cloud's people. They were at least two hundred."

The effort shortened his breath. Dan'l waited a moment.

"Your uniform. I don't recognize them insignia."

The captain grinned weakly. "That's because . . . you haven't seen a Continental Army unit yet."

Dan'l understood. "Did George Washington take command?"

The captain nodded. "Yes. Sent us out here . . . to make a treaty with the Shawnee and Algonquin. Looks like Gage got to them first."

Dan'l remembered fighting beside Washington at Fort Duquesne, the several long conversations they had had about the Britons, and how Washington would never fight with them again because he had been disillusioned with the Crown.

"You mean Rain Cloud's sided with the Brits?" Dan'l said.

The captain nodded. "There was a redcoat officer with them. Gage warned us to disband these army units or he'd attack them. I guess he kept his promise. Or Rain Cloud did, for him."

"This is a sad day," Billy said, rather to himself.

"How the hell could he do that?" Dan'l asked. "After what happened at Fort Stuart?"

The captain grinned a harsh grin and coughed. A worm of blood appeared at the corner of his mouth. "Oh, you didn't know? He thinks colonial militia did that."

"What!" Dan'l said, anger flashing in his blue eyes.

"Some English trapper is spreading the story through these parts. He met a war party and told

148

Rain Cloud's son that Carolina militia burned Fort Stuart. Led by the trapper Dan'l Boone."

Dan'l's face tightened in hot anger.

"The story was taken to Rain Cloud, and he believed it. He says now that he'll drive all settlers out of the area. Might even join up with his old enemies, the Shawnee."

Dan'l turned to Billy. "It's that son of a bitch McKenzie!"

Billy nodded. "Yes."

Dan'l turned back to the captain. "I'm Dan'l Boone."

The captain squinted at him. "I'll be damned."

"It waren't me and no Carolina militia at Stuart."

The captain's face was white from the effort of speaking. "We know that. We heard it was some renegade British officer."

"The son of a bitch caused this, Captain. Him and him only," Dan'l said.

The captain shook his head and coughed again. "I . . . can't see you. What's happening . . . to me?"

Dan'l sighed heavily. "Lay quiet, Captain."

"You have to . . . stop him, Boone. He's causing more trouble . . . than most people will ever know."

"We know," Dan'l told him. He realized that Boonesborough itself was well within Rain Cloud's striking range. "Just don't talk no more. We'll try to get you to—"

But in that very moment, the captain jumped

visibly on the ground, gagged on some blood that came up into his throat, and died.

Dan'l reached down and felt for a pulse. He looked over at Billy. "He's gone," he said.

Billy was somber. "This is a bad day for the Algonquin nation," he said heavily. "Rain Cloud was always a hothead. Now he has been deluded by a silver-tongued killer."

"I wonder if he took McKenzie in," Dan'l said. "The trail is leading in that direction."

Billy shook his head. "No. Rain Cloud has never allowed a white man into one of his villages. He has the belief that the spirits would be offended."

Dan'l stood up, and Billy did too. "Let's get moving, Billy. We got a lot of ground to cover, and things is getting worse every minute."

"I am with you, Sheltowee."

"It looks like McKenzie's headed through Logan's Station," Dan'l said, looking down again at the dead captain. "We'll report this there, and ask for somebody to come out here and take these bodies back. Let's go."

They left that scene of death and mayhem soberly. McKenzie was becoming even more of a problem than Dan'l had anticipated.

They had to do something about him.

And time was running short.

It was just three hours later that they rode into Logan's Station.

The settlement was like several recently built

ones that had no stockade wall for protection. The more settlers that came into Kentucky and Tennessee, the less concerned they all were about Indian attacks. The Shawnee had mostly moved west in recent years, and there was almost never any serious threat from them. The resettled Algonquin had caused nobody any trouble, until this attack on the military. And the irony was that Rain Cloud did not even know he was attacking the military force of a new and emerging nation. The Brits had told him the small unit was of a weakened Carolina militia, and that there would be no repercussions in the eastern cities.

Logan's Station was a bustling small town, about the size of Boonesborough, and was growing every year. Dan'l had been there on many other occasions, and had personally known the explorer and guide the town was named for. Like Dan'l and John Findley, he was one of the frontier's renowned pioneers.

Dan'l and Billy rode in just before dusk. There was still a central square, as in the fortified towns, but there were also several side streets going off in all directions, with hundreds of residences built on them. On the central square were two trading posts, a general store, an inn with a drinking establishment on the first floor, a livery stable, and a couple of public buildings. There was no military garrison, and that was causing some concern at the moment.

As they rode in, several men and women on the streets gave Billy a long look, knowing he was

Algonquin. Billy tried to ignore the looks, but there was a lot of hostility in them. Dan'l and Billy went right to the town constable, on the far side of the square, and entered his whitewashed office together.

The constable looked up from a scarred oak desk, and his eyes narrowed when he saw Billy.

"Well, what the hell is this?"

Dan'l kept his poise. "Evening, Constable. I'm Dan'l Boone, and this here is my friend, Billy Two Tongues."

The constable looked him over. He barely knew Dan'l's name, since he was a recent emigrant west from New England. "Boone, huh? Ain't you the one they named that town after, north of here?"

Dan'l nodded. "The same."

"Well, you sound like a man of substance, Mr. Boone. I have to wonder why you think you can bring an Indian into this office."

Dan'l's face settled into hard lines. Occasionally one individual would forcefully remind him why he liked to spend so much time in the woods and away from people.

"I come here on business," he said with strained patience. "We want to report a massacre out at Walnut Hills, south of here, in the valley. A military unit was attacked by Algonquin. Thought you might want to talk to both of us."

The constable rose from behind the desk. He was a thickset man with a slight potbelly and balding hair. He wore a heavy-looking one-shot pistol on his belt, and had a star-shaped badge on his vest.

"I don't think I made myself clear, Boone. Get this redskin outside, and then you and me will talk."

Billy was becoming uncomfortable. "I'll leave, Dan'l. I can meet you at the public house."

But Dan'l was not listening. He walked over to the constable, reached for the man's face, and hurled him against the nearby wall.

The constable almost lost his balance, and barely kept from falling to the floor. Now Dan'l moved closer, looking bearlike to the other man.

"Are you some kind of goddamn pea-brain, mister?" he growled in a deep voice. "We're here to help you. Can't you act like a decent human being till we leave?"

The constable stumbled away from him, fear marring his face. "What the hell!" He fumbled for his gun, drew it, cocked it, and aimed it at Dan'l's chest. "You're under arrest, damn you!"

Dan'l shook his head slowly, and looked over at Billy. "You are something mister. Who the hell pinned that badge on you, some asylum lunatic?"

"You keep on, by God, and you'll be eating lead!" the other man said tensely.

Dan'l walked closer again, and the constable backed up a step, not even knowing he was doing it.

"There's a whole platoon of new federal infantry out there, laying dead in the weeds," Dan'l said. "They got to be buried, even if you ain't interested in details."

The constable held the gun on him. "We know about the attack. We ain't got no personnel to go gallivanting around burying the military. They can wait for the Army."

Dan'l narrowed his eyes. "What kind of man are you, anyway? Ain't you got no sense of decency atall?"

"I know better than to bring a bloodthirsty red man into a town with civilized folks," the constable said evenly. "There's innocent women and children here, by God. And maybe you didn't know it, but this devil's people killed them soldiers in the valley."

Billy decided to speak up. "I am Algonquin. But I am not of Rain Cloud's village. I was at Fort Stuart."

"Goddamn! He talks better English than us!"

Dan'l sighed. "If your brain was gunpowder, you couldn't blow the top of your own head off."

The constable's face flushed. "I don't know what you're up to, Boone. But you better just cool your heels in my jail till I figure it all out. And I'll just turn your Indian friend over to the locals to do what they want with him."

"If you fire that thing," Dan'l said in a low, brittle voice, "you better kill me with the first shot, mister. Cause if'n you don't, I'm going to cut your liver out and have it for breakfast tomorrow." He slowly removed the war knife from the belt that

Gray Fox had given him. Billy did likewise with his own knife.

The constable eyed the knives and their razor edges, and swallowed hard. He stood there, not knowing what to do.

"Well," he finally said weakly, "I won't throw you into a cell. But I want you out of here early tomorrow. Or I'll round up some boys and come after you."

Dan'l shoved the knife back into a beaded leather sheath. "I guess you ain't hickory-stump dumb after all, Constable. Thanks for your hospitality." He turned to Billy, who opened the door to the street.

The constable called after them as they left, "You better keep that Indian out of sight, though!"

It was a short walk down the street to the Frontier Inn, where they hitched their mounts outside. They had decided not to stay the night, but would have some food and drinks and inquire about McKenzie, and then ride on out to make hardship camp out under the stars.

They climbed three steps and entered through a door with real iron hinges. The sign hung at the side of the entrance read: "STOUT AND ALE, One Shilling a Glass."

Inside, they found the usual drinking establishment, very similar to the one McKenzie had raised hell in when he met Spencer and Weeks. There was a long counter with two barkeeps behind it, and a dozen tables where customers were served. A forest tapestry imported from England hung on the wall behind the counter, showing deer and green trees. A small stately castle could be seen in the background, standing behind the trees. On a rear wall was a dart board, and a cracker barrel stood on a wall to their left. There were two tables of customers who were drinking ale and talking quietly among themselves.

Dan'l and Billy walked to a table fairly near the entrance and sat down. Immediately, all eyes turned to them.

Billy could have dressed more like Dan'l and not attracted so much attention, but he felt it was beneath his dignity to try to impersonate a white man. His hair hung wild to his shoulders, and he wore a band of beaded deerskin across his forehead. His rawhide shirt was delicately worked with beads and paint, and he wore moccasins below his rawhide trousers. From his belt hung the long knife, and his facial scarring showed ugly in the bright oil lamps' light.

"What the hell," the taller of the two barkeeps said, staring hard at Billy.

Finally, the man came over to their table. He leaned down and whispered harshly to Dan'l, "You can't bring him in here."

Dan'l grabbed a handful of his shirt and pulled him down close to his face. "Now, listen good. We want two bowls of your best stew. I seen your sign when I come in. We want some homemade bread to go with that, and two pints of ale, dark."

"You don't understand," the barkeep said tightly, looking over his shoulder at his other customers. "I can't serve him."

Dan'l held onto him. "Can't?"

"It's against the rules."

"Well, maybe you better change your rules, skunk-weed. Now, you going to get that stew, or do I turn my redskin here loose on you?"

The barkeep glanced fearfully toward Billy, then nodded. "All right."

The fellow returned to behind the long counter, and he and his partner dipped up some stew, casting dark looks toward Dan'l and Billy, and toward their other customers. When he finally brought the food and drink over to Dan'l's table and served Billy, two men at a nearby table got up, threw some money angrily onto their table, and stormed out of the place.

Now the only other customers present were three men at a table at the back, dressed in eastern clothing and playing cards. They kept looking toward Billy and talking among themselves, but did not break up their card game.

Dan'l ate voraciously, unmindful of any of the others in the room. The episode with the wildfire had been more unsettling for him than it should have been, because he had still been recovering from his injuries at the hands of McKenzie. Billy ate slowly, keeping a watchful eye on the men at the far table, and wishing they had not bothered to ride into this white man's village.

When Dan'l finished the stew and bread, he

called the same barkeep over.

"Now, you see? That waren't so painful, was it?"

"Please hurry and leave," the fellow said. "We have a reputation to maintain here."

Billy smiled. "We'll be leaving soon, don't worry."

The barkeep looked at him wide-eyed. "He speaks English, for God's sake! What is this, some kind of trick?"

The men at the far table turned to look again.

"Ain't you never heard of an Indian talking your language?" Dan'l said easily. "This boy could teach you to write your name proper, mister!"

The barkeep ignored the insult. "Well, that don't make him no white man. I hear they can teach monkeys to imitate human speech too."

Billy stopped eating and threw a diamond-hard look at him. "Is that what your daddy was? A monkey?"

Dan'l coughed on the ale he had just swigged.

The barkeep's face grew red. "Just finish your damned drinks, and get out!"

Dan'l wiped a hand across his mouth. "Not so fast, barkeep. I want to ask you a couple questions before we go."

"I don't have to answer any of your questions."

Dan'l let out a long breath and his voice hardened. "Oh, yeah. You do."

The barkeep stood there, uncertain, seeing the look on Dan'l's face. "What's the question?"

"We're on the trail of a man named McKenzie," Dan'l said. "He's riding with four other men. McKenzie talks with one of them British accents."

"Yes?"

"Well?" Dan'l said. "Have they been in here? In the last day or two?"

The men at the other table had stopped playing cards, and had turned to watch. One of them wore dark clothing, and had a gold chain hanging from a vest pocket. A second man was completely bald, but with thick brows that met in the center of his face. The third was very thin, with a pale, emaciated face. They were all land investors from the east, sharpers who specialized in grabbing up land from desperate people, or fearful ones, to make a big profit later. Every one of them carried a side arm.

Billy noticed that they were paying more attention to them now, looked them over, and immediately named them in his head: Gold Chain, Thick Brow, and Ghost Face, in the Indian way.

"Yeah, there was men in here like that. The one you call McKenzie had a Scottish accent. There was one real big man with them, I remember. They all had guns. Now, will you please leave?"

"When were they here?" Dan'l asked him.

The barkeep sighed heavily. "Last night. I think they're probably gone now. They stayed here, and left early this morning."

"Did they mention which way they was headed?"

159

"You ask a lot of questions, mister."

Dan'l looked into his eyes. "This is important. Real important."

The barkeep shrugged. "Oh, hell. They mentioned Danville, north of here. Now, get out."

"When we done finished our drinks, barkeep."

While the barkeep still stood there, the three men at the other table stood up, one by one, as Billy watched them. The tallest one, Gold Chain, walked casually over to their table. Thick Brow and Ghost Face fanned out on either side of him, flanking Dan'l's table.

"Are you hard of hearing, farm boy?" Gold Chain said. "The proprietor wants that Indian out of here."

Dan'l looked up at him. He wore a European-made flintlock revolver across his belly, so that it was the first thing you saw as he approached you. It was an announcement to the world, Dan'l knew, that he was good with the weapon, and that he would use it to resolve disputes.

"Who says every innkeeper on the frontier gets just what he wants, when he wants it?" Dan'l said easily.

The tall fellow laughed quietly. He looked Billy over arrogantly. Then he turned back to Dan'l. "I say it," he finally said.

A hush fell over the place. The barkeep backed away a few paces, to get out of the way. Dan'l swigged some ale, slowly, then looked back up at the tall man.

"Don't push it, dandy."

Gold Chain's eyes hardened. "Are you calling me names, farm boy?"

"I'm calling what I see. A Boston mama's boy, out on the frontier playing with guns. You ought to be real careful, you might shoot yourself in the foot."

Gold Chain was suddenly huffing and puffing. "Why, you backwoods son of a bitch!"

Billy had stopped eating. He looked down at the edge of the table, and focused on an iron bar he had seen there before. It rested in iron loops at the table's edge, and was used to hinge two tables together when more surface was needed. It was four feet long, and very thin. Billy reached and slid it out of its loops.

Gold Chain saw the move, and drew the revolver from his belt. "That won't help you now, red man." He aimed the cocked revolver at Billy's scarred face. "You're a dead Indian."

His finger squeezed the trigger.

Dan'l was closer to him than Billy, and in the last second, Dan'l leapt to his feet, knocking the table sidewise, and shoved upward on the tall man's arm.

The gun went off, but the chunk of lead missed Billy's head by an inch, burying itself in the front door behind him.

A lot happened in the next few seconds. Dan'l grabbed Gold Chain in a fierce embrace, like a grizzly bear. Behind Gold Chain, Thick Brow drew his gun also, and aimed at Billy. But Billy was on his feet now, and hurling the iron rod at him like a war lance. The rod hissed through the air and punched through Thick Brow's chest almost without slowing down. It stove in his sternum, ruptured his heart, and broke his spine exiting. When it finally stopped, a foot of it stuck out behind him.

While all of that was happening, Ghost Face drew his own gun, cocked it, and aimed at Dan'l. Dan'l saw it, though, and turned Gold Chain into the line of fire, still hugging him tightly. Ghost Face's revolver fired, and the slug ripped into Gold Chain's back.

His eyes saucered, but he was still struggling in Dan'l's grasp. Dan'l grabbed his head, twisted hard, and snapped his neck audibly.

The lights went out on Gold Chain in that terrifying moment, and he collapsed in Dan'l's arms. Dan'l let him slump to the floor as Thick Brow staggered forward a couple of paces, holding the end of the iron rod in both hands, as if he would not die if he did not let go. Then he plummeted to the floor. His leg kicked a chair and knocked it over.

Ghost Face looked even paler now, standing there by himself, looking unbelieving at his two dead comrades on the floor. He turned the revolver over in his hand, as if it had somehow betrayed him by shooting the tall man. When he looked back up, Dan'l was standing in front of him. He flinched noticeably.

"You got to prime it to use it again," Dan'l said in a low, hard voice.

Ghost Face threw the gun to the floor quickly, as though it were a scorpion that could sting him.

"There. I'm not armed," he said.

Dan'l grabbed him by the arm in an iron grip that made Ghost Face wince, then dragged him clear across the big room, as he stumbled and flailed, to the front door. He tore it open, and hurled the thin man into the street outside. Ghost Face went tumbling down the three steps and into the dirt below, then lay there awkwardly, bruised and breathless, but feeling very fortunate.

Dan'l turned to the barkeep. "*Now* we'll go," he said. "Come on, Billy. We got a trail to ride."

Chapter Nine

One of the two men who had left the Frontier Inn before the shooting started was a drifter named Baines, who had been drinking with a local he knew from previous trips through the area. Baines was just passing through, and intended to make a lot of miles yet that evening on his way to Danville.

The local had gone on home when they left, to rile his brother and son about the Indian that was eating and drinking at the public house. But Baines had hung around outside for a short time, sensing that there was going to be trouble. He heard Dan'l, therefore, inquire about McKenzie, and the barkeep's reply, through the partially open doorway. In fact, he was there through the shooting, and then rode off in a hurry, not wanting to be identified as a witness.

Baines wanted to get to Danville early the following day, and rode hard that night before he made a small camp for himself. That put him, unknowingly, only two hours behind McKenzie, and in mid-morning of the next day he caught up with the McKenzie gang.

Baines had no idea he was riding into the camp of the man Dan'l had inquired about in Logan's Station when he saw the campfire that cool morning in the early part of May.

McKenzie had risen late, and the group was just getting ready to ride into Danville to get ammunition and supplies, and to sell hides they still carried with them. He planned to spend a day or two in town, and inquire about the next stage to come through there. If the timing was right, they might stick around and ambush it on its way into the settlement. One haul from that could make up for a lot of trail robbery and poaching traps.

Baines rode into the camp warily, but not with real fear. He had come upon many travelers, singly and in groups, since leaving Carolina a week ago, and quite often they would share coffee or even food with him.

McKenzie was saddling his gray stallion when Baines rode in, and was still not really awake. Suggs was throwing sand on the low fire, with Weeks helping. Spencer, looking very primitive in his bearskin cap and hair shirt, was hitching the wagon horse to the hide wagon, which still held a couple dozen buffalo hides and some newly poached beaver pelts. Ian Quinn was tethering his mount to the back of the wagon. They had sold the buggy.

McKenzie saw the rider first, and stopped to watch him come up to the perimeter of the camp. Baines looked at him and tipped his dark hat.

"Good morning, boys. Mind if I stop to jaw a little?"

McKenzie wondered if he had anything to steal except for the scrawny horse he was riding. "Suit yourself, laddy," he said in his Scottish brogue.

The others heard the exchange, and turned to watch Baines walk his mount into their camp. Suggs and Weeks exchanged a look between them.

"What the bloody hell do you want, stranger?" Suggs said.

Baines eyed him narrowly. He looked around, counted them. Then he remembered the questions asked by Dan'l back at the inn. About a man named McKenzie.

"Not a thing," Baines finally said. "Unless you still got a cup of coffee you might want to offer a fellow traveler."

"Get your coffee in Danville," Weeks said sourly.

Quinn, though, was looking him over. "Wait. I still have a dollop in my cup over here on the wagon, mate. It's yours if you want it."

He caught McKenzie's eye, and McKenzie nodded. Baines smiled and dismounted. He figured he had information that might be valuable to them. "Much obliged, gents." He went to the wagon, picked up Quinn's cup, took a swig, and nodded. "Damn fine coffee. It's appreciated."

"Hell," Suggs mumbled.

Spencer came over to Baines, and looked him up and down. "Heading for Danville, are you?"

Baines inspected his shirt with his eyes. "That's right. Hoping to get a job there. Maybe at the livery."

McKenzie walked to his horse and studied the saddlebags. "If you're carrying any cash, we'd like to sell you some hides."

Baines met McKenzie's hard look. "Would you happen to be the man called McKenzie?"

McKenzie's eyes narrowed and he glanced quickly at Suggs, who was nearby. "Now how would you know that, my lad?"

Baines shrugged. "I heard your name mentioned. In Logan's Station. You was there just before me, I guess."

"Who the hell are you?" Spencer said slowly.

As they gathered around him, Baines put his hands up defensively. "The name is Baines. But I'm not here to cause you any trouble. I don't care what you done."

"What we done?" Suggs said menacingly. "What the hell do you think we've done, laddy-buck?"

Baines looked a little tense. "Why, I didn't mean anything by that. It's just that when somebody's chasing after you, it's natural to think there might be a reason."

"Chasing after us?" McKenzie said in a hard voice. "What the bleeding hell are you blithering about, man?"

Baines hurried to explain. "In Logan's Station. Those men that were asking about you."

McKenzie glanced over at Quinn, then at Suggs. He moved closer to Baines. Looking directly into his eyes, he said to Suggs, "Have a look in his bags."

"Hey, just a minute—"

"Yes?" McKenzie said carefully.

Baines noted his steely eyes. "Well. If you insist."

Suggs looked through the saddlebags, and found nothing to identify Baines further. There was also nothing worth stealing.

He turned and shook his head at McKenzie.

McKenzie smiled. "Don't fret yourself for nothing, bucko. We're civilized fellows here. So long as you don't wear a badge."

He laughed, and Weeks and Suggs did too.

"Now, laddy," McKenzie went on more seriously. "Just who were these blokes that were asking after me?"

Baines studied their faces before speaking. "I . . . thought that might be worth something to you."

"Oh, hell," Suggs said. "Let me have him for a couple of minutes."

Baines glanced quickly at the big, ugly man.

"No, no," McKenzie said in an oily voice. "It's a perfectly reasonable request, Suggs. What were you thinking of in the way of compensation then, Baines?"

Baines shrugged. "Whatever you can afford. A few shillings. A sack of coffee."

"Ah," McKenzie said. "Well, then. How about something much bigger than a few coins? How about your life?"

Baines suddenly wished he had never ridden into this camp. He tried a smile. "I've already got that."

"Have you, then?" McKenzie said.

Baines swallowed back his new fear. "Well, of course, if you haven't got anything for payment, I could tell you anyway."

Spencer was taking his cavalry revolver out, and preparing it for use. Baines saw him and quickly continued.

"I heard them talking to the barman at the Frontier Inn. It was Dan'l Boone, I've seen him in Salisbury. He had an Indian with him, I think an Algonquin."

"Bloody hell!" McKenzie growled. He turned to Quinn. "You *said* those were moccasin tracks in camp."

Quinn nodded. "It was an Indian that set him loose."

"That one must be the only one in these parts what ain't looking to put an arrow in a paleface," Weeks said with a grin.

But McKenzie found nothing humorous about all this.

"He's coming after you," Baines told them. "That was pretty clear."

There was a momentary silence. Quinn looked even more sober than McKenzie. He had always worried that McKenzie's little games would cause them trouble. They should have killed the hunter as soon as they caught him.

"I could join up with you boys," Baines said. "That would be payment enough. I'm looking to find something out here."

Spencer caught McKenzie's eye, and McKenzie nodded almost imperceptibly. Spencer aimed the revolver at Baines's head, and as Baines's eyes widened, fired.

The lead entered Baines's skull through his right eye and blew a hole in his head. His head whiplashed violently, and bone and matter flew onto Weeks's shirt. Baines collapsed to the ground as if a rug had been pulled out from under him.

"Son of a bitch!" Weeks yelled out, wiping stuff off him.

Spencer rubbed a hand across his broken nose, and examined his revolver. His earring shone in the bright sun. "I still think this thing shoots to the left."

McKenzie turned to Quinn, who was staring hard at the new corpse. "Yes, it was necessary," McKenzie told him. "He would have turned us in for a farthing."

Quinn nodded doubtfully. "Righto," he said.

"Now what?" Spencer said. "Do we change our

plans and not go to Danville?"

"Because of some backwoods farmer?" Suggs asked loudly.

"He's no farmer," Quinn answered.

They all looked over at him.

"Quinn's right," Weeks said. He was standing near Quinn, and looked a lot like him in build, except he was taller. His thin face showed concern. "He could be trouble."

"You should've let me kill him," Suggs said darkly to McKenzie.

McKenzie sighed. "All right, all right. So I underestimated Mr. Boone. There's no cause to panic, lads. There's only two of them, isn't it? But we won't sell the hides at Danville."

"Oh, shit!" Suggs said.

McKenzie explained, "He knows we're going to Danville. It's a large place. If they found us there, they could stir up some law against us."

"So we let Boone dictate where we go and what we do?" Suggs said angrily.

"Of course not. We just pick our own ground to fight on. Let him catch up to us on our terms, where it's just him and us. Then, my lads, I assure you there will be no game-playing this time around. I'll cut his bloody heart out and stake it to a tree."

Suggs seemed placated. Spencer was replacing the gun in an oiled holster. "I like the sound of that."

"Since we're not going into Danville, though, we're going to have to make for Harrodsburg.

There's a big market there. Maybe we'll come onto some more pelts on the way," McKenzie told them. "Or even a stage."

"We need supplies," Quinn reminded him. "Food, ammunition. I need shoes, and so does Weeks."

"Very well then," McKenzie said. "We'll send one man into Danville. He should escape attention. Buy our supplies and meet us on the trail to Harrodsburg. That should put things right, most likely. What about you, Weeks?"

Weeks was still cleaning the mess off his shirt. "Me?"

"And why not? You look as if you could use some clean articles. Maybe have yourself a wash—you're beginning to smell."

Weeks frowned at him.

"We'll send you in with a few coppers to spend."

Weeks nodded glumly. "Right," he said. He stepped casually over the corpse of the unfortunate Baines as he went for his horse.

That same morning, at the village of Chief Rain Cloud, the volatile chief was in a private palaver with a shaman who would have been familiar to Dan'l and Billy. He was Running Wolf, the middle-aged medicine man of Gray Fox, who had given his people orders to nurse Dan'l back to health a few days ago.

Running Wolf had resisted that decision by Gray Fox, and it had caused an argument between them after Dan'l and Billy were gone. Hearing that Rain Cloud's shaman had just died of the white man's pneumonia, Running Wolf had ridden to Rain Cloud's village and offered himself as replacement. Running Wolf and Rain Cloud had known each other in Pennsylvania, and had always been bound together by their absolute hatred for all white men, whether they were British, French, or colonials.

Just the evening before, Rain Cloud had announced that Running Wolf would replace their dead shaman.

Rain Cloud had already heard the McKenzie-spread rumor that it was Carolina militia who destroyed Fort Stuart, and that they were led by Dan'l Boone, and was perfectly content to accept that story. But when Running Wolf arrived, he maliciously confirmed the rumor because of his anger at Dan'l for intruding into Gray Fox's village and duping Gray Fox into treating him like a brother. Running Wolf knew Dan'l had had a run-in with McKenzie, but chose to believe that McKenzie was the innocent in the episode, and not Dan'l.

"I hear that McKenzie is still working for the redcoats," Running Wolf told Rain Cloud on that sunny morning. "He would, therefore, be the enemy of Sheltowee."

"Ah, that is why Sheltowee was captured by him," Rain Cloud said. "So you believe McKenzie?"

Running Wolf nodded. "I do. And I believe

your decision to make war on all settlers in this area is correct, Great Chief."

They were sitting cross-legged on the floor of Rain Cloud's Great House. In contrast to the makeshift appearance of the village of Gray Fox, where Dan'l had been nursed to health, this village had been built more like the ones where the Algonquin had come from. Like the Cherokee, the Algonquin were now building residences that were more sophisticated, square-shaped dwellings of woven logs and branches, with thatch roofs, intended for long-term use. Rain Cloud had even erected a brush wall around the perimeter, for defensive purposes, not unlike the stockade fences of some colonial settlements.

The Great House they sat in was such a sophisticated structure. It had buffalo robe rugs on a dirt floor, and wood shelves around the perimeter, with fetishes and decorations on them. A low fire burned in the center of the big room, with stones arranged to contain it, and a hole at the roof's center allowed the smoke to escape.

Running Wolf looked very much the way he had at Gray Fox's village. He had decorated his body with dyes, including his face, because of this serious palaver with his chief. He did not wear the wolfskin on this occasion, but covered his rather heavy body with an ermine cape, a symbol of his great wisdom. He wore three raven feathers in his graying hair.

Rain Cloud was a rather young chieftain, muscular and hard, and his eyes had a deadly look.

He almost never smiled. It was not in his character to find amusement in much of anything. He had brought his people to southern Kentucky to get away from the paleface, only to find that there was more hatred on the frontier than where they had left, as evidenced by the slaughter at Fort Stuart. He had decided he would move his people no farther. He would make war on the colonials, and drive them out of the area. If the militia came, they would find death, as had those in the valley recently. And if it suited his purpose to allow British advisors to guide him to militia expeditions, and to militia garrisons, he would not refuse to do so. It was not the British who were farming the Indian's native land and ruining it for hunting, and for his own small-scale cultivation. It was the colonials.

"You have spoken much of going against nearby settlements," Running Wolf said to him. "I think it is time that we quit talking, Great Chief, and took our warriors into the field."

Rain Cloud had done a lot of blustering, but had hesitated to actually plan attacks on white villages. The battle with the militia unit had happened because the officer of the unit had challenged the Algonquin to lay down their arms, and they had chosen to fight rather than to do so.

"You are probably right, Shaman," Rain Cloud said.

"The bloodthirsty paleface will overrun you here if you let him come in greater numbers," Running Wolf went on conspiratorially. "You must teach him a lesson, Great Chief. You must show him the Algonquin do not accept the kind of treatment they received at Fort Stuart."

Rain Cloud nodded more assertively. "Yes, I think you are right, old friend. We must go on the attack. Or we will be seen as victims, as our brothers were."

Running Wolf smiled. "You are very wise, Rain Cloud. May I suggest our first battle be waged at the nearby settlement called Richmond? They have no garrison there."

Rain Cloud agreed. "It should afford a great victory."

"And perhaps after that, we might consider Boonesborough, the home of the man who may have led the attack at Fort Stuart."

The chief sat straight-backed, looking very regal. He wore a modest breastplate of finely worked leather, decorated with rows of multi-colored beads, and a headband displaying several eagle feathers.

Finally, he allowed a taut smile, a rarity for him. "That seems a thing that would please the Great Spirit," he said quietly.

It was almost high noon when Dan'l and Billy rode into Danville.

After breaking camp that morning, McKenzie had purposely ridden through a wide area of pure rock, to try to throw Dan'l off his trail. When Dan'l and Billy had come to that place, and lost all the tracks but those of Weeks, who had headed into Danville on the dirt trail, Dan'l decided they would go on into the settlement.

"It could take us hours or days to pick up that main trail again," he had told Billy. "Let's follow this fellow here. It might be more productive."

"It isn't McKenzie, Sheltowee," Billy had pointed out. "The tracks aren't deep enough. This horse was ridden by a slight man."

"That would be the one called Quinn," Dan'l had said. "Or maybe that drifter Weeks. No, I'll settle for one of them. For now."

So they had ridden on toward Danville.

Like Logan's Station, Danville was a bustling frontier community. It had never been fortified, and it had real dirt streets, and stores, and even a small bank.

There were a lot of people on the streets when they rode in. Everybody was out enjoying the spring weather, despite the fact that news had come to them of the Indian attack on the military unit down near Logan's Station. There were women in long gingham dresses, and men in eastern-style suits, and a lot of farmers on horseback or driving wagons.

Dan'l and Billy looked for Weeks at the local inn first, but he had not been there. Next they inquired at a store, and spoke to a man with rimless spectacles on his nose.

"There was a fellow in here about an hour ago that fits your second description," the storekeeper said.

Dan'l looked at Billy. "Weeks," he said.

"He bought some flour and coffee. Bought himself a shirt too. Best Georgia cotton."

"That was an hour ago?" Billy asked.

The storekeeper looked him over. "Say, you aren't supposed to be in here," he said. "We don't sell to Indians."

"He ain't buying anything," Dan'l said sourly. "Did this fellow say where he was going?"

"Hmm. Yes, I think he asked the location of the livery stable. Wanted to get a shoe replaced on his horse by the hostler."

It was a short walk to the stable, down a side street, so they left their horses tethered at the store. When they arrived at the stable, with its odors of leather and manure, a few minutes later, a muscular, wiry little man was just finishing shoeing Weeks's horse.

Dan'l walked over to the hostler, but did not speak to him. He put a hand on the black and white mare and examined it.

"Yeah, one of them had a horse like this," he said to Billy. "He's here, all right."

"What can I do for you, stranger?" the hostler asked sarcastically. He looked over at Billy, and spat on the ground.

"Who left this horse with you?" Dan'l said without preliminary.

The hostler appeared offended. "I don't see how that could be any of your business."

Dan'l stood there trying to remain patient. "He's a killer," he said.

The hostler frowned. "Are you the law? We got

a constable here, you know."

Dan'l made a face. "No, I ain't the goddamn law. The name is Boone. I'm after Jock McKenzie. This man rides with him."

"You're Boone? Dan'l Boone?"

Dan'l glared at him.

"Why, I been hearing about you for years. Hey, you're a kind of hero hereabouts, since you burned that Indian village out down south!" He looked at Billy. "Is this a slave you keep with you?"

Dan'l and Billy exchanged a dark look. "You ain't answered my question," Dan'l said, coming up close to the other man.

"Oh, hell. He said his name is Weeks."

Dan'l nodded. "That's what I thought."

"He's just out back. With his saddlebags. I was just about to tell him his horse was ready."

Dan'l turned to Billy. "Let's go," he said.

"Wait. I don't want trouble here. Go get the law, Boone, if you want to make trouble."

Dan'l ignored him. He and Billy left the place, and walked around to the back. There were tall weeds back there, and a few hollyhocks. Weeks was leaning against the building, tipping a small bottle of liquor to his lips. Suddenly he turned and saw Dan'l and Billy.

His face went ashen when he recognized Dan'l, and the bottle slipped from his fingers and fell to the ground.

"Boone!" he whispered.

Dan'l had not brought his Kentucky rifle, but

Billy had carried his old musket from the store. He had readied it for firing as they rounded the building, and now held it trained on Weeks.

"Well, well," Dan'l said.

They both walked up close to Weeks, and Weeks looked into Dan'l's eyes and felt a chill skitter along his spine. "It wasn't me that done that to you," he said to Dan'l. "It's McKenzie you want."

"Yeah, but we got you," Dan'l said.

Weeks glanced from Dan'l's face to the scars on Billy's. He was breathing hard. He had worried, when McKenzie sent him in alone, that Dan'l might be closer than they thought.

"Look, I don't want no trouble. I split from McKenzie. I'm on my own now."

Billy came and touched Weeks's dirty hair under his dark hat. "Interesting color. I don't think I have one that color, Sheltowee."

"Huh?" Weeks said.

"He's talking about your scalp," Dan'l said.

Weeks looked at Billy again, big-eyed. "I know my rights. You got to turn me in to the law. I ain't hurt nobody. I get a court hearing."

"You get what we give you," Dan'l said.

"What is the white man's law?" Billy said to Dan'l. "If I bring a man to justice, do I get his horse? I mean, if he's dead?"

Weeks swallowed. "Look, you can have my mount. And everything on it. You don't want me, Boone."

Dan'l grinned. "You mean, everything on your

180

horse's irons? Including all that flour and coffee, and all that powder and lead?"

Weeks nodded uncertainly.

"What was you up to, Weeks?" Dan'l asked. "You going to start a war somewhere, all by your lonesome?"

"I . . . can sell it to hunters. For a profit," Weeks said lamely.

"Maybe you're taking it to McKenzie," Billy said.

"Oh, no. I told you. I'm done with him."

"You going to meet him out on the trail somewhere?" Dan'l asked.

"Hell, no," Weeks replied quickly. His Ferguson rifle was with his horse, inside the stable. But Spencer had lent him the British cavalry pistol for this foray into town, and Weeks had stuck it into his belt at the back, where it was not visible now. He remembered it at that moment, and knew it only had to be cocked to be ready to fire.

Dan'l rubbed a thick hand through his dark beard, then reached forward casually, grabbed Weeks by the head, and lifted him off his feet, a low growl starting in his throat.

"Hey!" Weeks yelled, his legs dangling and kicking. "Don't!"

Billy marveled at Dan'l's iron strength, considering how he had looked just a few days ago.

"Now, you son of a bitch!" Dan'l gritted between his teeth, "you tell us where to find McKenzie, or I'll turn you over to my friend here. He's pure Algonquin, and he'll skin you alive and then eat parts of you for supper."

Weeks's eyes rolled to the side, to try to see where Billy was. Billy suppressed a smile. He put the muzzle of the long gun up to Weeks's ribs. "We don't have to shoot him first, do we?" he said to Dan'l.

"No, wait!" Weeks cried out.

"Yeah?" Dan'l said, holding him off the ground as effortlessly as if he were a rag doll.

"I'll—I'll tell you!"

Dan'l let him down, but kept one hand clamped on Weeks's face. "Go ahead."

"Let me go. I can't—talk like this."

Dan'l remembered that night when McKenzie had done his little dance around him, kicking and mauling him with such pleasure, and Weeks had stood off to one side and watched. He grimaced bleakly, then released Weeks.

Weeks coughed and sputtered. "Damn!"

"We're waiting," Dan'l said.

"He's on his way to Harrodsburg. Just past that rocky area, he'll join the trail coming from Danville. I'm meeting them there."

"You *was* meeting them there," Dan'l said.

Weeks eyed him sheepishly. "Yeah. Was."

"Maybe we'll let you show us where," Dan'l said.

Weeks's eyes got big. If he showed up leading Dan'l Boone to McKenzie, he would not survive the day. Either he would be killed in the fighting that followed, or McKenzie would kill him later.

"No, I can't do that!" Weeks said fearfully.

182

"The hell you can't," Dan'l said.

"He'll kill me!"

"We'll kill you," Billy spat out.

Weeks sighed heavily. "All right."

Billy said to Dan'l, "I'll get his horse."

Dan'l nodded, and Billy started away. Dan'l turned away from Weeks to face Billy, who was five paces from them.

"And pay the hostler with flour. I don't want—"

Weeks had already reached for the pistol, and was fumbling with the cocking hammer while Dan'l was distracted. Billy saw what was happening and interrupted Dan'l.

"Sheltowee!"

Dan'l turned to face the gun, and his very posture and look terrified Weeks, and made him hesitate.

"You'd have to put three in me to kill me," Dan'l grated out. "And before you can do that, I'll cut you open from stem to stern."

Billy had the musket trained on Weeks's chest now, and it was cocked. Weeks hesitated some more, not knowing what to do.

"Now I'm going to take that away from you," Dan'l said, "and use it on you."

He meant that he intended to beat on Weeks with the pistol, but Weeks did not take it that way. He looked at Dan'l, and then at the musket Billy held, and suddenly turned the muzzle of the pistol to his own temple and squeezed the trigger.

There was a loud report and Weeks's brains ended up on the weathered side of the stable, mixed with blood and bone.

Weeks stood there for a long moment, then slipped to the ground, his trousers wet at the crotch, his jaw still working.

Dan'l and Billy just waited there until the corpse was still, then looked at each other.

"What a damn mess!" Dan'l sighed.

"Yes," Billy agreed. "And he ruined the scalp too."

Chapter Ten

Fortunately, the hostler had come outside to see what was happening, and had just rounded the corner of the building when Weeks shot himself. So he was able to verify for the local constable Dan'l and Billy's story that Weeks had committed suicide.

The trouble was, it took until mid-afternoon to clear themselves with the law.

When they finally got out to where they figured McKenzie and his men should be, they were gone. There was evidence that they had built a fire there, beside the trail, while they waited temporarily for Weeks. But it was obvious that McKenzie had grown impatient and headed on out. McKenzie was not a man who waited for things to happen. And he was as unpredictable as a cougar.

Dan'l figured McKenzie did not care whether Weeks ever caught up with them or not. They would cut down on provisions and keep moving.

McKenzie knew, Dan'l reasoned, that Dan'l was after him.

The terrain was still rocky where the Danville trail joined McKenzie's, so it was no easy task to pick up on it. Dan'l and Billy rode on opposite sides of the trail to Harrodsburg, trying to find tracks that matched what they knew of their quarry. Finally, in late afternoon, Dan'l identified McKenzie's spoor in an area of damp ground. There were deep tracks made by Suggs's mount and light ones by Quinn's, and McKenzie's had a special kind of shoes.

"You are good, Sheltowee," Billy smiled. "I had heard you were good, but you are better than that."

Dan'l shrugged and grinned. "It ain't science, like Ben Franklin does with them lightning rods. You just got to know the ground under your feet."

Dan'l was looking better now. There were no bruises on his bearded face, and his hair was caught in back of his head in a kind of pigtail, smoothly combed. His black, wide-brimmed hat was brushed clean, and his rawhides looked neat from the river washing.

The only thing that bothered him now was the side wound from McKenzie's ambush, but it was healing every day and giving him less trouble.

When they got into high country again, Dan'l was surprised to see that McKenzie's tracks left the main trail to Harrodsburg and headed off to the south. Dan'l reined in and studied the ground for a long moment.

"I wonder if he's taking a shortcut," he said to himself. "Or decided maybe not to go to Harrodsburg."

"It is always difficult to know what is in a white man's head," Billy said, then smiled at Dan'l. "Maybe we should split up for a while, Sheltowee. It appears that their tracks find the same direction as the main trail. At least for some distance. If you get too far off, fire your rifle, and I will come to you. If I want you, I will do the same."

Dan'l nodded. "I reckon a redskin can have a right idea once in a while."

Billy saw the slow grin, and returned it. They had begun to like each other. A fast friendship was forming, and it helped both of them get through this mission they had embarked on.

"If I follow this for a half hour and it don't come back to the main trail," Dan'l said, "I'll join you on it."

"Very well, my friend."

They rode off separately then, Dan'l headed to the south of Billy. Dan'l had to keep sight of McKenzie's tracks, so it was slower going for him than Billy, who only had to follow a track in the ground worn there by previous travelers.

They were headed into high rocks, and Billy had not been on the track for five minutes when he heard a sound in the boulders above his head, and then a low snarl, and he knew immediately it was a cougar.

There were not many in these eastern mountains, but when hunters encountered them, they usually tried to back off, because cougars were deadly when aroused.

Billy pulled the musket from its saddle boot, watching the rocks, not seeing the cat yet. He wished that he had not split with Dan'l, because the lion would not be as likely to attack two riders. He fumbled with powder and lead, loading and priming. He knew that Dan'l was just a hundred yards away, to his left, but there were rocks in between them and Dan'l was not in sight.

After several tense moments, the gun was cocked and ready. It weighed ten pounds, and was cumbersome to handle on horseback. Billy decided to dismount, and began walking ahead of his horse, leading it through the rocks, the reins in one hand, and the musket in the other.

No further sounds came from above. Billy walked slowly, looking up. He was not quite sure which side of the trail the sounds had come from. Overhead, a turkey vulture wheeled and pirouetted, and made him nervous.

He walked twenty yards, and there was nothing. Maybe he had been hearing things that weren't there. He relaxed.

The cougar snarled loudly from a high rock

and leapt savagely onto him.

It all happened so fast, Billy hardly had time to raise the gun to fire. The furry body plummeted down at him, the teeth bared, the yellow eyes wild with primordial hatred. Billy fired the musket just as the animal hit him, and the lead only grazed the big cat's shoulder.

Then the animal was on him.

Billy went down hard under its weight, and then he was on the rocky ground, looking into that red, fanged mouth, and feeling the claws rip into his arm. He held the weight of it off him with the musket as he heard his mount gallop off, terrified.

The next moments were all snarling, ferocious struggling, with the cat's open mouth in his face, and the smell of the pelt strong in his nostrils. Claws were ripping through his clothing, and making long gashes in his shoulder and arms.

The animal had frenzied strength, and Billy was weakening. In just seconds it would be over. The cat would get past the long gun and tear him to pieces.

He heard rocks falling nearby and got just a brief glimpse of Dan'l there, up above him. Then there was the roar of Dan'l's rifle, and the cougar's skull exploded in his face. The animal leapt high off him, twisting as it went, and fell heavily to the rocks, thrashing wildly for a moment. Then it was still, lying in a pool of its own blood.

Billy lay there breathing hard as Dan'l climbed down to him. Billy slowly sat up and examined himself. His rawhides were slashed up some, but his flesh wounds appeared rather shallow.

"Are you all right, partner?" Dan'l said, kneeling beside him.

Billy met his concerned look. "Yes, I think so. But I am pleased, Sheltowee, that you are so accurate with that gun. The cougar's head was very close to my own."

"Hell, that was just the chance I had to take," Dan'l grinned, standing up. He pulled Billy Two Tongues to his feet and looked him over. "You need a couple bandages. I'll go round our horses up, and we'll get you fixed. I don't want you getting no infection and dying on me. Our job ain't finished yet."

"You are such a sentimental white face, Sheltowee," Billy said acidly.

By the time Dan'l rounded up the mounts, the day was gone. Dan'l figured now that even if McKenzie went to Harrodsburg, he would probably be gone by the time he and Billy ever got there. It was beginning to look as if McKenzie could elude them forever, if he just kept on the move.

They made camp in a small valley not far from where the cougar attacked. Dan'l put more permanent bandages on Billy's arm and shoulder, where the claw wounds were deeper, and they made a fire and had a meal of dried beef and hardtack, washed down with coffee. Neither of them was very hungry.

When the meal was finished, they sat side by side against a heavy log near the fire, Billy lighted up a long, decorated pipe, and they smoked it together.

"How are the wounds?" Dan'l finally asked him as they stared into the flames.

"They burn like fire. But I do not mind, my friend. Suffering is good for the soul, and wins the Great Spirit to your side, if it is borne well."

"Do you really believe that?"

Billy handed the pipe to him for the second time, and looked into the fire. "Do you not?"

Dan'l shrugged. "I always tried to keep the misery to a minimum," he admitted. "And I could never see no good in hurting."

"Sometimes the Great Spirit does not let us see beyond our noses," Billy said.

Dan'l grinned. "Now ain't that true." He took in a deep breath, and let it out slowly. "One of them lions jumped me one day when I was out in Tennessee scouting around for farming land. I got my skinning knife out in front of me, and he just jumped on it. Ripped hisself open the whole length of his belly, but he still damn near killed me. They thought I was going to die for a week 'cause of the infection."

"A cat wound is touched by demons," Billy said quietly. "They must be prayed over. I will do so when you are asleep tonight."

"That's something to look forward to."

Billy smiled at him. "The praying will be in my head, Sheltowee."

Dan'l grunted. "Give my thanks to the Great Spirit for that." He handed the pipe back to Billy. Behind them, one of the horses guffered quietly, and out in the brush somewhere, there was a slight rustling.

"Coon," Dan'l said.

Billy sucked on the pipe, and blew out white smoke. "How can you know that?"

"How do you walk north without a compass?"

There was a silence then between them.

"I was raised at Fort Harmer," Billy said after a while.

Dan'l looked over at him.

"It was bad. I was taken in by a man and his wife. Not as a son. They took me for the work I could do. I was just in my tenth year.

"I was put to cleaning floors, weeding fields, feeding and tending animals. Nothing I did was right for them. The woman would beat me through the day, and when the man came in from the fields, he would beat me. Only he beat me with whips and his belt."

Dan'l shook his head. "What happened to your parents? Your clan?"

"My parents were both killed in an attack on our small village by white settlers. I was abducted and taken to Fort Harmer and sold there to the white couple."

"No wonder you're so ornery," Dan'l said.

Billy looked at him, and he was grinning.

"Slaveholding was common in Salisbury," Dan'l finally said. "A few Indians, but mostly Africans. It's agin' our religion, us Quakers. We don't think any man ought to be owned by another man."

"The Algonquin do not think in that way," Billy said. "We have made slaves of captured enemies. The Cherokee, the Mohicans. They have done likewise. In the old days, we ate the vital parts of dead enemies also. It was a practice accepted by several tribes. We believe it allowed us to take on the powers of our slain adversary."

"Adversary? Where the hell do you get words like that?" Dan'l wondered, shaking his head.

"I learned English from a schoolmaster. He was very smart. For a white man."

Now it was Billy's turn to grin.

Dan'l kicked at the fire. "My Paw come upon a Salisbury man whipping his Negro slave one day. I was with him. We come into town for victuals.

"That poor black fellow had dropped a heavy sack of salt that was too big for him, and the sack busted. We saw it happen, just before we come up on them. The owner was lambasting that African something fierce, tearing the shirt off his back with that buggy whip. Paw stood there and waited for the fellow to stop, but he wouldn't. Finally Paw grabbed that whip out'n the other fellow's hands, and knocked him right on his ass. You never saw such a look on a man's face. But Paw wasn't through. When the fellow yelled at him, Paw took that whip and started on him."

Billy laughed softly.

"He didn't quit till that man looked almost as

193

cut up as his slave. Then he throwed the whip down on top of him, and delivered a sermon about treating all folks with respect. He was acting constable at the time, and he freed that African right on the spot."

"I can see you are proud of your father."

"I guess I am."

Billy gazed into the fire. "The last memory I have of my father is when he tried to fight off the white settlers in their attack on our village. They were shooting women, and he was very angered. He went into the fight with only a tomahawk. He pulled one man off his horse, a fellow who had shot a running woman, and split his head open with one blow. Then, as I watched, a rider came up and shot my father in the face."

A long, heavy silence.

"When I went to him, he was trying to talk. It was he that told me my mother had been killed a few minutes earlier. Then he died trying to tell me to run and hide."

Dan'l looked at him. "I'm right sorry about all that, Billy."

Billy nodded. "When I could accept the beatings of my owners no more at Fort Harmer, I escaped. They came after me with dogs, but I had a big head start. I lost the dogs in a wild part of a river, and they gave up on me.

"I wandered through the wilderness for weeks, and finally luck shone upon me. I came to the village of Chief Longhair, who was a cousin of my father. He took me in, and I was used by him as a translator for several years. When you came to arrange for our movement to Fort Stuart, you did not speak with me, because Longhair knew you speak Algonquin."

"You was pointed out to me," Dan'l said.

"And you to me." Billy smiled.

"You was awful lucky, there at Stuart," Dan'l said quietly. "McKenzie was real thorough. He must've thought you was dead."

"Lying in your bed, in your home," Billy said, "I vowed to kill McKenzie, if I ever came upon him."

Dan'l caught his gaze.

"I could have killed him that night I took you from their camp," Billy said. "I would have given my life for it, and it did not matter to me. But I knew I had to bring you out of there. You had shown me a kindness I did not know the white man possessed. You treated me like a brother."

Dan'l waved a hand as if to ward off the compliment.

"We have cared for each other, and fought together," Billy said. "And now we have smoked the peace pipe together. We are brothers of the heart, Sheltowee."

Dan'l liked that. He nodded. "Yes."

"Do you really think the two of us can stop McKenzie, Sheltowee?" Billy wondered, knocking ashes out of the long pipe.

"I know I won't give up on it till it's finished. One way or the other. Trouble is, we got the Algonquin up in arms now, riled by McKenzie, and they ain't thinking straight. At least, Rain Cloud ain't. They could get in the way of our hunt."

"We must try to avoid Rain Cloud's people," Billy said.

Dan'l appraised Billy's sober face. "Billy, it looks like Rain Cloud believes the lies that's been told about me and the militia. If you get caught with me by Rain Cloud's warriors, you know what they'll do to you."

Billy smiled sourly. "They will not treat me well."

"You maybe ought to think about splitting up, Billy. I can always recruit somebody else to go after McKenzie with me."

Billy looked into his blue eyes. "One who would have my resolve, my brother?"

Dan'l grunted. "No. I don't think so."

"Then we are one until this is finished. When that time comes, and our mission is completed, my plan is to return to the village of Gray Fox and make my home there. I believe I can help his people."

"You're all right, Billy."

"And so are you, Sheltowee."

On a low bluff overlooking Boonesborough, Chief Rain Cloud reined in and held his hand up for the assembled warriors behind him to stop.

Running Wolf sat beside him on a smaller mount, wearing his fearsome wolfskin and head. His face and body were painted in war paint, as were Rain Cloud's, and Running Wolf wore a bone necklace for victory and had smeared his hands with the blood of a badger.

They had changed their plans yesterday, and decided to start their war at Boonesborough.

Lined up behind them were three hundred warriors, all in war paint, most with some kind of gun. They were fierce-looking in their gear and war paint, and they were ready to kill white men.

Rain Cloud turned to his troops.

"Today we will avenge Fort Stuart!" he cried out to his men. "Today we will restore the honor of the Algonquin nation!"

There was a roaring outcry in response, and Running Wolf wore a wide smile on his hard face. "Death to the whites!" he called.

Rain Cloud held his hand up again in preparation for a charge down the slope toward the settlement.

Down in the town, Dan'l's father, Squire, heard a knocking on the door of Dan'l's house, and went to answer it. He and Dan'l's mother, Sarah, had traveled all the way from Salisbury in Carolina to be with Rebecca at the birth of her baby when they had heard that Dan'l might not get back to her in time. Sarah was in the kitchen with Rebecca and her cousin, who had the same name as Dan'l's mother. Uriah Latham had just dropped by earlier that morning to see how Rebecca was doing and to meet Squire.

When Squire answered the door, it was Latham again. He looked very excited.

"Squire, it's the Algonquins! We just seen them

up on the bluff! They're coming in, and they got war paint on!"

Squire looked toward the stockade wall, a couple of blocks away, and now he could hear them, yelping and whooping, coming down the grade, though they were hidden from sight by the high wall.

"Good God!" he muttered.

"There ain't no gates nowadays," Latham said. "They'll be swarming inside the wall in just minutes." He thought of the tents and cabins outside the walls, and realized they were being overrun even as they spoke.

"God spare us," Squire said hollowly.

Latham had a rifle under each arm. "I'll stay and defend with you, if you want me."

Squire nodded. "Come on in, Uriah."

They bolted the door behind him with a long, thick bar of wood. Then Squire ran into the kitchen, armed with Latham's second gun, while Latham bolted windows.

"We're under attack by Indians," he said in a tense, low voice. He was sturdily built, like his son, but age had bent his back slightly, and his hair was silver. He dressed in black, like many Quakers.

Rebecca gasped loudly, and her hand went automatically to her fat belly. The younger Sarah yelped an abrupt cry of fear, while Dan'l's mother just stood there looking very serious. Graying hair hung alongside her still-pretty face.

"What shall we do, Squire?" she said quietly.

"Uriah is battening up. You women go to the bedroom and stay there, no matter what happens. You understand?"

Rebecca was breathing hard. She nodded. "Yes."

Now they could hear the yelling and screaming from the streets outside as the Indians came in on horseback, shooting and hurling lances at anyone caught out in the open.

"Oh, my God," Rebecca's young cousin kept saying as Squire herded them into the nearest bedroom. "Oh, God in heaven!"

Once in there with the door closed, the women sat down on the beds and huddled, the elder Sarah with her arm around Rebecca.

"Oh, God! Dan'l!" Rebecca cried.

Out in the big part of the house, Latham had thrown open the shutters at two windows, and he and Squire manned them with their guns. Outside on the street, Indians were riding past loudly, their horses' hooves thundering in Latham's ears, their battle cries curdling his blood. He saw men shot in the head, and women run down with horses, then scalped alive. The tiny militia garrison was responding, and being cut down.

"Don't fire at them unless they attack this house!" Squire yelled at him. "We got a pregnant woman in here!"

Latham nodded, and kept his rifle aimed at the street. They were both very tense, and Squire had never been more scared in his life. He found himself wishing Dan'l were there.

Outside, there was a bloody melee. Men had now run from their homes, and from buildings at the central square, and were returning fire to the Indians. But Rain Cloud's small army was overwhelming in its numbers. Squire saw Indians falling off their mounts, in the street and in the square, but there were always more of them, swarming through the village like locusts, killing and maiming. One of Rebecca's neighbors ran from a house across the street, and an Algonquin warrior threw a lance that sliced all the way through her and impaled her to the ground. Her legs continued to kick at the dirt, as if she had not given up trying to escape. Another Algonquin tore a baby from its mother's grasp, and bashed its brains out on an open door.

The carnage was unbelievable. Men were falling all around, skulls split open, or holes in their chests. Tomahawks flew through the air, and there was some hand-to-hand fighting, with blood flying. The militia was wiped out quickly.

Latham found it difficult to follow Squire's suggestion, seeing all the mayhem before his eyes and knowing it was going on all over town. But then several warriors rode right at the Boone house, hurling flaming lances. One threw a long lance right into the window where Squire stood, and the weapon sliced past his head within an inch, and hissed across the room, burying itself into an opposite wall.

Squire and Latham began firing immediately,

and they both knocked Indians off their mounts. But as they reloaded, others were banging at the front door, and in just a moment the heavy beam holding it secure cracked under the battering. The door flew open, and three Algonquins rode right into the wide parlor, still mounted, waving muskets and tomahawks and yelling savagely.

It was a wild moment. Squire fired at the closest Indian, and hot lead punched the fellow off his mount, and he fell, crashing to the floor, shot through the heart. But then a second warrior fired and hit Squire in the high chest, slamming him back against a wall.

Latham, getting his gun cocked finally, fired at that Indian, and blew the crown of the fellow's head away. Before he could fall, his horse turned and ran back through the front door. The third Indian jumped off his mount and onto Latham, and split his head wide open with a tomahawk. Latham's eyes stared widely, and he hit the floor dead.

The other horses stomped around the parlor, then followed the first one out onto the street. The remaining Indian ran to the bedroom door, threw it open, and stood there before the three women, looking like a demon from hell.

Rebecca's cousin screamed hysterically, and Dan'l's mother clutched Rebecca to her and closed her eyes, waiting for the worst. But suddenly Rebecca broke free of her, and rose to stand, still clutching her belly. To the elder

Sarah's astonishment, she had a look of defiance on her pretty face.

"This is the home of Sheltowee!" she said loudly.

The warrior had raised his tomahawk above his head to attack. Now he lowered it slowly. He knew the name well, and was not one of those who had believed that Dan'l was involved at Fort Stuart.

"I am carrying Sheltowee's child," she continued in broken Algonquin, which Dan'l had taught her. "If you harm any one of us in this room, and particularly Sheltowee's unborn child, he will come after you."

The warrior stood there, eyes flashing.

"He will kill you and all of your kin," Rebecca said. "He will burn your villages. He will leave nothing standing. He will not stop until the Algonquin is no more. He is Sheltowee!"

The warrior stood there for another instant, then raised the tomahawk and hurled it toward the women. But it sailed past them and thudded into the wall behind the bed. The young cousin screamed again, and both Rebecca and Dan'l's mother flinched, but did not cry out. The Indian then let out a series of war whoops that could be heard clearly out on the street, and turned and ran out on foot.

Squire had fallen to the floor, and was semi-conscious, and the warrior did not even notice him again as he left. Out on the street, he was

killed immediately by one of the last shots fired
by the defenders.

Moments later, Rain Cloud recalled his troops,
and they rode on out of the settlement.

Carnage and destruction lay in their wake.

Several houses and buildings were aflame,
with black smoke curling into the sky.

Corpses littered the streets.

Rain Cloud felt avenged for what had happened at Fort Stuart.

Dan'l and Billy, following McKenzie's trail,
were just a half day's ride from Boonesborough
when all of that happened, and Dan'l had wondered whether to detour home to see how Rebecca was doing. But he had rejected the idea,
hoping that persisting now might get him home
quicker in the end.

The events of that afternoon, though, changed
his plans. While Rain Cloud was attacking
Boonesborough, a separate, five-man war party
was out on the trail at the chief's direction, looking for a one-wagon military transport that was
supposed to come through on its way to Harrodsburg. The Indians did not find the wagon,
but ran onto Dan'l and Billy in late morning.

They had been told by Running Wolf that Dan'l
was in the area, and that an Algonquin was traveling with him. Their orders were to treat them
as deadly enemies.

The frontiersman and his partner were on the
Harrodsburg trail, crossing a meadow ringed by

high hills, when Billy spotted the war party. It had just crested the hill to their right, and Billy reined in fast when he saw it.

"Sheltowee! Look, up there!"

Dan'l had already seen them, and had stopped his mount beside Billy. He studied the small knot of riders gravely. "Damn," he said. The last thing he wanted was trouble that would distract him from McKenzie.

"They are Algonquin," Billy said, squinting up at them.

"And they've seen us."

"Can we make a run for it?"

"I don't think so. Them ponies of theirs look fast."

"They probably know who we are," Billy said.

"That's what I'm afraid of," Dan'l replied. "Come on, let's get to that dry creek bed up ahead. That'll give us some cover."

Even before they reached the narrow, weed-choked slit in the ground, the Indians were riding down on them.

Dan'l and Billy dusted to a quick stop in the gully, and pulled their mounts off their feet, making them lie on their sides in the high weeds. Then they loaded and primed their guns just as the five Indians swooped down across the meadow.

"Here they come!" Dan'l called.

The Indians thundered toward them, yelling and brandishing guns, their hair flying in the wind. They were a splendid sight to Dan'l, and he hated to spoil it. He sighted along his long rifle.

"They are too far!" Billy exclaimed.

Dan'l fired and three hundred yards across the open meadow, the lead Indian was knocked savagely off his racing horse.

As Dan'l reloaded quickly and smoothly, Billy looked over at him. "I have never seen a shot like that."

"You ain't seen nothing yet. Now you get one."

As Billy aimed the Indians were a hundred yards away. He could see the angry looks on their faces. He fired, and a second Indian went pirouetting off his plunging horse. Dan'l finished priming, and cocked the Kentucky rifle. The Indians were fifty yards away. He fired without aiming, and a wild-looking warrior was hit in the chest, high. Then their hot lead was thunking around Dan'l and Billy as they rode on over them, jumping the narrow gully. The last one hit slid off his horse right at the gully, and Dan'l saw he was hit in the stomach and that it was not a fatal hit. The Indian rose to his feet just a short distance from Dan'l, limped over to him with a short lance, and raised it to hurl it into Dan'l's chest. The other two warriors were turning their mounts to ride back over the gully.

Dan'l jumped to his feet and met the wounded Indian halfway as he charged with the lance. Dan'l caught the arm with the weapon, and they grappled. Billy rose to help Dan'l, but Dan'l had already reached for the Algonquin knife on his belt, and now shoved it past the Indian's arm and into his ribs.

The Indian's eyes widened, and he collapsed beside Dan'l. In the same instant, the riders came swarming over the gully again, whooping and yelling. One of them fired a second time, grazing Billy's left side with a shallow flesh wound, and the other one hurled a lance at Dan'l that missed him by a fraction of an inch and thunked into the dirt bank behind him.

But the Indians had had enough now, seeing three of their party down. With more yelling and arm-waving, the last two rode off across the high grass again, and disappeared over a low hill.

"Are you hurt?" Dan'l asked Billy, breathing hard.

"It is a scratch only," Billy said, touching his side.

Dan'l looked down at the dying Indian at his feet. The fellow caught Dan'l's gaze. He spoke slowly in Algonquin.

"You are lucky again, Sheltowee. But Boones-borough dies today."

Dan'l narrowed his eyes. "What?"

The Algonquin managed a weak smile as a ribbon of crimson appeared at the corner of his mouth.

"Dead. Your village is dead."

Dan'l reached down, grabbed him, and shook him. "What the hell do you mean?" he demanded, forgetting to speak in Algonquin.

The Indian hung limp in his arms.

"Damn you, talk to me!"

He felt a touch on his shoulder, from Billy.

"He is gone, Sheltowee."

Dan'l released the warrior, and the still figure fell back to the ground. Dan'l stood there, just staring at it.

"Son of a bitch," he said quietly.

Chapter Eleven

Dan'l's horse had run off in all the shooting, and Billy had to go run it down for him. While he was gone, Dan'l just sat there in the gully and thought about what the Algonquin had said. When Billy returned, he had made up his mind.

"Done got to find out, Billy."

Billy led their mounts over to Dan'l.

"I got to go see what happened back home."

"I understand, Sheltowee."

"It's less than a day's ride. This is the closest we'll be. I got to know about my family."

"I would feel the same, my brother."

They were standing in the gully, face to face. Dan'l clapped a hand on Billy's shoulder. "There ain't no use in your going. Let that wound heal proper up at Brady's Cabin. It's up ahead on the

Harrodsburg trail about twenty miles. An abandoned cabin where travelers stop. I'll meet up with you there in a few days."

Billy grimaced with pain when he moved. "I would prefer to go with you, Sheltowee. You might need me."

"The hell you will. Put a poultice on that rib, and just set for a couple days. Maybe somebody will come past from Harrodsburg and give you news about McKenzie."

Billy smiled. "Maybe, old friend."

"I'm lighting out now, Billy. You got enough victuals to last you several days. I'll be back."

Billy nodded. "Good luck to you, Sheltowee."

A couple of moments later, they rode off in different directions.

Dan'l rode hard that day, pushing his Indian horse harder than it liked. By the time he arrived at Boonesborough, in late afternoon, the animal was frothing on its flanks.

Dan'l rode in slowly. There were still wisps of smoke rising from several burned buildings. Outside the stockade, there were still some corpses on the ground.

He saw men collecting the last corpses off the streets. There were lances stuck into building walls, and bloodstains on the ground, and on doors. With his heart in his mouth, Dan'l rode to his house, just off the main square of the old fort.

He saw arrows stuck into the exterior wall, and the front door broken off its hinges. He dismounted in dread, and walked to the doorway. A militia officer with a bandage around his head met him coming out.

"Your wife's all right, Dan'l."

Dan'l felt a quick lump rise into his throat. "Thank God," he muttered.

"All the women are fine."

"All?"

"Your parents were here. Your father is hurt, Dan'l. And Uriah Latham is dead, defending your house."

"Oh, Jesus."

"It was Algonquins. That goddam hothead Rain Cloud. He killed half of my men and a lot of villagers. I heard some of them yelling about revenge. I know a few words of their language."

"They think colonials did that thing at Fort Stuart," Dan'l said. "It's a long story." *With Jock McKenzie at the center of it.*

"I'll let you go see your wife."

"Thanks for stopping by, Lieutenant."

Dan'l stepped through the doorway as Rebecca was just coming out of the kitchen. When she saw him, her eyes misted over. He went to her without speaking, and embraced her above her swollen stomach.

"Oh, Dan'l!"

"I'm sorry, Rebecca. I'm sorry I waren't here."

The other two women, hearing voices, came in too. The older Sarah came and hugged Dan'l. "We're so glad to see thee, son. Thy family has missed thee this day." She often lapsed into the Quaker form of speech when speaking to Dan'l.

"Where's Paw?" Dan'l said.

"He's in the second bedroom. The doctor said he's going to be all right. But he'd like to see thee."

Dan'l kissed Rebecca gently, then went into the bedroom, through a hallway. The women left him alone with Squire.

Dan'l looked down on Squire, resting in bed. "I heard your voice out there," his father said with a grin. "Glad you could get here, Dan'l."

Dan'l knelt beside the bed and hugged his father. Squire was surprised. When Dan'l released him, he was smiling. "You don't have to worry none about me, boy. The lead didn't even collapse my lung. Give me a week or so, and I'll be fit as a fiddle."

"I should've been here," Dan'l said heavily.

"That ain't so. You got a big job to do, boy. If that evil man ain't brought down, there's going to be even more of this. And somebody's got to do it."

Dan'l sighed. "I hear Latham got it."

"He went down fighting like a man. He was a friend to be proud of, Dan'l. They took his body down for burial, along with all them other ones."

"Is Rebecca really all right?" Dan'l said.

"She seems to be. But this might bring that baby out. I reckon it's good you're here."

Dan'l stood up. "You rest, Paw. I'll want to talk to her."

Squire nodded. "She needs you, Dan'l."

Dan'l went back out into the parlor, where all

the women were seated, waiting for him. Young cousin Sarah went and laid a kiss on his cheek, and Dan'l smiled at her.

"We hoped you would come," young Sarah said.

"I heard about it from an Algonquin," Dan'l said. "I never thought Rain Cloud would go this far. He's been listening to a lot of lies."

"There's over a hundred villagers dead or dying," his mother told him. "It was awful, Dan'l."

"I got to see Rain Cloud. Him and me met once, right after he come to this area. Maybe he'll listen to me."

"You can't go to him, Dan'l!" Rebecca said fearfully. "He might kill you."

"This has all got to be stopped, Rebecca. Back east the colonials are making war on the British. Now the Indians is getting riled agin us too."

"It's not your business to put everything right," Rebecca said loudly to him. "We need you here."

The other women kept their silence. Dan'l took a deep breath and looked at his wife. "Come help me put some gear away," he said quietly.

She rose and went to him. "All right."

He excused them, took her into their bedroom, and closed the door behind them. She turned to him, grim-faced.

"I love you, Rebecca."

She tried a smile. "I know."

They lay down on the big bed, and he leaned over and listened at her belly. "How is my son taking all of this?"

She shrugged. "I feel different, Dan'l. Since they came in here. Things are different inside me."

"He's . . . all right, ain't he?"

"I think so. But this all jarred us something fierce. He might want to come out sooner."

Dan'l lay back beside her. "It ain't safe here now. Not with Rain Cloud making war."

"We've been in fighting before here at Boonesborough," Rebecca said.

"It's different now. The Shawnee never come at us in big numbers."

"It's all right," she said. "As long as you're here."

"I want you to return to Salisbury with Maw. Just till you have the baby."

"I'll have the baby any day! You want me to have it out on the trail?"

Dan'l sighed. "Well, even if you went to Danville, it might be safer."

She touched his bearded face. "I'm having our child right here, Dan'l. In our home you made for us. No damn Indian is driving me out!"

Dan'l grinned. "You always was a right spunky wench."

"I faced down one of Rain Cloud's warriors right here in my own bedroom," she said, sticking her chin out.

Dan'l nodded. "I guess that gives you the right to deliver just about anywhere you want."

"I guess it does."

"I'll stay till it's finished, Rebecca." He thought

of Billy, out there by himself. And McKenzie, raising hell all along the frontier. "But then I'll have to leave again."

"Oh, God, Dan'l. Let somebody else do some of it. You're going to be a father."

"Don't rile yourself, Rebecca."

She looked away. "Well. At least maybe you'll get to hold your child in your arms before you saddle up again. I guess we can all be thankful for small favors from above."

Dan'l smiled at her. "A real spunky woman," he said.

Dan'l helped the women clean the place up that evening. After supper, after he took his father's food tray away, he went back in and changed his bandage.

Squire was glad to have him there, if only briefly. Dan'l hardly ever got to Salisbury these days. He had been very busy taking groups of settlers into Tennessee and western Kentucky, and mapping out new territories. He was very rarely at home.

"You figuring on staying till the baby comes?" Squire asked him when Dan'l had sat down in a rocking chair and stoked up a corncob pipe, a habit he rarely indulged in.

Dan'l sucked on the pipe, and blew out a stream of white smoke. From the waist up, he was wearing just his long underwear. He tended to get warm fast when indoors.

"I reckon I have to," he said slowly. "In case

she gets into any trouble."

"I know how you must feel, boy," Squire said, propped on a pillow at the bed. "You want to be out on the trail, tracking down that devil Mc-Kenzie."

Dan'l met his look. "Billy's out there alone, Paw. Waiting for me. I should've brung him back here with me."

"Uriah told me about him. When I let you set in on them trading sessions with the Cherokee in Salisbury, when you was just a stripling, I never thought you'd end up riding the trail with a red man."

"Billy's not your ordinary Indian. Him and Jake Medford is two of the best friends I ever made. And I got one of them killed already."

"That waren't no fault of yours, son," Squire said. Dan'l had told his father about his capture. "Don't take too much on yourself."

"I just want to get back out there," Dan'l said heavily.

Squire regarded him soberly. "I hear you had some trouble here when you took that boy in. That Billy Two Tongues."

"Yeah, Paw. There's always a few hotheads in any settlement."

Squire smiled. "We sure had our share back in Salisbury, remember? It's better there now. But I hear tell there's some men here, including militia, what think you done sided with the British and Indians against them."

Dan'l shook his head. "Rain Cloud thinks I

burned the fort at Stuart."

"That's what happens when a man tries to keep peace by standing in the middle," Squire said.

"Hell, don't they know I'm carrying a militia commission to hunt down a man that's an enemy to all colonials?" Dan'l wondered. "Captain Emery set right out there in my parlor and recruited me."

"There ain't no fairness sometimes in the way men think. I reckon that Billy you're riding with has got a lot to do with it."

"And they know I rode over to Duquesne and talked to Colonel Hopkins," Dan'l said. "But, hell. I just went there to register a complaint about McKenzie."

"They say he tried to recruit you."

"He did. I turned him down."

"Captain Emery ain't here no more, Dan'l. It's some new fellow. Same rank in the Continental Army. The Virginia and Carolina militia is obsolete. New people joined up, a lot of hotheads. It's different now. The colonies is talking about declaring their independence from England."

"I know," Dan'l said. "Hell, maybe it's for the best. They tell us what we can and can't do, even out here on the frontier. Land would've been opened up a lot quicker if we was on our own."

"Well, just be careful while you're here in town. You got some enemies in your own settlement."

Dan'l nodded. "But I got more important things on my mind, Paw. There's McKenzie, and there's Rain Cloud. Soon as that baby gets here,

I'm breaking camp. On my way to Billy, I might just make a stop with the Algonquin."

"I heard you mention that. But Rebecca's right, son. It could be mighty dangerous."

"It's got to be done, Paw. And I reckon I'm the one to do it."

In the middle of that night, while Dan'l was asleep beside Rebecca, and the house was quiet, she woke him suddenly with a look of concern on her pretty face.

"Dan'l. I think it's starting."

"Huh?"

"I'm having contractions."

He sat bolt upright in bed. "Oh, hell!"

"Get Maw and little Sarah. I'm going to need them."

Within fifteen minutes, the whole household was up. Even Squire got painfully out of his bed to help get things together. Dan'l went for the doctor, and the two other women fussed about, boiling water and getting towels and cloths together. Rebecca wanted to get up and move around, but Dan'l's mother would not allow her to. She was right too, since the contractions began coming faster almost immediately, and it was clear that Rebecca was going to have a premature delivery that night.

Dan'l arrived with the doctor just as Rebecca was delivering, and Dan'l had to go outside where he could not hear her cries of pain so clearly. She did not have a bad time of it, though, and soon Dan'l heard some high-pitched squalling from inside.

When he rushed into the bedroom, he saw the elder Sarah holding her grandson. Rebecca lay fatigued on the big bed, smiling at Dan'l.

"You got your wish. It's a boy."

Dan'l went and looked at the wrinkled, red-faced baby, and a swelling of pride thrust into his chest. "James," he murmured to the child. "We'll call you James."

Surprisingly, Rebecca was up and about by midday, and by supper time wanted to help the other women with cooking. Young James was treated like a frontier prince, and Dan'l could already see himself taking the child out hunting with him, and showing him the backwoods that he so loved.

At the end of the next evening, Dan'l told Rebecca he was leaving.

"For God's sake, Dan'l!" she protested.

"Listen to me," he said quietly, in the privacy of their bedroom, with little James sleeping in a crib only twenty feet away. "When this is all finished with McKenzie and the Algonquin, there'll be plenty of time for us. I promise that, Rebecca. But right now, time is agin us, you understand? I got to make the most of what I got."

"Damn it, doesn't your family ever come first?"

He sighed. "What do you think I'm doing out there? It's for you, Rebecca. For us, and all the settlers in this valley. And it can't wait."

She averted her eyes. "I'm sorry, don't pay me

no mind, my love. I just want you to get to know your son."

"I will," Dan'l said. "You can count on it."

They embraced then, and she held onto him tightly for a long time.

That night, she had a nightmare in which Rain Cloud ran a lance through Dan'l, and then stood over him laughing loudly. When she woke with a start, Dan'l was breathing heavily beside her in bed and James was fast asleep.

The following morning, Dan'l saddled up a new, fresh horse he had purchased at the local livery, and headed out to meet Billy Two Tongues. But he had made up his mind to visit Chief Rain Cloud on the way.

Dan'l said his good-byes quickly, so it would be easier, and rode off with Rebecca standing in the open doorway, holding his new son in her arms.

He took a long look, because he knew there was no guarantee he would ever see them again.

The Algonquin village was almost on Dan'l's direct route to Billy, if in fact Billy was still at Brady's Cabin.

Dan'l rode hard that day on the new mount, a big, strong chestnut stallion that, as it turned out, had belonged to Captain Emery before he was transferred to Philadelphia in the new army by wagon train. He had sold the horse to meet travel expenses.

Dan'l rode through some beautiful Kentucky

countryside on that sunny May morning, and he wondered how long all of this would look so peaceful if a revolution really developed in the coming months. Maybe he could slow it all down, if he could bring down a troublemaker like McKenzie. And maybe convince some area Indians that their future lay with the colonials, and not the army of King George.

Dan'l passed through thick forest most of the morning, and had his rifle ready at all times. Ambush was easy in thick woods, and Rain Cloud had apparently passed a death sentence on him.

The hours went by without incident, though, and in late morning Dan'l crested a low hill and looked down on the large Algonquin settlement, covering many acres.

It was the largest one west of Pennsylvania.

Dan'l immediately spotted two sentries on high ground overlooking the village. They had both seen him. They were armed with what appeared to be Brown Bess muskets, which Dan'l figured they had gotten from the British.

Dan'l rode on down the hill toward the camp. One of the sentries flashed a message to the village with a trade mirror. Neither one threatened to fire on him as he walked his mount between them, but they looked very hostile.

When Dan'l arrived at the village edge, children ran out to look at him, and several braves came on foot and lined the path he took. There were combative stares, and a young man yelled out at him in Algonquin, "Killer of women! You dare come here!"

Dan'l rode on in, and a crowd gathered around him and his horse, and followed alongside him. One woman spat at him, and a small boy hurled a stone that struck him in the back. He made no reaction to any of it.

Soon he was at the central clearing in the village, with a ring of larger mud-and-wattle buildings surrounding him. It was a real town, obviously put up before Rain Cloud had had any thought of war. It was a permanent settlement.

A door opened in one of the larger structures, used as the Great House, and Running Wolf came out, glaring at Dan'l. Behind him came Rain Cloud himself, staring hard.

Dan'l dismounted, and was immediately surrounded closely. He was completely unarmed, and had even taken the war knife off his belt. A couple of women yelled obscenities at him, but he ignored them.

Running Wolf walked over to him. He was unadorned, and looked even more hostile than he had in Gray Fox's camp.

"You are too bold, child slayer."

Dan'l met his gaze levelly. "You know I wasn't at Fort Stuart, damn you!" he said. "What are you doing here? Do you want a war with the settlers?"

Rain Cloud came up beside his shaman, looking grim. "The great Sheltowee," he said caustically. "Have you come to surrender yourself to our justice?"

Dan'l used his hands as he spoke in Algonquin, to make his intent more clear to those who watched. "I have come to talk peace with the great chief," he said slowly. "Now that he has attacked my own village and wounded my father."

"Peace!" Running Wolf exclaimed. "It is too late for peace, white face!" He turned to Rain Cloud. "Take him prisoner. He must face our justice."

Rain Cloud hesitated. "He came to us openly and unarmed. I must listen to him."

Running Wolf's face darkened with renewed rage. "He is the enemy!"

Rain Cloud scowled at his shaman. "Your counsel is heard, Running Wolf. Sheltowee, you will accompany me into the Great House."

"Thank you, Great Chief," Dan'l said.

They walked to the communal building. Running Wolf followed behind them, but Rain Cloud stopped him at the entrance.

"You will wait outside," Rain Cloud told him.

Running Wolf scowled fiercely. "You will exclude me from this palaver?"

"I know your counsel," Rain Cloud said. "Please. Be patient."

There was some muttering among the assembled Indians as Rain Cloud and Dan'l entered the building alone, ducking low through the entrance.

Inside, Rain Cloud invited Dan'l to sit, and they both seated themselves before a low fire of burning coals. The chief did not light a pipe, and Dan'l knew that was a sign that Dan'l was not a wanted guest.

Dan'l noticed that on the many shelves or benches around the perimeter of the floor there were polished skulls of cannibalized enemies from the past.

"Now." Rain Cloud got down to business without preliminary. "Say what is on your mind, Sheltowee."

Dan'l nodded, and replied in almost perfect Algonquin, "You have been lied to, Great Chief."

The chief frowned. "Yes?"

"By a man named McKenzie, and by Running Wolf. Perhaps others."

"You accuse my shaman?"

Dan'l looked at the fire. "Running Wolf heard the true story of Fort Stuart from a survivor. Billy Two Tongues. He knows who burned the fort."

"And that was?"

"Jock McKenzie, and his British company of regulars."

"McKenzie is not a soldier. He is a spy for the British."

"He is neither," Dan'l said. "But he *was* a soldier. He was cast out because of the dishonor of Fort Stuart."

"This is true?"

"You can ask Colonel Hopkins at Fort Duquesne. McKenzie now spreads lies across the frontier. To cover his own lawlessness and to cause trouble between your people and the colonists."

Rain Cloud hissed between his teeth. "I have never spoken with this man directly. I would have seen the truth in his eyes."

"You would have seen evil," Dan'l said.

The chief looked into Dan'l's eyes, and he saw no deception there.

"I helped put Longhair at Fort Stuart," Dan'l told him. "To settle his people peaceably among ours. I was very angry when I found out what had happened there."

The chief let out a long breath. "We met briefly only once, Sheltowee. I am from a distant place. I did not know what to believe."

"I understand, Great Chief of the Algonquin. But I invite you to ask about me among the Cherokee, and even my enemies the Shawnee. They will tell you that my word is true."

"I have listened to false stories and made war needlessly."

"Running Wolf is a good shaman," Dan'l said. "But he has a hatred for the white man. This is not good, if we would live in harmony in Kentucky."

"I should have lighted a pipe for you."

"It is all right, Great Chief."

"I am sorry about your father."

Dan'l shrugged. "We do not seek revenge on the Algonquin. We hope that understanding will lead to peace."

Rain Cloud nodded sagely. "You are wise, Sheltowee."

"It is but a small stream beside Rain Cloud's mighty river."

Rain Cloud smiled. "I will heed your counsel, Sheltowee. I will persuade my people to keep peace with the white settler while he resolves his dispute with the Great White Father, King George."

"You sit beside the Great Owl in majesty," Dan'l said.

"This McKenzie. We could help you find him."

Dan'l paused, then shook his head. "Your help could be misunderstood. There are but four men. Billy Two Tongues and myself will hunt them. With luck, we will impose the white man's justice on them."

"I pray that it will be appropriate."

Dan'l nodded. "So do I."

As Dan'l rode out of Rain Cloud's village, he left with the satisfaction that perhaps he had turned things around between the Algonquin and the settlers of that area. Now he could get on with finding McKenzie.

He understood what Rain Cloud meant when he indicated his hope that the white man's justice would be appropriate for a man like McKenzie. Dan'l was not so sure himself that traditional punishment was right for such a felon. McKenzie had slaughtered hundreds, white and red. He had caused dissension and trouble everywhere he went. He was indirectly responsible for the killing at Boonesborough.

Mere arrest and trial could fall far short of what had to be done with McKenzie, and Dan'l was very aware of that. He knew that Davison would prefer that course, to make an example of McKenzie. But Dan'l figured things had gone beyond his acting like a frontier policeman now.

McKenzie's lies, in fact, were about to cause Dan'l even more trouble. When he was only two hours out of the Algonquin village, on the Harrodsburg trail, he met a three-man squad of Boonesborough militia-turned-army soldiers who had left Boonesborough not long after him, to deliver documents to a garrison at Danville, and were now returning home.

They came upon him quite unexpectedly at a curve in the trail, in a wooded grove.

Dan'l reined in quickly, not recognizing who they were for a moment. He reached for his rifle, then relaxed.

"Oh. You're militia," he said. "Ain't you from the Boonesborough garrison?"

The threesome were a sergeant, a corporal, and a private. They all wore the insignia of the Continental Army on their uniforms.

The sergeant spurred his mount forward. "That's right. And you're the goddamn traitor Boone, I reckon."

Dan'l felt something heavy drag at his chest. He was very weary of all of this. "I'm Dan'l Boone," he said evenly.

"You just talked to them damn Algonquin, I

bet," the corporal said to Dan'l. "We know you was riding out here."

"Is that all you know?" Dan'l said.

The private's horse guffered softly, catching the new tension. "What do we have to know, damn you? You side with them savages, and you run to Duquesne now and then to tell Hopkins what our strength is. You tell Rain Cloud he can attack our garrison, because we ain't at full company. Ain't that enough?"

Dan'l shook his head. "Who told you them lies?"

"They ain't lies."

"I never told Hopkins nothing," Dan'l said easily. "And I just got Rain Cloud's promise to cool his braves down, and take the war paint off."

"We don't hardly believe that," the corporal said.

"Well, I guess I'll just have to live with that," Dan'l said. "Now, I got trail to cover."

He started guiding his horse around them, but the sergeant blocked his way. Dan'l gave him a hard look.

"Maybe we ought to show you what we think of Indian lovers," the sergeant said. He dismounted, and gave his reins to the corporal. "Why don't you just stay a mite?"

Dan'l looked down at him. The sergeant was a big man, and big men always had the idea they could challenge Dan'l, who was not much above average height, but very powerfully built. "I ain't got time for this, Sergeant," he said patiently.

The sergeant grabbed the reins of Dan'l's

mount, up by the horse's nose. "Maybe you ought to just make time."

Dan'l sighed heavily, and climbed down from his horse. The other soldiers stayed mounted to watch. The sergeant put his fists up as if to fight. "If our officers won't do nothing about you, maybe we can make you wish they had." He grinned harshly. "You ain't got that famous rifle in hand now, Boone. What are you going to do without it, big hunter?"

Dan'l threw a vicious punch at the sergeant's head that came so fast the sergeant did not even see it before it smashed into his jaw and fractured it loudly. The punch had sliced between the sergeant's fists without even touching them, and hit his face like a bag of lead balls.

The sergeant went down hard.

He hit the ground on his back, out cold. The other two soldiers looked down on him unbelieving.

"Oh, damn!" the private said.

The corporal looked at Dan'l as if seeing him for the first time.

Dan'l took a canteen of water off his belt, removed the cap, and poured some water on the sergeant's face. The sergeant moved, then shook his head and muttered on obscenity. His eyelids fluttered open, and he looked up at Dan'l. He started to say something, then yelled in pain. He grabbed at his jaw.

"You—broke my jaw, you—son of a bitch!" he mumbled between his teeth.

"You want me to keep on?" Dan'l said nicely.

The sergeant averted his gaze.

Dan'l looked up at the others. "You boys get down here and put this non-com on his horse."

They just sat there for a moment, but then dismounted, one after the other. They dragged the sergeant to his feet, and he stumbled over to his horse, holding his jaw. They helped him into his saddle.

Dan'l stood holding the reins of the sergeant's mount. "Now listen to me, you stupid bastards," Dan'l said sternly. "I'm out here under orders of Colonel Davison. When you went Continental, so did I. I'm carrying a temporary rank of captain. I just stopped this boy from attacking a superior, a by-God court-martial offense."

They glared at him angrily. He grabbed his mount's reins, and climbed back aboard it. Then he looked down on them.

"Try to get this straight when you get back to the garrison. I just come from a big palaver with Rain Cloud. He knows now he was lied to, and he wants to make peace with all whites in the area. Can you remember that?"

The corporal nodded. "Yeah."

"And you tell your new commander I ain't coming back till I got McKenzie's scalp in my saddlebag. He'll know what I mean."

"All right."

"Now, if you ain't got no other complaints, I'll be riding," Dan'l concluded.

He rode off without further comment, with the three soldiers staring after him with bleak faces.

Chapter Twelve

Jock McKenzie had never reached Harrodsburg.

He and his men had met a trader on the way there, at a small trading camp, who had bought all of their hides and paid top dollar for them. At that same encampment, McKenzie learned why Amos Weeks had not rejoined them yet, with the provisions they sent him after. A hunter brought the news that Weeks had committed suicide at Danville, and that the death had been reported by none other than Dan'l Boone.

McKenzie realized that there must have been a confrontation between Weeks and Dan'l, and that Dan'l was somehow responsible for his loss of Weeks.

For the first time since he had heard of Dan'l

Boone, McKenzie was not grinning when his name was mentioned.

He was angry.

After a day at the small rendezvous camp, he decided to turn back on his pursuers and kill them. That same evening, before he could leave, Aubrey Suggs brought a hunter to their fire.

It was a cool night, and the hunter was wearing a big bearskin coat and a coonskin cap. He had a foot-long handlebar mustache decorating his lower face, and carried a British cavalry officer's saber on his belt. He was a very odd-looking man.

Suggs appeared quite excited. "I got a chap here I'd like you to meet," he told McKenzie.

McKenzie, Spencer, and Quinn were all sitting quietly around the fire, and McKenzie had been telling them they should try to find out where Dan'l was at the moment. All around them were the tents and fires of area traders who met at this trail juncture a couple of times a year to buy and sell furs, hides, liquor, and supplies for woodsmen. Next year they might hold the meeting at Harrodsburg, which wanted the business, and whose town fathers insisted they could supply the facilities to house everybody and feed them.

The hunter started talking without being introduced. "I been hunting these woods almost as long as Dan'l Boone hisself," the fellow was saying as McKenzie focused on him. "I shot over fifty quail in an hour once. I took thirty buffalo hides in one shoot, down in the north of Tennessee. I got the best pelts in these parts, boys. Maybe you'd like to see some?"

"Who the bloody hell is this?" McKenzie said to Suggs.

Suggs jumped in quickly, standing beside the hunter. "His name is Dodge. He just came from Brady's Cabin, south of here."

"So what's the blinking point?" McKenzie said.

Quinn was shaking his head.

"He says there was an Indian there. Billy Two Tongues."

McKenzie sat up straight. "Are you sure?" he said to the hunter.

"That's what he called hisself. He had this scarred face. Awful ugly to look at."

"Tell him what he said to you," Suggs said impatiently.

"Said he was from Fort Stuart originally. He was there when that place was burned to the ground."

"No, you blinking sot!" Suggs said. "The other. About Boone!"

The hunter gave Suggs a hurt look. "Oh, that. I asked him why he was camped out there. He told me he was waiting for somebody."

"Yes?" McKenzie urged him.

"Said he was waiting for Dan'l Boone."

McKenzie turned and exchanged a dark look with Quinn.

"Said Boone had went home, but was coming to meet Billy soon now. Said he wouldn't leave till Boone got there."

"Damn!" Quinn said.

"When was this, Dodge?" Spencer asked.

"Just yesterday. I guess you know Billy, huh? He's probably still there."

McKenzie rose and placed a shilling in the hunter's hand. "Appreciate the news, old chap. Now bugger off."

The hunter squinted at McKenzie, then shook his head. "Nice to talk to such friendly folks."

He gave them a sour look, and turned and left.

Suggs hurried over to McKenzie. "Well? A spot of luck, wouldn't you say, governor?"

McKenzie nodded absently. "Pound to a penny the Indian is still there."

"It's only a three-hour ride," Spencer said.

Quinn stood also. "Maybe Boone will be there too. We could get them both, by Jesus! And this running would be finished."

"Who the hell is running!" McKenzie exploded.

Quinn blanched. "Well. I meant, having them on our backs."

"I don't run from any man, you bleeding pus sac!" McKenzie yelled at him.

Quinn turned away.

"He don't mean nothing, Captain," Suggs said, suppressing a small grin.

Spencer intervened, to calm McKenzie. "If we rode out of here early, we could be back there before noon tomorrow."

McKenzie withdrew his glare from Quinn. He nodded. "Yes, and we bloody will be. I'm flaming tired of having these two traipsing around the countryside behind our backs. I'm going to put a goddamn end to it."

"I want that Indian myself," Suggs growled.

"We could get them both," Quinn said quietly.

McKenzie just gave him a cold look.

The next morning, the foursome rode back along the Harrodsburg trail to Brady's Cabin.

McKenzie was hoping Dan'l would have arrived, and they would catch the pair there. But that was not to be. Dan'l had camped out on the trail, expecting to arrive at the cabin in early afternoon of that same day.

Billy was still there by himself, and running out of provisions. He had expected Dan'l back a day or two ago, and now was becoming impatient, and a little worried. In early morning, though, just about the time McKenzie and Dan'l were making their way toward him from different directions, but with Dan'l much farther away, a diversion occurred.

A trapper rode up and dismounted, and walked over to greet Billy.

"Morning. Do you speak English?"

Billy scrutinized him from the doorless front entrance of the cabin. The trapper was a lean, lanky fellow with a graying beard and soiled cloth trousers and shirt who wore a greasy-looking beaver hat atop his head. Under his arm he carried a German Jaeger rifled musket, a newer gun that some British troops were using now.

"That depends," Billy said easily.

"Hey. Ain't you that Billy Two Tongues? That escaped the fire at Fort Stuart?"

Billy nodded. "I was at Fort Stuart."

"God, what a mess. Say, I thought you was riding with Dan'l Boone."

"I am," Billy said.

The fellow looked around. "Where is that old trail-buster? I ain't seed him in a coon's age!"

"He is not here. But I expect him any day. He returned home."

"Oh, hell, yes. That attack at Boonesborough!" He laughed a high laugh. "You don't want to show your face around these parts much, do you, Billy? I mean, being Algonquin and all."

Billy did not smile. "I am not hiding. I am waiting."

"Oh, sure. I didn't mean that." He saw that Billy was holding a cup of coffee in his hand. "By the way, you ain't got another cup of that somewheres, do you?"

Billy stepped out into the sun, and handed the cup to him. "I have not started it."

"Why, much obliged." He took the cup and swigged the coffee while Billy watched. "My name's Hadley, by the bye. Been trapping out here almost as long as Dan'l. Met him in Salisbury, right after the Frenchie War. Best damn shot I ever seed."

"I know," Billy said.

"Say, what are you two doing out here?" Hadley said, drinking the coffee in the sun.

Billy hesitated. Everybody that passed wanted

to know their business. "We're looking for a man named McKenzie. Do you know of him?"

Hadley shrugged. "Can't say as I do. Is he running from the law?"

"He is the murderer of Fort Stuart."

Hadley squinted. "Good Jesus!"

"Sheltowee is commissioned to find him."

Hadley swigged the last of the coffee, and went and hung the cup on a square nail on the wall of the broken-down cabin. Then he came out to face Billy again. "Is they a bounty?"

Billy smiled to himself. "No. No bounty."

"Oh."

"We do not do this for money."

Hadley nodded. "I see what you mean. Look, you mind if I wait here with you? I mean, till Dan'l gets here? I think I might like to join up with you boys. I mean, hunting men is always more fun than running down buffalo or such." He laughed that high laugh.

"You can ask him," Billy said doubtfully.

Hadley was standing facing the cabin, his back to the hills behind him. Billy was only a few feet away, his back to the cabin. Hadley was just in the process of explaining his abilities to Billy, when it happened.

"Dan'l knows I can take care of myself. He seen me take a shaggy down at three hundred yards. I think I'd like to go after the son of a bitch that—"

Suddenly his face exploded right in front of Billy. Just flew apart in a hail of bone and gray matter, with stuff spattering all over Billy's own face and shirt. Billy felt a pain in his left earlobe at the same instant, and then came the sound of the shot that had hit them.

Hadley stumbled forward, his whole head shattered, his face gone, and fell into Billy's arms. Billy made a sound in his throat, and stepped away from Hadley's corpse, letting it fall to the ground at his feet.

Then Billy was punched hard in the low chest, as if by a hickory walking stick, and thrown up against the doorjamb of the cabin as the sound of the second shot came to him. He hung there, looking down at the blood on his shirt, and then up at the hills, where he saw a dull flash of light, and realized they had been shot from long distance.

"McKenzie!" he gritted out as he slid to the ground outside the cabin.

As he sat there holding his rib cage, he saw the four riders come down the hill toward him. Only one carried a long gun, and that was McKenzie himself. When they came closer, Billy saw a grim smile on his square face with its long scar over the left cheek and its wild eyes.

They came on up to the cabin warily, looking about, McKenzie in their fore. Suggs and Spencer were right behind him, and Quinn brought up the rear.

"Where is he?" McKenzie said to Billy as he reined in. "Where's Boone?"

At a distance, McKenzie had allowed himself

to believe that the other man with Billy might be Dan'l. But he realized as soon as they started down the hill that he was not.

Billy glared at him, but did not reply.

"Are you hard of hearing, then, red man? I know you talk the King's English, so don't be coy with us."

Suggs moved his mount up beside McKenzie's. "You're lucky you didn't kill him," he said gruffly.

McKenzie dismounted, satisfied that they had shot the only two men at the cabin. The others followed suit, and stood around Billy in a loose semi-circle.

"What an ugly bastard!" Spencer spat out.

Quinn was still looking around. He had more fear of Dan'l than the others.

"Luck had nothing to do with it, laddy," McKenzie responded to Suggs. "I could have hit him in his redskin heart if I'd chose."

"Sheltowee could have made that shot at twice the distance," Billy said to McKenzie, glaring up at him.

"Ah, the red man has some spunk left, chappies. That's a bloody good show." McKenzie walked through the open doorway. "Bring him inside. The yelling won't carry as far."

Suggs looked over at Quinn, then shrugged. "Whatever you say, Captain."

Suggs and Quinn caught Billy under the arms, dragged him inside, and propped him against a busted-up bunk. He was in a lot of pain, and was losing blood. He looked at his captors, and knew this was the last day of the world.

McKenzie came and stood before him. He pulled his hat off and dusted it on his knee, and his long hair looked wild.

"Well, now."

Suggs went and leaned against a wall. Quinn sat on the busted-down cot, and regarded Billy glumly. Spencer looked around the cabin, and made a face.

"What a pigsty," he said to himself.

McKenzie faced Billy. He squatted down now, so he would be on Billy's level. "So you're the one escaped from Fort Stuart?" he said in a pleasant voice.

Billy glared at him, his breath coming short. He was having difficulty remaining conscious. Don't come now, Sheltowee, he said in his head. It won't matter.

"Do you think it was worth it, then?" McKenzie said to him, grinning through a long stubble of beard.

Billy remained silent.

"All Boone has caused you is trouble, lad. And now look at you. Wouldn't it be better if you'd burned up in the fire?"

Billy glared at him.

"You were ruddy talkative outside. The haggis is in the flames now, bucko. If you ever used your King's English to advantage, now would be the best time. It would be marvelous wise, you might say."

"I have nothing—to say," Billy grated out.

"Ah. He hasn't lost his second tongue, after all. Your name is Two Tongues, isn't it?"

Suggs laughed. Spencer walked to the doorway and looked out toward the hills, bored.

Billy grimaced in pain.

"Ah, the wound is giving you trouble. Well, of course we could dig that lead out of there. If you cooperate."

Billy sat there.

"Tell me, lad," McKenzie said more seriously. "What black deed did you inflict on poor Weeks, to have him stick a gun to his head?"

No response.

"Or did you shoot him, then put the rotting gun in his hand?"

"He was a coward," Billy said. "He shot himself."

Spencer turned and gave Billy a deadly look, suddenly interested again. "Can you imagine? An Indian talking like that about a white man?"

"It's by-God disgusting," Quinn said quietly.

"No, no, lads," McKenzie said. "The lad is just being honest. We want him to be honest, old chaps. He can say King George is a water bug, if it please him." He laughed easily.

Oh, bloody hell, Suggs said to himself. But he did not voice the thought aloud. He did not want any more trouble from McKenzie. McKenzie was still being curt with Quinn.

"Do you think King George is a water bug, then?"

McKenzie was leering into Billy's face, and

Billy realized in that moment how much he hated the man.

"Algonquins do not—think about your king—at all," he managed, breathing hard after the effort.

"Bloody hell!" Suggs said, aloud this time.

But McKenzie was not offended. He had no loyalty to King George III whatever, nor to England. This had been sensed by British troops, and had caused him occasional trouble in the past.

"So what did you do or say to Weeks that made him want to blow his brains out?" McKenzie persisted.

"We said we were—taking him to you."

McKenzie looked puzzled for a moment, then laughed a loud, boisterous laugh. "Did you hear that, lads? Weeks was more afraid of me than he was of Boone!"

Spencer cast a dark look at McKenzie. Quinn tried a laugh that did not come off, and Suggs just stood there, thinking about that.

"You're waiting here for Boone, lad, are you not?" McKenzie said to Billy, and suddenly his voice was low and hard.

"Boone is in his home. Taking care of—his family." Sharp knives of pain sliced through his chest, and almost blacked him out.

"You already told that hunter Dodge that you're meeting Boone here, Billy. So don't start lying now, lad."

Billy eyed him bleakly.

"When do you expect him, Billy? Save your own life, lad, that's a good chap."

Billy could hardly think through the pain. "His wife—is with child. She is due. He may not come at all."

McKenzie rose to his feet and stared down at Billy. "You were so honest about King George."

"Let me have him for a time," Suggs said.

McKenzie paced the room before Billy. "Shall I tell you what will happen to you, lad, if I turn you over to Suggs?"

Sitting there on the cot, Quinn remembered Dan'l, and a small fear crept into him as McKenzie spoke.

"Or maybe you'd prefer it was a surprise?" McKenzie said.

"I told you—the truth."

McKenzie turned to Quinn. "Tie his hands behind him, Leftenant."

Quinn almost said, "Yes, sir!" before he caught himself. "All right," he grunted.

He pulled Billy forward and used a short length of coiled rawhide on his belt to tie Billy's hands. Billy almost passed out in the process.

"There," McKenzie purred. "Are you comfortable, then?"

Billy gave him a somber look.

"Then let's try again," McKenzie said. "I shall inquire slowly, so you don't miss a word. When is Boone meeting you here at this bloody cabin?"

Billy knew that Dan'l must be on his way. But he did not intend to tell this killer that. He resolved to give him false information. But it had to look as if McKenzie was forcing it from him.

"I—won't tell you more."

"I see," McKenzie said.

"Let me have him," the sadistic Suggs said, rather breathlessly.

"You can't make an Indian talk if'n he don't want to," Spencer said in a hard voice. "I've tried. Shoot him in the head and let's get to Harrodsburg. I want to get a good meal under my belt."

McKenzie turned to him, straight-faced. "Are you content to allow me to do this my way, laddy?" he asked in a soft, menacing voice.

Spencer shook his head. "Go ahead. Have your little game."

McKenzie glared at him. "So you think it's game-playing, is it? Do you want Boone on your back trail all bloody summer?"

Spencer nodded weakly. "You're right, do what you have to," he said just to get away from McKenzie. He turned and stepped through the doorway, into the sun.

McKenzie stared after him for a moment, then turned back to Billy. "Do you see the trouble you cause, lad? Do you wish to make more for me?"

"I told—you what I know," Billy said.

But he had already planted the idea in McKenzie's head that there was more, and McKenzie had taken the bait.

"Suggs," McKenzie said.

Suggs came forward, a dull grin on his beefy face.

"Why don't you probe the wound? To see where the lead went. It made just a wee hole in his chest."

Suggs broadened the grin. He took the long knife from the sheath that he always carried, and knelt before Billy. "Now, red man. Let's see what you're made of."

Suggs then slowly shoved the point of the knife directly into the gunshot wound, a quarter-inch at a time.

Billy's eyes went wide, and a loud scream tore itself from his throat. Suggs turned the blade slightly, and Billy screamed again.

McKenzie put his hand on Suggs's shoulder, and Suggs removed the blade from the wound. Billy hissed in shock, then sat there trying not to faint. Blackness welled up on him, then edged back away. He was breathing raggedly.

"Did you find the ball?" McKenzie said pleasantly to Suggs.

"Not that time," Suggs said. "It must be deeper."

"That's—enough," Billy gasped out. "Let me die."

"When you've told us *all* you know," McKenzie smiled.

Billy nodded weakly. "I am sorry, Sheltowee," he whispered, putting on an act for them.

"Well? Go on," McKenzie said.

"Boone told me—to wait here till—the moon is full."

Suggs scowled. "That's almost a week off!"

244

Billy was losing ground. The gunshot was almost directly over his previous wound, which he had not fully recovered from yet. He was in bad shape, and knew it. The only thing he could do now was try to save Dan'l from ambush.

A second one might prove fatal.

"His home has been—attacked by Algonquin," Billy grated out slowly, between gasps. "He did not even know—his family was alive—when he left."

McKenzie and Suggs exchanged a look. That confirmed the story they had heard about the Algonquin war-making from the hunter Dodge.

"He might not—come at all," Billy concluded. "I was to go looking—if the full moon—did not bring him."

McKenzie stood there and absorbed that.

"He's telling the truth," Quinn said, speaking up.

McKenzie sighed slightly. "Maybe."

"We can't wait around here hoping the bloke shows himself," Suggs said to McKenzie. "We have things to do."

McKenzie looked through the open doorway, past Spencer to the hills beyond. He had hoped to get both of them here.

"Yes, yes," he finally said. "You're right, of course."

Quinn let a breath out. He was glad to get out of there. "Let me end it for him," he said.

McKenzie looked down at Billy. "No. Suggs, you can do it. Make it last a bit."

Billy heard the remark and cast a dark look at his tormenter. "Sheltowee will learn of this."

McKenzie looked at him and grinned. "I'll be outside, Sergeant."

As he left the cabin, Suggs turned to Billy with the long knife before him, smiling.

Billy waited for the inevitable.

Dan'l arrived at Brady's Cabin three hours later, an hour after high noon.

He pulled his fresh mount to a halt at the edge of the clearing.

Things looked different to Dan'l immediately.

For one thing, he could not spot Billy's mount. Also, the cabin had a dead look to it.

Dan'l slid the Kentucky rifle from its saddle scabbard and loaded it. He used the new paper cartridges that were now available on the frontier, and had been in use for some time in the east. It made loading much easier and faster. Then he primed and cocked the long gun, watching the surrounding hillsides. Something was wrong. He felt it in his gut.

He rode on down the hill and approached the cabin. "Hallo in there!"

No response.

"Oh, hell," he murmured.

He looked around the cabin, and saw all of the fresh hoofprints. He dismounted carefully, and took a closer look.

"McKenzie!" he whispered to himself.

He looked at the open doorway. "Billy?"

A hawk screeched out a hunting cry, high above the hills. Otherwise, silence. Dan'l looked up and saw the lone vulture, circling high overhead.

He stepped to the doorway and looked inside. There were drag marks on the ground, leading up to the door, and there were dark stains in the dirt. The first thing he saw inside the cabin, near the door, was the corpse of the trapper Hadley, with its head destroyed. Big blue-green flies were buzzing loudly on it, and a rat had come in from somewhere and was eating at an arm. It scurried out of sight when it saw Dan'l.

Dan'l stepped inside, out of the sunlight, and his eyes adjusted to the lesser light. Then he saw Billy.

Billy still sat against the far wall.

More buzzing of flies came from that direction. Dan'l moved closer, and squinted down. Then his jaw dropped slightly open.

Suggs had done a job on Billy. First he had punched his eyeballs out, and their liquid was dried on Billy's cheeks and face. Then he had cut Billy's chest open. Slowly. By that time Billy was beyond hurting, but Suggs had not stopped. He had cut Billy's tongue out as a joke. The blackened tongue lay on the dirt floor between his legs, thick and bloated.

Dan'l knelt in front of him, and a tightness came into his throat.

"Billy," he said softly.

He had told his friend to wait for him here, in

this dangerous place. He had not returned. Now Billy was dead. Just as Jake Medford was dead.

Dan'l lifted his eyes to the roof of the cabin, his face twisted with grief, and roared out a gut-wrenching cry to the heavens, a cry that echoed chillingly across the encroaching hills on that sunny May morning, and sent furry creatures scurrying to their holes in abject fright.

Chapter Thirteen

He could not bear to look at Billy's body.

He left the cabin slowly, rifle dropped to his side, completely vulnerable. If McKenzie had been hiding in the rocks on the hillside, Dan'l would have been an easy mark. But the Scot was long gone, on his way to Harrodsburg.

Dan'l turned and looked in that direction.

"It's just you and me now, you bastard," he declared in a tight, emotion-filled voice.

"There won't be no more partners for you to murder, you sonofabitch!" he yelled at the hillside. "And there ain't going to be no arrest, no goddamn trial! Not now!"

His horse made a snorting sound and shied away from him when he went to it. He reached into a saddlebag, took out some primitive matches, and walked over to the cabin. After gathering some dry brush nearby, he piled it up against the cabin wall, then started a fire.

In moments it had flamed up and set the rotten wood of the structure ablaze. Dan'l led his horse away from the growing flames, stood back, and watched the cabin burn. Soon it was blazing brightly, with black smoke curling into the sky.

The Algonquin believed that Billy's soul would rise with the smoke and be free for eternity.

The fire had been his enemy at Fort Stuart. Now it was his friend.

Colonel Frank Davison looked up from his desk at his company headquarters in Salisbury, where he was doing some paperwork to effect the melding of his garrison into the new Continental Army. An aide had tapped on his doorjamb to get his attention, and now stood at attention before him.

"Sir!"

"Yes, Lieutenant?"

"There's news from Kentucky, sir. Boonesborough has been attacked by Chief Rain Cloud. Quite a few deaths, sir."

"Damn," Davison said, putting his quill pen down. "That devil McKenzie's poison has stuck in the red man's gullet, it appears. I wonder how many other tribes will do the Brits' work for them before this is finished."

Back east, the Committee of Public Safety had

raised enough money to support fifteen thousand men as a permanent army, and many militia units were being swallowed up whole into it.

"Do you want to send a detachment out, sir? The garrison at Boonesborough is depleted now. The town is probably almost defenseless."

Davison shook his head. "I can't spare a man, Lieutenant. They say we may be fighting the king's troops at Charleston or Savannah soon. General Washington foresees actual shooting engagements, now that Gage has declared anybody a traitor who carries a gun. There's talk of convening the Continental Congress shortly, in preparation for real hostilities with the mother country."

"Good heavens, Colonel. Are we really to end up firing on British troops? I have cousins in the royal forces."

Davison nodded. "So do many of us, Lieutenant. And I'm certain many of them feel the same way. It's a damn shame. But now there's the bloody Restraining Act to fuel the flames of resentment again, telling us we can't trade with any country but Britain and Ireland."

"What would we do if we gained independence, like some are talking about?" the lieutenant wondered. "We're not really fit to govern ourselves, do you think, Colonel?"

"Well. I guess we'd muddle through somehow. It's all just a damn shame. We need a conference with the king's envoys, to try to resolve all this peaceably. But that seems more and more unlikely."

"I'm glad we're out here away from it. For a while, at least."

"I suspect it will be a very short while," Davison told him.

"Sir, what about Dan'l Boone? A couple of us were wondering. You and Captain Emery sent him out after that renegade Jock McKenzie."

"Yes, I haven't forgotten. We gave him a commission and an aide. Medford, I believe his name was. We figured the frontier would be a lot quieter without that bastard McKenzie in it."

"Does his commission carry over to the Army now, Colonel? Should we be trying to get in touch with him, to find out how his mission is going?"

Davison sighed. "I've just been addressing that situation, Lieutenant. Unfortunately, I have a message back from Charleston that militia personnel on temporary assignment will not retain rank in the Army. Also, all militia assignments and orders are hereby canceled. Boone is on his own."

"But he probably thinks his commission carried over," the lieutenant said.

"I know. But we have no idea where McKenzie is, or Boone. I'd like to be able to tell him to return home and take care of his own family. But I don't know how. I may not even be able to get him the pay I promised him. It's damned unfair. But I don't make the rules."

"He's out there, Colonel," the lieutenant said, "risking his life on a mission that's been rescinded, for God's sake."

The colonel nodded. "I feel just as badly about it as you, Lieutenant. But there is this. The need to bring McKenzie to justice is still there. The cause of peace on the frontier is being served by Boone's being out there and *not* knowing. I know that sounds hard-hearted, but that's war, by Jesus."

"Yes, sir."

The door was still open, and they heard a commotion and excited talking coming from the outer office.

"Would you see what that is, Lieutenant?" the colonel said tiredly.

The lieutenant went out, and in a moment came back in with a wide-eyed corporal who had just ridden in from the east.

"There's more news, Colonel," the lieutenant announced. "From another direction. Why don't you tell him, Corporal?"

The corporal saluted, snapping to attention.

The colonel returned the salute casually. "Yes, yes, Corporal. Report."

"It's war, Colonel!" the young man exclaimed excitedly. "In Boston! General William Howe demanded that colonial troops disarm there, and they wouldn't. There was a shooting engagement at Bunker Hill, with thousands of casualties. The British made the colonials flee for their lives!"

Colonel Davison just sat there for a long moment, absorbing the news.

"Are you sure about all of this, Corporal?"

"Oh, yes, sir. It came from Army headquarters in Charleston."

Davison nodded absently. He had feared it would come to this, and soon. Now there was probably no going back. Now it was more important than ever that the frontier be pacified, and that the Algonquin, Shawnee, and Cherokee be kept under control. A devious man like McKenzie could do incalculable harm.

"Don't let him escape us, Dan'l," he said to himself.

"Beg pardon, sir?" the corporal said.

"Oh, nothing, Corporal. Nothing anybody in Charleston would understand."

Over at Fort Duquesne, where the British colonel, Hopkins, had just heard the same news, the conversation was on the same topic, but was taking a much different turn. Hopkins sat in a small conference room just off his private office, talking privately with his young adjutant, the one who had greeted Dan'l Boone when he visited the fort to talk about McKenzie. The long, lanky Hopkins, with his aquiline face, looked moody now as he sat at an oval table, rolling a pen in his fingers. His adjutant watched him carefully.

"Well, the bloody fat's in the fire now," Hopkins said to the younger man. "We'll be getting marching orders very soon now, I'd wager. We're going to be hurtled headlong into a real war, Captain."

The fuzz-faced youngster looked curious. "But, Colonel, surely these ill-trained colonials can't put up a real fight against seasoned British troops. If they really want a war, it should be over in a matter of weeks."

Davison regarded him soberly. "Remember what happened at Lexington. They don't fight like we do, Captain. They fire from ambush, like the French used to do. They all learned it from bloody savages, of course. It's disgraceful, really."

"I'm sure King George will send as many troops as it takes to put down these rebels," the adjutant said. "And some of the Indian tribes are showing signs of friendliness toward us now, and willingness to fight on our side. Just like they did with the French. They say their fight was never with us. It was with the colonial farmers who take their land. The Algonquin in New York and Pennsylvania have already made overtures toward us. And, of course, Rain Cloud attacked Boonesborough on his own, without any encouragement, and reduced the garrison there to less than a company."

Hopkins nodded. "I know. I hope Dan'l Boone's family was safe. He's a moderating force out there. We may need him before this is over. To help stop the shooting."

"There's a rumor that he went out after McKenzie on his own, Colonel. I guess maybe it's something personal."

"I suspect Boone just wants this all over." Hopkins smiled. "So he can get on with expanding the frontier westward. I don't think he cares whether King George is in charge or not, so long as his life work isn't disrupted."

"Maybe we should be looking for McKenzie," the adjutant said, watching Hopkins's face closely.

Hopkins looked over at him. "And why would that be, lad?"

The adjutant shrugged. "The Shawnee, for instance, don't know what McKenzie did at Fort Stuart, I'm sure. And if they knew, they wouldn't care, since the Algonquin are their deadly enemies. Some say McKenzie got Rain Cloud all riled up before he attacked Boonesborough. If we really want Indian allies in the coming war, maybe we could use McKenzie, out there on the frontier, to do some recruitment for us. Despite the fact that he thinks all Indians are sub-human, he seems to have a way of getting to them. Maybe we need him."

Hopkins held his look. "God. Have we come to this? Must we use a cold-blooded killer for our own purposes?"

"Cold-blooded killers win wars, Colonel," the young man said flatly. "I wouldn't invite McKenzie into my home, but out here in the wilderness, he may be just the man for a dirty job."

"I suppose there's truth in that," Hopkins said heavily.

"With your permission, sir, I'll put somebody on it. I'm sure McKenzie can be found out there.

And the bastard will do anything for money, we know that."

Hopkins sighed. "Unless Boone gets to him first."

The adjutant nodded.

"Well. Let me think on it, lad."

"Don't think too long, Colonel. Things are happening fast now."

"I know, Captain. I know."

At that same time, out on the trail to Harrodsburg, Dan'l was riding hard to pick up McKenzie's spoor, and by late afternoon, he had found traces of the four horsemen. They had left the main trail, to throw him off in case he was following them, but came back onto it within twenty miles of Harrodsburg.

Just after Dan'l found their trail, he got a small surprise. Two Shawnee were crossing the main trail just ahead of him, and when they spotted him, they halted and allowed him to approach them.

Dan'l rode up to them warily. There were not many Shawnee left in the area now, because most had moved west. But the ones that were left were still as hostile toward all white settlers as they had ever been, and were as cruelly savage.

Dan'l slipped his rifle out and held it cocked and ready to fire as he reined in just a short distance from the mounted Indians.

Dan'l had not seen a Shawnee out on the trail for over a year, and the sight of them made his pulse quicken. They were magnificently fierce-looking, with their scalp brush and painted torsos and their war lances hanging boldly on their mounts' irons.

The nearest one held his hand up in greeting, and Dan'l responded. They were both tough-looking warriors, but the one who initiated the greeting was slightly larger.

He was studying Dan'l's face closely.

"You are Sheltowee," he said in Shawnee.

Dan'l nodded, and spoke in their own language. He was almost perfect in Shawnee. "Yes, I am Sheltowee. And you are of the great Shawnee nation."

The warrior's horse neighed softly. Dan'l looked at its riding blanket, and the dyed rawhide reins, and realized that this was the animal of a person of importance.

"Sheltowee," the first warrior repeated, looking Dan'l over. "I thought you would be . . . older."

Dan'l made a face. "I'm not forty yet."

"I meant no insult. But you fought against my father. At Fort Duquesne. I am the youngest son of Blackfish."

Dan'l smiled through his beard. Even though he had killed many of Blackfish's warriors in battle, Blackfish had such respect for him that he had offered to be Dan'l's godfather at one time.

"It does me honor to meet a son of the greatest of all Shawnee chieftains," Dan'l told him.

"We have heard through the drums that your home village was attacked by Algonquin," the muscular warrior went on. His more youthful companion made no attempt to join in the dialogue.

"This is true," Dan'l told him.

The warrior gave Dan'l his name, a long Shawnee one. "I am war counselor to a village to the west of Harrodsburg. There we tell tales of the bravery of Sheltowee at the two battles of Fort Duquesne."

Dan'l was pleased. "It is an honor to be so remembered. And the people of Boonesborough tell stories of the great bravery and war powers of Blackfish."

"The Algonquin are enemies from the Nether World. They eat human flesh and defile their own holy ground. Now they move west like the white settler, and kill any Shawnee they find in their path."

"I have heard of this," Dan'l said soberly. Rain Cloud, for instance, had slaughtered a small village of Shawnee when he first moved into southern Kentucky. But the Shawnee had done terrible things to his people. It had been that way for a thousand years or more.

But this man was right about cannibalism. The Algonquin had reverted to the practice after a raid on one Cherokee village, down south of there, even though the habit had been largely abandoned. Billy Two Tongues abhorred the idea that his people had ever done such things, and had told Dan'l so.

"If Sheltowee wishes it," the Shawnee told

him, "I will recommend to my chief that we will join forces with the militia, to drive the hated Algonquin from this hallowed land of Ken-Ta-Ke."

Dan'l looked down for a moment. "The Shawnee offer is heard with great appreciation. There is no braver warrior in battle than the Shawnee. But the people of Boonesborough have resolved to try to live in peace with the Algonquin. They were lied to by other white men, and the lies caused the trouble. I will settle with these other men."

"You make a mistake of judgment, Sheltowee," the Indian told him, "in trusting the Algonquin."

"I do not think so," Dan'l said. "If we can stop the lies between whites and the red man."

The Indian nodded. "So be it. Good wishes follow you, Sheltowee."

"And mine follow you."

A moment later, Dan'l was alone on the trail again.

It was one of his few encounters with Shawnee that had been friendly.

He was relieved that, as at Rain Cloud's village, it had not come down to killing.

There would be enough of that, he reckoned, when he caught up with McKenzie.

Dan'l had no way of knowing it, but McKenzie had stopped for the night, out on the trail, just ten miles ahead of him. His group had ridden steady after leaving Brady's Cabin, but decided to have one more meal on the trail before riding into Harrodsburg that same evening.

They had settled down at a small fire, and had finished eating, when McKenzie started talking about their future. He was sitting on a boulder ten feet from the fire, sipping a cup of coffee.

"I told you Boone wasn't coming. He's too busy at home, probably." He grinned. "After that lovely wee attack by the ruddy Algonquin."

"You pulled a bracing good trick on them, Captain," Quinn said, piping up. He was back in McKenzie's good graces now, and wanted to stay there.

"Krikey!" Suggs offered. "We got rid of the blackguard without firing a bloody shot!"

"I hope so," Spencer said, sitting beside the fire with the other two. His broken nose looked very bony in the firelight, and his earring shone dully in its glow. "I'm tired of looking over my shoulder. I say we should have waited at the cabin for a few days. If he showed, it would be over."

"But he might never, lad," McKenzie reminded him. "And I've got more important things to think about than putting in a tedious wait at that smelly rat's nest."

"It puts me right off to think on the malodorous pigsty!" Suggs agreed, making a face.

McKenzie set his cup down on the boulder beside him.

"Remember what we were talking about the other day? About getting a few pounds ahead, and heading back east? I've been thinking more and more about that, laddies."

"We've got enough now," Suggs suggested.

"Not really. When we ride into Philadelphia, or Boston, I want to arrive in high style," McKenzie said. "Have enough of a bankroll to live comfortably while we make plans. Things will be in a state of chaos, my buckos. A perfect situation for well-heeled thieves. Soldiering will be a large priority for a long time to come. Some constables will leave for various battlefronts. You and me, lads, will find easy pickings. Rich men's houses. Fancy emporiums. Maybe even a bank now and again."

"I agree with Suggs," Spencer told him. "Let's go now. I've had my fill of the goddamn frontier. Let's go east and live in style."

"Now, now, chappies," McKenzie said, clucking his tongue. "Impatience never got the hen's eggs. Let's look for a really bonnie opportunity. In Harrodsburg, or Bardstown. There may be too large a militia at Harrodsburg. But one of the two places should afford a bonnie target for us. A pub, perhaps. A place that keeps a lot of money on hand. Then, once our pockets are bulging, we'll turn tail and ride east. Maybe take a stage box or two on the way, and blame it on the Algonquin. That should heat things up again, and take the focus off of us. In a week, we'll be sleeping on soft beds in one of Philly's finest inns."

"God, you're fearful wise," Suggs said, then belched loudly.

Spencer looked over at him, and wondered if he had made a smart decision in joining up with this odd assortment of humanity. Now that

Weeks was gone, he felt a little more out of place with these Europeans.

"Ride it out with me, my buckos, and you'll have your pockets bulging with gold," McKenzie grinned. "All at the expense of these blithering colonials. Is it not a thing to make a man giddy with expectation?"

"We might get a medal from the king after all," Quinn suggested, laughing.

Spencer had not heard them express political attitudes before, and now their remarks made him feel even more apart from the others. "Not all colonials are so laughable," he said suddenly. "Weeks was a colonial. So am I."

His voice cut into their joviality much like a sharp knife into a flank of venison. A quick silence fell over them for just a moment. Then McKenzie recovered.

"I chose you to ride with us because you're not typical," McKenzie explained. "I thought you understood that, lad."

Spencer nodded. "Right," he said. But he began to feel differently toward his new comrades. If the war had not come upon them so unexpectedly, he knew, he might have been more tolerant of them. But now he felt a little like a traitor to his own people, riding with these men. And to Spencer that was worse than being a thief and murderer.

"In the end," McKenzie went on, "it's not a matter of Brit or colonial, is it? It's whether a bloke is smart enough to take what he wants,

when he wants it, and how he wants to take it. If
chaps like us are put upon, it's us against the rest
of them. Brit or colonial. Am I right, pray you?"

"You're bloody well right!" Quinn said quickly,
looking over at Spencer.

"You're marvelous bright, McKenzie," Suggs
cooed in his gravel voice.

They all turned to Spencer.

Spencer tried a smile. "Hell. Forget I mentioned it."

Dan'l arrived in Harrodsburg the following
morning, about twelve hours after McKenzie's
gang, because he had elected to spend the night
on the trail. His horse had needed the rest.

Harrodsburg was about the size of Boonesborough, with several hundred families crowded
into a stockaded area, and some scattered residences outside it. When Dan'l rode into the village, there seemed to be a lot of activity on the
main square, and the center of it was a group of
men who were gathered outside a small inn, talking loudly and angrily. Dan'l rode up to listen.

"She don't deserve nothing better."

"Hanging's too damn good for her."

"Did you bring the rope, Ed?"

"Let's go bring her out here."

Dan'l could not know it, but these men were
worked up about a local whore that Dan'l knew
from his single days, just after the French and
Indian War. Her name was Little Betty, but she
was as large as most men, and a completely un-

inhibited young woman. She had had the temerity to take a half-breed to her bed two nights ago, and that had angered a lot of the drinking men of the town. Then, last evening, when McKenzie and his people had stopped in for a few ales, Suggs had partaken of her charms before they left the establishment. When Suggs was finished with Little Betty, he had refused to pay her, and when she had complained, he had knocked her around some. Men had run upstairs to see what the ruckus was about, and Suggs had lied to them, saying that Betty had stolen his money. They'd wanted to believe him because they were already very angry with the whore, and when Suggs "recovered" a few silver coins from under her pillow that he himself had stashed there, Betty had received a further beating. Now, they had determined to tie her up, set her on a pole, and tar and feather her. If she survived that, she would be ridden out of town.

They expected no opposition, since the local constable was out of town and the garrison commander paid little attention to goings-on in the village.

Dan'l stopped a short distance down the length of the square, and focused on the men.

"Go fetch the tar buckets, Burt, and make sure they're hot."

"We'll go bring her down."

Dan'l dismounted and walked over to a storekeeper who stood watching the proceedings. The air was damp, and heavy thunderclouds hovered over the town.

"Morning," Dan'l greeted the apron-clad older man.

The fellow just looked him over, without replying.

"What's going on?"

"Oh, nothing much. They're going to tar a local whore. She stole some drifter's money."

"You say a drifter?"

The other man looked impatient. "That's what I said. Who the hell are you, mister?"

"The name's Boone. Dan'l Boone."

The man's face changed. "You're Boone?"

Now it was Dan'l's turn for impatience. "Who was this drifter?" he said.

"I'm sorry I didn't recognize you, Mr. Boone. You're practically a legend in these parts."

Dan'l scowled at him.

"Oh. The drifter. God, I don't know who he was. A big, ugly man. Was in the pub last night with three other men. I hear a couple of them talked with an English accent."

Dan'l nodded to himself. "Are they still here? These four men?"

"Somebody said they rode out just about an hour ago. Some was glad they did. They looked kind of rough."

"Son of a bitch," Dan'l said.

"Was you looking for them?"

"Anybody hear where they was headed?"

"I don't know. You might ask them men that's

making the noise down the street. Some of them were in the pub last night too."

At that same moment, two men came bursting out of the pub door with a heavyset blond woman in tow. She was kicking and yelling obscenities at them.

"You bastards! I didn't steal nothing! Get your dirty hands off of me!"

"We got her," one said. "Let's get on with it."

Dan'l's eyes narrowed on her. One dark night many years ago, when she had been rather good-looking, he had paid for her services, and enjoyed them. That was before he had even met Rebecca, or had any thought of marriage. He had liked Little Betty then, and had seen her on a couple of recent trips through Harrodsburg, but had rejected her offers of intimacy.

The men were tying Betty onto a long pole in a straddled, sitting position, and a couple of fellows had brought up two pails of steaming tar and a box of chicken feathers.

"I'll be damned," Dan'l said to himself.

"I never seen this done to a woman," the store-keeper said. "She might not last through it."

The gang of a dozen men were pulling at Betty's clothing now, tearing it off. A local woman came up to them and demanded they stop, but they shoved her away. Other citizens would not interfere. Betty was down to some scanty under-clothing, and when one fellow insisted that was enough, they brought up the hot pails of tar.

Betty eyed them with sudden terror. "Don't do this! I ain't no thief!"

"You're a goddamn liar!"

"Goddamn Indian lover!"

Dan'l slid the Ticklicker from its saddle sheath, and loaded and primed it. The storekeeper looked at him warily. "I wouldn't interfere, Boone. Some of them been drinking already this morning."

Dan'l nodded. "Thanks for the advice. Now, keep out of the way."

Dan'l walked down the street with the rifle hanging loose under his arm. A fellow called Burt, the one who had started this whole thing, was picking up a pail of tar, in preparation to dumping it all over Betty.

"Throw it on her!"

"Let her scald in it, by God!"

"No, please!" she yelled.

Dan'l came up behind them and raised the muzzle of the Kentucky rifle. "What the hell do you think you're doing?"

His low, hard voice caught their immediate attention. They all turned to him. There was often a core of men like this in most towns, Dan'l knew. They usually ended up in jail.

"Who are you?"

"Keep out of this, stranger."

"Hey. That's Dan'l Boone."

Betty turned and saw him. "Dan'l! Please do something!"

Sobriety settled over several faces in the

crowd. "Dan'l Boone," somebody repeated.

"Put that bucket of tar down. Now," Dan'l told the man named Burt.

Burt set it down carefully, as if it were a crate of eggs. Then he rested his hand on a revolver at his hip. "I don't care if you're the goddamn governor. This woman's getting what she deserves."

"This does it for me," one man muttered. He turned and walked away.

Dan'l walked up to them. He looked at Betty, who was scratched and bruised, with a lot of her ample flesh showing. "Was the man with you last night called Suggs?" he asked her.

"Yes, and a brute he was too!" Betty said, her eyes moist now. "He wouldn't pay, and when I complained, he began beating on me."

"That sounds like Suggs," Dan'l said.

"He put that money under the pillow. To take the blame off himself."

"You're saying he was lying, you damned whore?" Burt said. He was a rough-looking fellow wearing dark clothing.

"That's right!" Betty said defiantly.

"Who the hell's going to take a whore's word against a paying customer's?" Burt said fiercely.

"A whore that sleeps with redskins!" another man piped up.

"I believe her," Dan'l declared.

They all looked toward him again, and saw that the muzzle of the rifle was pointed in their general direction.

"Aubrey Suggs is a killer and a liar," Dan'l said

in a deliberate, level way. "This woman ain't."

A deep silence. Quite a few town people had gathered about now, watching quietly. Two of the assembled troublemakers looked at each other, then turned and left their companions without another word. A third one, seeing them leave, also walked away.

"Hey, what the hell is this?" Burt called after them. "We come here to get a job done, by God!"

"Untie this woman and get her off that pole," Dan'l said quietly.

Tension now hung over the square like a night fog. Burt had grabbed the butt of his revolver. It needed only cocking to fire.

"You go to hell, Dan'l Boone or whoever you are," Burt said loudly. His grip tightened on the gun.

Behind him, out of sight of Dan'l, a companion of his already had a one-shot pistol out, primed, and cocked. He eased out from behind Burt now.

"I won't ask you again," Dan'l said to Burt.

"Hell, Burt," somebody said nervously. "What's the difference? She had a good scare."

"Nobody's telling us how to run our town, I don't care who he is," Burt said in a hard voice.

In that instant, the fellow behind Burt stepped clear of him and aimed at Dan'l's chest.

But Dan'l had seen him, and as the other man squeezed down on the trigger of his weapon, Dan'l fired from the hip.

The rifle roared with an ear-shattering blast, and picked the gunman up off his feet as if pulled on a wire and hurled him out of the knot of men, knocking one down as he flew past. He hit the ground hard, a hole in him from front to back, his heart exploded like a ripe Kentucky squash.

There were gasps of shock, and then Burt was drawing the revolver and cocking it. Dan'l stepped forward in a quick movement, swung the rifle around in a wide arc, and smashed it into Burt's skull.

All present heard the distinct fracturing of bone; then Burt fell to his knees, his jaw working. He knelt there for a long moment, with blood running down from his right ear, then collapsed onto his face. His left fist punched at the dirt spasmodically once, and he was dead.

A couple of men still close to the action backed away, looking terrified now. Betty sat stunned on the pole. She had never seen a situation turn around so quickly, and so violently.

"Now I ain't in no mood to ask again," Dan'l said in a low growl. "Who wants to volunteer?"

A small man came forward, untied Betty, and helped her off the pole. She came and leaned weakly on Dan'l.

"You," Dan'l said to the bystander woman who had tried to stop them. "Take her back inside."

The woman got Betty, and guided her back into the building. When they were gone, Dan'l turned back to the remaining men. As they watched, he reloaded and primed the long, heavy rifle.

"Now," he said, in a hard, menacing voice. "Let's talk some more about Suggs."

Chapter Fourteen

Of the several men still standing there around the two corpses on the ground, only one was defiant enough to talk back to Dan'l.

"You just killed two of us," he said belligerently. "Why should we tell you anything?"

Dan'l decided he was the one to talk with. He spoke to the others without looking at them.

"The rest of you get," he said simply.

They hesitated, looking at each other. Then they slowly moved off without argument.

"Hey! Don't let him tell you what to do!" the remaining man said to them as they left.

Dan'l focused on him. "Did this Suggs have a man named McKenzie with him?"

The man's face showed some fear, but he tried to hide it. "So what if he did?" He looked into

Dan'l's hard eyes. "Sure, there was four of them. Seemed like real friendly people."

"And they rode out this morning?"

The fellow paused a moment. "That's right."

"Do you know which direction they was going?"

"Maybe," was the sly response.

Dan'l came up close to him, and spoke into his face. "Do I have to commence on you?"

The other man swallowed back the tension. "All right. I heard the one you call McKenzie talking to Suggs when they was saddling up. He said he wanted to be back in Danville as soon as they could."

Dan'l frowned. "Danville? That's where they come from."

A shrug. "That's what he said. I can't tell you nothing else."

Dan'l breathed out a long sigh. "All right. Now get your goddamn tar off the street, mister."

The fellow looked hard at him, but picked up the pails and walked off with them. He looked back over his shoulder once, and then was gone.

Dan'l had already been delayed, and was itching to get on McKenzie's trail. But he wanted to make sure Betty was all right. He went inside the public house and found her sitting at a table, looking washed-out. Another whore was sitting with her. Nobody else was in the big room. When they saw Dan'l, the second woman excused herself, and left Dan'l and Betty alone.

Dan'l went over and sat down with Little Betty.

She smiled weakly at him.

"I don't know how to thank you, Dan'l."

"It waren't nothing," he said. "Just cleaning the stable of a couple of varmints."

"Are they really . . . dead?" she asked.

Dan'l looked out through the open doorway, to where a couple of undertakers were loading the bodies aboard a small wagon.

"I reckon they are," he said. He looked into her blue eyes. "You ain't going to fret none about that, are you?"

"The constable will think it's all my fault."

"I don't reckon so. There was plenty of witnesses. You probably wouldn't 've lived through what they had in mind."

"The yellow bastards," she said.

He touched her hand. "There's a time to move on, Betty. Maybe this is that time for you."

"Maybe."

"If'n you're all right, I got to be riding."

"I'm all right now. Why don't you . . . come upstairs for a while, Dan'l? We could renew old acquaintances."

Dan'l grinned. "I'm married with a family, Betty. But I'm much obliged for the offer. Anyway, I got some more varmints to deal with."

"The one called McKenzie?"

He nodded.

"I thought I heard that fella tell you they was headed south. Toward Danville."

"That's what he said."

Betty shook her blond head. "That's not true, Dan'l."

He held her gaze. "How do you know?"

"I heard them talking this morning. Before they left the inn. They're headed for Bardstown. To the north."

"That bastard," Dan'l said. "I wondered about that."

"He just wanted to cause you some trouble," Betty said. "Because of what you done out there."

Dan'l nodded. "This makes more sense. You helped out a lot, Betty." He rose, the rifle still in hand. "I'll be going now. Think over what I said."

She smiled. The other woman had thrown a shawl over her, because of her partial nudity, and she looked almost domestic sitting there. "I am. I got a cousin back in Richmond. I might go stay with her for a while. She don't know what I been doing out here on the frontier."

"Good luck to you, Betty," he said.

Then he left the place.

Out on the street, the local commander of the militia had just walked down to ask questions about the shooting and the deaths. He had spoken to two witnesses, who had told him the whole story. Now he approached Dan'l as he went to his horse.

"You're Dan'l Boone, I reckon."

"Aye, Captain," Dan'l replied warily.

"I heard what happened out here. I just want you to know I'd have done the same. If I was able."

"I'm glad to hear that, Captain."

"I'll report it on to the constable, when he returns," the officer said. "Just the way it was told to me."

"I'm much obliged for that. Them boys wanted a fight. There didn't seem to be any other way to handle it."

"I don't like whores," the young captain told him, looking neat in his blue uniform. "I try to keep my men away from them. But those fellows had no cause to treat one that way. No matter what she'd done."

"I felt the same," Dan'l said.

The captain stood there. "I hear you're looking for that Jock McKenzie."

"That's right. Under orders from Colonel Davison."

"You been in touch with him lately?"

Dan'l shook his head. "Not for a spell."

"The word is that all special orders are rescinded. I just wonder how that might affect you."

Dan'l stared past him for a long moment. "It probably means they won't pay me when the job is done."

The captain sighed. "I'm sorry if it works out that way," he said.

"Captain, I don't give a tinker's damn about the money. It ain't about money now. I guess it never was."

"If I'd known they were here last night, I'd have arrested them," the captain said. "I heard about

Fort Stuart. I'm sorry I couldn't have been some help."

"It's all right," Dan'l told him. He put a foot in a stirrup and mounted the brown stallion.

The captain looked up at him. "I can't spare any men to help you go after him," he said. "Except maybe I could give you one for a limited time. Say, one week."

Dan'l shook his shaggy head. "No, Captain. You never know when you'll be facing a unit of British cavalry. I'm going it alone now. I guess that's the way it always had to be."

"Very well. May God be with you, Quaker."

Dan'l smiled. "The same for you, Captain."

McKenzie's gang had been on the trail for three hours when McKenzie stopped them and dismounted, looking over the terrain ahead. His gray horse pawed the dirt beside him, while he held the reins in one hand and shielded his eyes with the other. He had stopped shaving entirely now, and was slowly growing a reddish beard.

"Are you sure we took the right fork in the trail back there, Spencer?" he said.

He turned to face the other three.

Spencer was out front with McKenzie, because he knew the country in these parts better than the Brits he was riding with.

"I only been to Harrodsburg once, and that was a few years back," he replied. "But I'm pretty sure this is the trail."

"*Pretty* sure?" McKenzie said sourly. "Is that a

bit like pretty dumb and pretty bloody incompetent?"

McKenzie had noted Spencer's cooling toward him since Brady's Cabin, and he resented it. He thought any man allowed to ride with him should regard it as a great honor. After all, he was the Mad Scot, the most talented fellow the king had sent to the colonies in quite some time.

Spencer was angry. "Dumb? I'd say that word describes three goddamn Brits that wouldn't be able to find their own way back to Boston if they didn't have a colonial along with them holding their goddamn noses to the ground!"

McKenzie's eyes closed down to hard slits, and he just stood there and held Spencer in a blood-chilling look. Suggs stared at Spencer as if he had suddenly gone crazy.

"You flaming sot," Suggs sputtered at him.

"Hell," Quinn said, shaking his head. He did not want any dissension at this point. He still felt Dan'l's breath hot on the back of his neck.

"Well, you have got your back up proper, then," McKenzie said, grinning a black grin. But there was menace in his voice.

Spencer knew he had gone too far. "Look. I'm doing my best, damn it. This is mostly new to me too. Maybe Suggs had it right. We don't need Bardstown."

McKenzie walked up to his horse and took hold of the reins. "Don't ever speak to me that way again, laddy."

Spencer averted his eyes. He looked burly in

the fuzzy shirt, and with his thick brows. He was getting grubby, the bearskin cap soiled, his face coarse with trail dust.

"Do you understand, then, mate?"

"Oh, for God's sake, McKenzie."

"Do you understand?"

"Yes! I understand!"

"Good. That's good. Because I wouldn't want to have occasion to blow the crown of your head off now."

Spencer just looked at him.

McKenzie turned to the others. "I suppose we'll go on, lads. If we're on the wrong track, we'll find out soon enough. In the meantime—"

He stopped, seeing Suggs looking past him. He turned and saw that an Indian was riding toward them from a stand of trees. Beside the mounted man walked a squaw, carrying a baby.

"What the bloody hell," Suggs said. "Look at this."

The young Indian rode up fairly close to them, greeting them with his hand as he stopped. The squaw watched them warily. The Indian thought they were colonial trappers. He dismounted and came up to McKenzie.

He knew only a few words of English, so he spoke in his native tongue. "Greeting, white face friends. I am Algonquin, on my way to the village of Rain Cloud. We have run short on food and ask if you can spare flour. Or cornmeal."

"What's the bleeding monkey talking about?" Suggs said.

"I think he's begging," Quinn offered.

"I know a few words of Algonquin," Spencer told them. "He needs food. Wants to know if we have any extra."

"What bloody cheek!" Suggs said belligerently.

McKenzie grunted a small laugh. "It's food you want, is it, then?" He put a hand to his mouth. "You're bloody hungry?"

The Algonquin looked from his face to the others. "Yes. We need food. If you can spare it."

McKenzie turned to Spencer. "Ask him if this is the way to Bardstown." He took the Mortimer repeating pistol from his belt, and casually primed it. The Algonquin watched him carefully, and his squaw, a young, slim girl, looked suddenly afraid. She held her child tightly.

Spencer gave it a try. "We go—Bardstown. It—this way?" He pointed.

The young brave nodded vigorously. "Bardstown, yes." He pointed in the same direction.

"Good," McKenzie said, understanding. "Do you see that bulging bag on his horse, lads?"

They all looked.

"I'd wager there's something worth taking in there," McKenzie grinned. "And, of course, that's a fine-looking animal he's riding too."

"Hell, Indians don't carry no—"

But Spencer's mild protest went unfinished. McKenzie cocked the side arm, aimed it at the Algonquin, and fired the weapon point-blank into the Indian's face.

The gun roared, and the lead exploded through

the red man's head, passed on through, and hit his mount in the left temple. The horse let out a sharp cry, and went down with the Indian.

There was a big commotion on the ground. The horse kicked and flailed, raising dust, as McKenzie stepped back quickly, out of the way. The squaw was kicked in the leg, and went down too, screaming loudly.

"Damn!" McKenzie muttered, looking at the horse.

The horse stopped kicking and died. The Indian was dead when he hit the dirt. The squaw lay there moaning now, still hugging her squalling baby.

Oh, Christ, Spencer thought.

"Damn!" Quinn exclaimed hollowly.

Suggs was the only one who enjoyed it. He laughed softly. "Well, that was blinking easy!"

McKenzie turned to Spencer. "It looks like you found the right trail after all. Now let's see if you can do as good a job on them."

"Huh?" Spencer said.

"You heard me. Take the woman and child over in the trees. You know what to do. Or shall I spell it out, lad?"

Spencer frowned. "Let Suggs do it. It's his kind of thing."

"Hey. What does that mean, Yankee?" Suggs said.

"I want you to do it," McKenzie told Spencer slowly.

Spencer held his gaze for a moment. Then he

dismounted, went and grabbed the young woman, and pulled her to her feet. She began sobbing more loudly, hanging onto her yelling baby.

"Get it over with," McKenzie said. "The noise is getting dreadful loud."

Spencer gave him a somber look, then dragged the woman over to the nearby trees, while McKenzie went through two small bags on the dead horse's saddlery.

Quinn looked over there, and could see nothing. A shot rang out, and the woman's crying stopped abruptly. A moment later, the baby was silent too. Spencer had used a knife. In a moment he came back out of the trees, wiping the blade of the knife on his trousers.

"It's done," he said.

McKenzie looked up from the rawhide bags. "Would you believe it?" he said sourly. "Beads. And animal bones."

Suggs laughed. "No!"

"Beads and bloody bones," McKenzie said, shaking his head. "And look at the damned horse!"

" 'Tis a damned disgrace!" Suggs commented.

McKenzie rose. "Ah, well. Some days so bloody little seems to go right. It must be the dark of the moon. Look at this poor devil, for an instance. All he wanted was a pitiful crust of bread, or the makings. Doesn't life hand us a dirty pot sometimes?"

Spencer regarded McKenzie straight-faced. He

had never met a more soulless man in all his years on the trail. He walked over to him.

"We did some talking about where we're headed, back in Harrodsburg," he said to McKenzie.

"Yes? Is it worrying about that you're doing now, lad?"

"I don't worry," Spencer said evenly. "I look at things and see what they mean."

"Ah, I see. And what does it mean that we mentioned Bardstown, then?"

Spencer rubbed the back of his neck. "I've had a feeling ever since we left town. I used to get it when hostiles was about."

"Well. You have my full attention." McKenzie smiled. He stepped around the dead horse to get to his own. A fly was already buzzing over the head of the dead Algonquin.

"I'd like to retrace our trail some. While you go on toward Bardstown. I want to see what's back there, if anything."

"Boone?" McKenzie said.

"He could be. He might have found that Algonquin partner of his. If he did, he won't quit till he finds us."

"What!" Suggs said. "Risk his life for a bloody subhuman redskin?"

Spencer turned to him. "You Brits don't know us people on the frontier. Boone wouldn't do nothing less because the Algonquin ain't white."

"Well, that's downright queer," Suggs said.

But McKenzie just stood there, mulling that.

"I think you might be right, Spencer."

Quinn nodded to himself. "He is right."

"I thought I'd ride back for maybe five miles. I'll catch you by mid-afternoon. We'll feel a lot better if he ain't back there."

"*You'll* feel a lot better," McKenzie corrected him, grinning.

Spencer looked grim. "If you'd heard the stories about that hunter I have, you might feel his breath on your neck too."

"Here we go again," McKenzie grunted. "The Legend of Boone. Don't you remember how humble he looked in our sack? We could have killed him at any time."

"And should have," Spencer ventured. "He could sit off at five hundred yards with that Kentucky rifle, and pick us off one by one. Outside of our shooting range."

"You have Weeks' bloody Ferguson rifle," McKenzie said. "And you've been hunting since you were a boy."

Spencer laughed softly. "You really don't know, do you? You all think that gun-shot, battered devil you saw in your sack is Dan'l Boone?"

They all regarded him quietly.

"You ain't seen nothing yet," Spencer said. "You think I can match him with a Ferguson? Or a Kentucky rifle? Hell, you never seen shooting till you seen him. And he ain't wounded now, McKenzie. He'll have the strength of a grizzly, and the goddamn cunning of a cougar. You'd be better off having a whole damn war party of Algonquin or Shawnee after you than a healthy Dan'l Boone."

A heavy silence had fallen over them. Quinn looked somberly toward McKenzie, to see his reaction.

Suggs shook his big head.

But McKenzie just stood there, thinking. Finally he said, "All right, laddy. If you have such a bloody fear of this Kentuckian, ride back on our trail and satisfy your curiosity. We'll have one more camp on the trail before Bardstown. If you don't catch us before that, we'll wait there for you."

Spencer ignored the additional insult. You have to consider the source, he thought. He nodded acknowledgment. "I'll see you later in the day."

He mounted and walked his horse around the corpse of the Algonquin.

"Don't let any jackrabbits spook you back there!" Suggs called out as Spencer rode off, and then laughed loudly.

The threesome headed on down the Bardstown trail, and rode for another three hours before stopping for an early afternoon break. They sat around a hastily built fire and drank coffee and chewed on biscuits, while McKenzie told them about the small bank in Bardstown that was ripe for robbery. With the proceeds from that swelling their nest egg, they could return east ready for some really big operations.

They had been there almost an hour when

McKenzie finally decided it was time to move on. He wanted to get rather close to the settlement that night, so they would arrive there early the next day.

"Shall we move on, then, boys?" he said as he walked to his mount. "There's some hard riding ahead yet."

He had just finished saying that when he heard the rider coming through a stand of trees behind them. They all turned toward the sound at the same moment, and then Spencer burst out into the open and dusted to a sliding stop just in front of them. His mount was frothy, and there was excitement in his face.

"He's back there!" he called out to them. He dismounted quickly and ran over to McKenzie, eyes wild.

"What?" McKenzie said easily.

"It's Boone! I knew I felt him close! He's only five miles behind me, and coming on fast!"

"Oh, hell," Quinn said.

McKenzie stroked his growing beard. "Well, well."

"The bastard doesn't know when to quit!" Suggs exclaimed.

"No," McKenzie said slowly. "It seems he doesn't."

"I told you he'd come," Spencer said, wiping a hand across his mouth. "It's the way he is."

McKenzie caught his nervous look. "Did he catch sight of you, then?"

Spencer shrugged. "I don't know. I don't think so."

McKenzie nodded, and a glistening appeared in his hard eyes.

It appeared the game would resume.

"Good," he said softly.

"What the hell's so good about it?" Quinn said without thinking, risking McKenzie's ire.

But McKenzie just looked over at him genially. "Don't you understand? The stupid bastard will ride right into our second ambush. There was a bonnie good place back about a mile. Remember, where the rocks overlook the trail? It's a similar situation to the place where we caught him before, with that partner of his."

"I know where you mean," Suggs said excitedly. "It'll be perfect. We'll do it all over again!"

"Except this time," McKenzie said so all could hear, "the game will end there. On the trail. At the ambush site. This time I'll kill him."

Quinn relaxed some inside.

"Now that's what I bloody well like to hear!" Suggs said.

"I agree," Spencer said, getting his breath back. "You can't play with somebody like him. Kill him while we can. Then we'll be rid of him."

McKenzie knew he was being criticized for his previous handling of Dan'l, but he chose not to challenge Spencer now. He was fed up with this "American," as these people were calling themselves since the first seeds of revolt had been planted in their heads. But now was not the time to tell him that. He needed him for the job at hand. Then, later, when Spencer was least expecting it, he might just put a bullet in his head.

"I'm glad you agree, Spencer," he said in a smooth voice. "All right, lads. Let's saddle up."

Three miles behind them, on a rocky trail that meandered uphill indefinitely, Dan'l spurred his mount forward at a brisk trot, his eyes on the ground, reading spoor.

A couple of hours ago he had caught a glimpse of a man in the rocks ahead, watching him, and then saw the fellow disappear. He had thought the figure looked like one of the men with McKenzie, but he could not be sure. Not long after that, he had found the dead Algonquin and his shot horse at McKenzie's previous trail stop, and then he'd been more certain he was getting close to them.

He'd also realized that if the rider watching him at a distance had been one of them, he would have to be very cautious in the way he followed the trail.

As he rode into high rocks again, therefore, he slowed down, watching carefully, examining every high silhouette. Finally, he came to a place where there were rocks looking down on both sides of the trail.

He paused momentarily, and his chestnut horse snorted out a soft nervousness. Like Spencer a few hours before, Dan'l felt something inside him that made the hair on the back of his neck prickle. When you were a woodsman, you tended to pay attention to such feelings. They could save your life.

He studied the rocks ahead and saw nothing. He heard nothing, smelled nothing. But there was still that prickling along the nape of his neck. And there was his mount.

He slid the big rifle out of its scabbard, and loaded it with a paper cartridge and primed it. He squinted up to take another look. His eyes were as good, some said, as an eagle's. But he still saw absolutely nothing.

He spurred the horse slowly forward.

Up in the rocks just a few hundred yards ahead, McKenzie and Quinn hid quietly on one side of the trail—on Dan'l's right—and Spencer and Suggs crouched behind cover on the other side. They had seen Dan'l coming for a quarter mile, and now he was getting into range.

McKenzie was more excited than he would have admitted, even to himself. Ever since Billy Two Tongues had stolen Dan'l from their night camp, McKenzie had hoped for a situation just like this one.

Consequently, his judgment was affected by his growing hatred for Dan'l.

They were all to fire together, on his signal. And he now raised his arm to give the signal, even though Dan'l was still over a hundred yards away.

You son of a bitch, McKenzie was saying in his

head, watching Dan'l move slowly toward them. You know, don't you?

McKenzie's every muscle tightened as Dan'l's horse moved forward, one slow step at a time. McKenzie was suddenly afraid Dan'l would see one of them at any moment. His emotion got the better of him, and he brought his arm down in a violent movement.

He quickly aimed along a second Ferguson rifle they had recently acquired, took aim on Dan'l's chest, and fired just as the others did the same.

Down on his mount, Dan'l had seen a glint of metal at the last moment, as Suggs raised up to get a better shot. He quickly bent forward in the saddle, giving a smaller target, just as the four shots exploded in the shallow ravine.

In the same instant, he was peppered with lead. Because of his ducking down, McKenzie's shot hit him in the shoulder instead of the chest. In almost the same moment, Spencer's rifle shot grazed his arm, Suggs's musket lead hit the stallion in the flank, and Quinn's Mortimer pistol ball hit the dirt harmlessly at the horse's feet.

Dan'l's horse reared high, reacting to the hit, and threw Dan'l to the ground, then ran off away from the shooters.

Dan'l lay on his back, breathing hard. He was bruised from the fall, but nothing was broken, and he still had the rifle. He lay there assessing damage, and realized he was all right. The shoulder hit had not touched bone, and the arm wound was just a scratch.

He had finally had some luck with Jock Mc-Kenzie.

He had fallen behind a waist-high clump of brush, and knew he was not easily seen now from the rocks. They would probably not bother to reload to fire again, with four shots taken already. He lay very still, as if mortally hit.

Up in the rocks, Suggs was yelling happily. "We got him! We got the bastard this time!"

On his side of the trail, McKenzie wore a smug grin on his face. "It looks like we did," he said to Quinn. "Let's go down and put one in his head, for good measure."

The foursome started down out of the rocks on foot, leading their mounts.

"I'm going to put another one right between his goddamn eyes," McKenzie growled.

Dan'l lay there motionless, like a waiting cougar. He had heard Suggs's remark, and did not move. He saw them emerging, one at a time, and did not move. Seventy yards, grinning and laughing. He could not let them get any closer.

Dan'l raised from the brush in a quick movement that stopped them all in their tracks. Suggs was closest, and presented the easiest target.

On one knee, Dan'l took quick aim and fired the big rifle.

Standing there with the grin of victory dissolving quickly from his ugly, beefy face, Suggs took the lead squarely in center chest. The shot cracked bone and mauled flesh, pulling him off his feet and dumping him onto the ground.

The next moments were chaotic, with horses rearing and plunging, and McKenzie swearing loudly, going for the pistol on his belt. Seeing Suggs go down, the nervous Quinn panicked, and started mounting his horse to ride for cover.

Dan'l took advantage of the momentary confusion to reload. He could do it with the new cartridges in fifteen seconds. He ignored McKenzie's and Spencer's reaching for their side arms—Spencer had found an old one-shot pistol in the dead Algonquin's belongings to replace the one lost to Weeks—and readied to fire again.

Spencer, fear constricting his gut, dropped a flint in his haste, and also panicked when he saw Dan'l ready to fire. He grabbed his mount's reins and plunged toward cover. Quinn was mounted, and was turning his horse to run.

McKenzie was furious. "Stay and fight, damn you!" He got Dan'l in his sights with a snarl. "Die, you son of a bitch!"

Dan'l was beaten by McKenzie's side arm, so he hit the ground flat. McKenzie's gun roared, and the lead ripped a hole in Dan'l's sleeve, but missed him. Dan'l took aim as McKenzie swore loudly and mounted his horse. The horse got between Dan'l and McKenzie, and then McKenzie guided it into rock cover.

Quinn had gotten his mount turned and then spurred it hard, heading back along the trail the way they had come, even before McKenzie had fired at Dan'l the second time. Quinn wanted nothing to do with shooting it out with Dan'l in an open fight.

But he had made a fatal mistake. He had not headed for cover as Spencer and McKenzie had. He had ridden straight back along the trail, figuring he would be out of range before Dan'l ever noticed him.

Now, though, Dan'l swung the muzzle of the long gun around, and leveled it on the only target remaining—Ian Quinn. Quinn was riding hard, directly away from Dan'l, two hundred yards distant. Two-fifty. Three hundred. He began to relax thinking he was well away from the danger.

Dan'l rested the rifle on his knee, and waited until he had a good bead on the tiny figure on horseback that was swiftly diminishing in size with every second that passed. Then he carefully, coolly squeezed the trigger for the second time.

Three hundred and fifty yards away, the shot punched Quinn in the high back, tore through his aorta, and knocked him violently off his horse.

The horse just ran out from under him and kept going. Quinn hit the ground, rolled and somersaulted several times, kicking up dust, and ended up on his face. His jaw opened to speak, to protest his bad luck, but then he was dead.

Over in the rocks, Spencer saw Quinn go down, and could not believe it. "Good Jesus, did you see that?" he said to McKenzie, who had just reined up behind him, hidden from Dan'l by a large outcropping of rock. "I never ever seen a shot like that, without a tripod!"

"Marvelous wonderful," McKenzie said with vitriol. "Now reload, damn you! We can still take him down. We're two guns to one."

Spencer eyed him incredulously. "Have you gone crazy, man?" He glanced over his shoulder, as if Dan'l might somehow be there. "We had him *four* to one. Did that do us any good? You do what you want, I'm riding."

McKenzie had reloaded the pistol, and now he aimed it at Spencer with a dark look, his horse moving nervously under him. A sweat had broken out on his forehead, and McKenzie was a man who almost never sweated.

"You stay and fight, laddybuck!"

Spencer looked into the barrel of the gun. He shook his head slowly. "I'm not showing myself to that long gun again. You won't shoot me, McKenzie. You need me now."

McKenzie heard the resolve in his voice, as he held the gun steady on Spencer. He cast a quick glance toward the place up the trail where Quinn lay dead. He lowered the gun.

"You damned coward. All right, get riding. We'll take the trail we came on. After we're out of sight."

They turned the horses and rode them farther into the rocks, keeping Dan'l out of sight of them. Down on the trail, Dan'l was on his feet, the rifle ready to fire again. He heard the riders move off, beyond the rock cover, and ran to where he could get a better look. But they were gone, over a stony rise of ground. He would never get a good shot at them now, on foot.

He lowered the rifle and walked back down to the trail. His horse was nowhere to be seen, but Suggs's dark brown gelding stood over at the side of the trail, watching him nervously. Dan'l walked over to it calmly, and it let him grab its reins.

He slid the rifle into its empty saddle scabbard and mounted, and the horse quieted down. He rode over and took a quick look at Suggs, who lay in a spreading pool of his own blood. Then he rode up the trail, and stared down at Quinn for a moment. Quinn looked even deader than Suggs.

Dan'l looked up into the rocks. "You better ride hard, you bastard," he said in a low, guttural voice. " 'Cause I'm coming."

Chapter Fifteen

Trying to lose Dan'l, McKenzie and Spencer made a big loop off the trail, riding over rocks and hard dirt, passing through scrub pine terrain, and came back on the trail south of the ambush site, heading back toward Harrodsburg. They hoped that Dan'l would be confused and go on to Bardstown to find them.

But Spencer knew that would not happen. Dan'l Boone had never lost a trail in his life. By the time he was six, he had been taught well by Cherokee. When he became a man, he had surpassed all of his teachers. He could track better than any Indian, ride better than British cavalry, and outshoot any man on the frontier.

Spencer wanted to keep going when they reached Harrodsburg, in an effort to outdistance

Dan'l, and keep riding east, figuring Dan'l might quit when they left the frontier.

But McKenzie had other ideas.

"No, we'll stop at Harrodsburg," he said when they reined up at a hillcrest to get their bearings. "We'll wait for him there."

Spencer held his mount in check and looked over at McKenzie. "Wait for him?" he said caustically.

"You heard it, lad. Wait for him. Make him come to us, when we're ready for him."

"We were ready for him back there!"

McKenzie eyed him darkly, looking wild on his mount. His long, light-colored hair was matted now with sweat, and his growing beard looked gnarled. "This time it will be bloody different, laddy. He tricked us back there, making us think he was fatal hit. In the next go-around, he won't be able to manage that. And I've got some tricks of my own up my sleeve, Mr. Boone, thank you. No, it will go better in Harrodsburg."

Spencer acquiesced to McKenzie's plan to set a third trap for Dan'l, because he knew deep down that they could not outrun the wilderness man anyway, and he too wanted it all to be over.

They rode hard the rest of that day, and arrived in Harrodsburg while there was still some light in the sky. On the way in, they saw a burial taking place on the nearby cemetery hill, and Spencer wondered if *he* might be going into the ground soon.

They bedded their horses down at the livery

stable, then had a light meal at the inn. Spencer could hardly eat. McKenzie did not get them a room, because he had no intention of going to bed that night. Dan'l was too close behind them.

McKenzie had decided to stay put in the pub on the ground floor and plan his third encounter with the hunter. They had just ordered ales to wash down their meals, when a third customer walked in, a man McKenzie knew immediately he could put to good use. It was the third man Dan'l had confronted in the episode with Betty, after he had killed the first two in self-defense. Before McKenzie's group had left that other time, he had had a drink with them. His name was Walcott.

He saw McKenzie as soon as he walked in, and went over to his table. "Hey. I thought you boys was going off to Bardstown."

McKenzie nodded to him, but Spencer just scowled in his direction. "Well, we're back, lad," McKenzie said.

"That Boone fellow was asking after you, right after you left. Killed a couple of my friends, the son of a bitch. Just to save a whore. Hell, I just waited till he was gone, and went and shot her through the ear." He laughed. "That's her they're burying up on the hill right now."

McKenzie laughed quietly. "I guess that makes you a flaming local hero, is it, then?"

Walcott heard the sarcasm in his voice and frowned. "She was a no-good thief and Indian-lover!"

McKenzie clucked his tongue. "It's not my business to judge, man or whore," he said. "Can I offer you a drink then, Walcott?"

The thin, ugly fellow nodded. "Hell, yes."

A heavyset barkeep came and gave them all more ale, and then returned behind the long counter. He had liked Little Betty, and he now disliked Walcott very much. The law had done nothing so far about Betty's death, and the barkeep was angry about that, but had kept it to himself. He went to the rear of the room, and pretended not to be listening to them. But he paid close attention while he worked.

"So you don't like Boone, is that it?" McKenzie finally said to Walcott, after they had swigged some ale.

"That meddling bastard. He'll get his one of these days."

"How about tonight?" McKenzie said.

Both Walcott and Spencer looked at him curiously.

McKenzie met Spencer's quizzical look. "Do you think Boone lost our trail?"

Spencer thought a moment. "No."

"Do you think he'll camp out on the trail, knowing we're just ahead of him?"

"I wouldn't, if I was him," Spencer replied.

"Then he'll be here tonight," McKenzie said with a smile.

Spencer wiped a hand nervously across his square face. "Yeah. He probably will."

"What's this got to do with me?" Walcott said.

He remembered how Dan'l had humiliated him on the square, making him untie Betty, and then haul the tar and feathers away.

"How would you like to help us rid the world of him?" McKenzie said. "When he gets here tonight? And earn a few quid in the bargain?" He held a small bag of coins up for Walcott to see.

Walcott was interested. "How many quid?"

"Shall we say fifty? At job's end?"

Walcott thought a moment. "All right. What do I have to do?"

"I've got a boy watching for us. I think Boone'll barge right in here, if he knows for sure we're here. We'll be waiting for him."

"Oh, Jesus," Spencer said.

"Don't worry, lad. You'll be behind that door to the back room. Out of sight. Walcott, behind that counter over there. Also hidden from view. I'm the only one to confront him directly. I'll be sitting right here."

"I like it," Walcott said.

"When you hear me say his name, you two show yourselves and fire away. I won't be in your way, Spencer. We'll all have clear shots, and we'll all blast away at once. I want us all to have a backup gun, though. Primed and ready to fire." He looked at Spencer. "Not like out there on the trail."

"It should be a turkey shoot," Walcott offered.

"I'll have my Annely in hand under the table when he comes in, and the rifle lying on top. Spencer, you'll have the same where you are.

You, Walcott, bring any two guns you like. Just make certain they're good ones."

"I can be back in ten minutes," Walcott told him.

McKenzie nodded. "See that you are."

Walcott rose and left, and McKenzie looked over at the burly Spencer and swigged some dark ale.

"Now," he said in a low voice. "Let's see how you handle close quarters, Mr. Boone."

It was an hour later when Dan'l rode warily into town, through the big palisade gate.

It had been a warm spring afternoon, and he was sweaty and tired from the day's events. He had slapped a bandage on his shoulder, under his shirt, but had not bothered with his left arm. Both shallow wounds were scabbing over well, anyway. They did cause him some pain, though, and contributed to his fatigue.

It was dusk, and there was almost nobody on the streets. He rode past the inn, and saw lights inside. Down the way there was a boy that looked at him, then turned and headed quickly toward the inn. Dan'l watched him for a moment, then headed on down to the livery stable. There he found McKenzie's and Spencer's horses, already bedded down in stalls.

They were here, he knew now.

Dan'l took his rifle when he left the place, and loaded and primed it. He also took some extra cartridges with him. On foot, he walked past the militia garrison headquarters, and it looked almost deserted. He came on into the open square, and stopped at the constable's office there.

It was a small building, whitewashed inside, with a back room that served as a holding cell. The constable was sitting at a table, reading a Boston newspaper. He looked up with little interest when Dan'l came in.

"You need something?" he said.

Dan'l took off his black Quaker hat and dusted it on his knee. "I'm Dan'l Boone."

The constable put the paper down, and looked Dan'l over slowly. "So you're him."

"I'm here after a couple of killers. I think they might be in your pub. Maybe you'd like to help me bring them down." He paused. "I'm not talking arrest."

"You're talking about that fellow McKenzie, I guess," the constable said. He spat into a spittoon.

"That's right," Dan'l said. "He'll be waiting to kill me."

The other man shrugged. "They ain't broke no laws here yet, Boone. This ain't Boonesborough. We don't shoot men down for nothing. Like you done while I was gone away."

Dan'l grew a frown. "They was going to tar a whore. I killed them in self-defense."

"You shouldn't interfered. She's dead now, anyway."

Dan'l could not believe it. "What?"

"Shot in the head. Some drunk says Walcott

done it. He's the one you hoorawed after your killings."

"Son of a bitch!" Dan'l muttered.

"Course, I didn't arrest Walcott. It's just that drunk's word against his. I reckon it's you I should be arresting."

Dan'l regarded him angrily. All the law seemed to do nowadays was get in his way. He went over to the constable and yanked a one-shot pistol from the man's holster, making him jump.

"Hey!"

Dan'l looked at it and saw it was loaded and primed. "Thanks for the loan," he said. He stuffed the side arm into his belt, then looked around the room. He walked to a small, wood-burning stove, and lifted an ashes door off its cradle. It was iron, and slightly over a foot at its longest measurement. He unlaced the top of his shirt, and slid the iron plate inside.

"What the hell you think you're doing?"

Lastly, Dan'l grabbed a ritual tomahawk off the wall near him, a souvenir of the French and Indian War that had been given to the constable. Dan'l slipped it into his belt at the back.

"You goddamn thief! You can't come in here and steal me blind!" He had always been jealous of the stories told about Dan'l, because of his own shortcomings. "I'm the law here, by God!"

Dan'l went over to the table, scowling into the lawman's face. He adjusted the iron plate next to his flesh, and felt its heavy weight. "Is Captain Michaels at the garrison?" He did not want any interference now, from any source.

The constable glared at him. "He's gone for a few days. You won't get no help from there. You're on your own, Boone."

Dan'l came around the table and grabbed him by the throat. "You get in my way, Constable, and I'll kill you too."

The constable's mouth opened slightly, and he knew in that moment that he would not interfere with what was going to happen. Or try to arrest Dan'l if he survived.

Dan'l released him and strode out of the place, slamming the rough-hewn door behind him.

Out on the street, he just stood there looking toward the inn for a long moment. Then a voice came from behind him.

"They're there, all right."

Dan'l turned and saw the frightened face of the barkeep, a face he recognized from previous visits.

"McKenzie?" Dan'l said.

The barkeep nodded. "Spencer, I guess the other fellow is. And they got Walcott there with them."

"The one that killed Betty?" Dan'l said fiercely.

"The same. The damned coward shot her in the head. Not two hours after you talked with her in the pub. I hate that man."

"They're just sitting around in there?"

"They won't be when you get there. I heard them talking. McKenzie's going to hide the other two. Give you a big surprise, he thinks. I couldn't hear it all, but I think one of them will be behind the counter."

"Do they know I'm here?"

The barkeep nodded. "They had a boy watching for you."

"Do they know you come down here?"

"They know I left. But they think I went to the store before it closes. They think I'm coming right back."

"I'm much obliged," Dan'l said.

"Don't go in there, Boone. They'll for sure kill you."

Dan'l checked the priming on the Kentucky rifle. "Somebody's got to do it. And your constable is a goddamn coward. I'm going in. You keep away."

The other man rubbed a hand across his mouth. "Maybe I could help somehow."

Dan'l looked him over. "No. You already helped. Now just stay clear."

Dan'l left him there, and walked the short distance to the inn. It was dark now, and oil lamps inside made yellow squares of the two windows in the place. Dan'l climbed two steps to the entrance, and opened the big, heavy door.

The first thing Dan'l saw was McKenzie.

McKenzie sat at a table to the left of the door, about halfway back to the far wall. He was facing Dan'l, and his hands were under the table. He looked ready and dangerous.

Behind him was the door to a back room, and Dan'l noted it was slightly ajar. At that same moment, he heard a slight noise behind the counter, a whisper of sound that most men would have missed.

"Well, well," McKenzie said, in a low, oily voice.

Dan'l just stood there, looking the room over, the rifle in both hands, ready to fire. Both Dan'l and McKenzie were now so primitive-looking that it was like two bears facing each other down. The air between them crackled with electricity.

"You should've killed me before," Dan'l said in a hard voice. "When you had the chance."

"But it didn't turn out so dreadful, lad," McKenzie said nicely. "You've given me a bloody second chance, haven't you, then?"

Dan'l cast a glance at the slightly open doorway to the back room, and saw something move in the crack. Yes, he knew where they were now.

"And you give me one," Dan'l said. "I ain't taking you in to no militia, McKenzie. Not after Billy. You're going down."

McKenzie laughed gratingly. "The Mad Scot? Not a bit of it, laddy. It'll be you, you illiterate sot. I own you, remember?"

Dan'l's voice was brittle. "Defend yourself, you bastard."

Just as Dan'l raised the rifle, McKenzie fired from under the table. The shot struck Dan'l in the low chest, where the iron stove lid deflected the lead. But Dan'l was knocked off his feet by the impact, hitting the floor hard.

The back room door flew open, and Spencer

aimed at Dan'l. Behind the counter, Walcott also sprang into view.

"Kill him!" McKenzie yelled.

While the roaring of McKenzie's revolver was still ringing in all their ears, and with McKenzie now rising to his feet, grabbing the rifle that lay on the table, it was Walcott that got in the next shot. His first pistol exploded loudly from behind the counter, aimed at Dan'l. But he was very nervous about the legendary Boone, and he fired too quickly. The shot hit the wood floor beside Dan'l's head, and missed him completely.

Now Spencer was squeezing down on the trigger of his rifle, aimed at Dan'l's head. But Dan'l beat him, firing the Kentucky long gun from a supine position on the floor, without aiming. At the open doorway, Spencer was blown into the darkness behind him, a ragged hole through his chest, beside his heart. He crashed over stacked chairs back there and was dead before the noise of their busted-up clamor stopped.

McKenzie fired the heavy rifle now, stunned because Dan'l was not dead or dying. Dan'l was rolling off his back, though, and grabbing at the constable's pistol in his belt. McKenzie's gun roared in the confines of the room, and chipped wood between Dan'l's side and his right arm.

Dan'l returned fire, cocking and firing in one movement. The hot lead struck McKenzie in the high chest, and hurled him off his feet, and he knocked a table and chair down as he hit the floor by the wall.

Walcott was petrified now, and was having trouble cocking his second pistol. Dan'l came up onto one knee, and reached for the tomahawk just as Walcott aimed at him. Dan'l threw the war hatchet at Walcott just as the other man was finding Dan'l in his sights. The heavy blade turned twice in the air as Walcott squeezed down on the trigger, and struck him in center chest, cracking bone and slicing into his chest like a big scalpel, burying most of its wicked blade in his heart.

He was punched against a shelf behind him, arms spread, the gun firing into the ceiling, glasses and bottles crashing around him. His eyes were wide and staring at nothing, his mouth trying to form some response. But then he slid from sight behind the counter.

McKenzie was yelling, "Kill him! Kill the son of a bitch!" But he fell quickly silent when he saw his second gunman go down, and that Walcott's shots had gone wild.

McKenzie was still on his back, and trying to get up. Blood running down his shirt, he quickly but clumsily reprimed the repeating rifle. Dan'l reached in and lifted the chunk of iron out of his clothing, and hurled it against the wall, so he would have freedom of movement. Then he found the Algonquin knife in its sheath, and drew it out. It was the fourth weapon he had called upon in the skirmish.

McKenzie finally cocked the long gun, and quickly aimed it at Dan'l's head as Dan'l came at him. "Now, you backwoods devil!" McKenzie shrieked in his Scottish accent. "Meet your Maker!"

Just as Dan'l reached him, the gun went off for the second time, and hit Dan'l in the head.

Dan'l felt the impact like a club hitting him, and bright lights exploded inside his head. He slammed against the wall, and almost went down. Blackness welled up, but he did not lose consciousness. The lead had just grazed his skull, taking a small patch of scalp and hair off the side of his head. He shook his head and felt blood running down past his ear. He looked at McKenzie, and saw two of him. But he was not finished with the Scot. He still held the knife in his right hand.

"Ha!" McKenzie was saying. "Go down, damn you!"

But then the man McKenzie thought he had killed was lunging at him off the wall. Dan'l hurled himself down onto McKenzie, the knife in front of him, and buried the weapon in McKenzie's stomach as their bodies collided.

McKenzie issued a grating cry as the blade of the thin knife sank in to the hilt. Then Dan'l used all of his muscular strength to draw the blade upward, slicing McKenzie open from navel to sternum.

The Scot's bearded face blossomed openings— eyes, nostrils, mouth—that confirmed the awful damage to his torso, as his innards spilled out onto his clothing, and blood spattered upward onto Dan'l.

McKenzie's eyes locked on Dan'l, and Dan'l looked deeply into them.

"That's for Billy, you son of a bitch."

McKenzie heard those words, but then blackness overcame him. His whole body shivered violently in shock, and a foul stench came from between his legs and he was dead.

Dan'l rose off the corpse, leaving the dagger where he had put it. He stepped away from McKenzie, and stumbled and fell against the wall. He hung there for a long moment, until he felt a little better. His vision still was not good. But it was good enough.

The barkeep came in through the open front door, and looked around. Corpses littered the place, one of them unseen.

"Good Jesus! You did it! You really did it!"

Dan'l staggered to the center of the room, retrieved his Kentucky rifle, and slung it under his arm. He staggered unsteadily past the proprietor, fitting his hat back on his bleeding scalp.

"You're hit. I'll put you up for the night."

Dan'l shook his shaggy head. "No. I'll get my mount and leave. When I sleep tonight, I want to be gone from here."

The barkeep glanced at the corpse of Jock McKenzie. "What about them?"

"The captain will take care of them. But I don't want no markers on their graves. Tell him that."

The barkeep nodded. "All right, Dan'l."

Without looking back, Dan'l left the inn.

Algonquin Massacre

In an hour, he figured, he would be well away from Harrodsburg, and Jock McKenzie, and all the bad memories that evil man put in his head. That would make tomorrow almost nice.

A mighty hunter, intrepid guide, and loyal soldier, Dan'l Boone faced savage beasts, vicious foes, and deadly elements—and conquered them all. These are his stories—adventures that made Boone a man and a foundering young country a great nation.

DAN'L BOONE: THE LOST WILDERNESS TALES #1:

THE LOST WILDERNESS TALES DAN'L BOONE

A RIVER RUN RED

DODGE TYLER

The colonists call the stalwart settler Boone. The Shawnees call him Sheltowee. Then the French lead a raid that ends in the death of Boone's young cousin, and they learn to call Dan'l their enemy. Stalking his kinsman's killers through the untouched wilderness, Boone lives only for revenge. And even though the frontiersman is only one man against an entire army, he will not rest until he defeats his murderous foes—or he himself goes to meet his Maker.

_3947-8 $4.99 US/$6.99 CAN

Dorchester Publishing Co., Inc.
65 Commerce Road
Stamford, CT 06902

WHITE APACHE

Jake McMasters

Follow the action-packed adventures of Clay Taggart, as he fights for revenge against settlers, soldiers, and savages.

#7: _Blood Bounty_. The settlers believe Clay Taggart is a ruthless desperado with neither conscience nor soul. But Taggart is just an innocent man who has a price on his head. With a motley band of Apaches, he roams the vast Southwest, waiting for the day he can clear his name—or his luck runs out and his scalp is traded for gold.

__3790-4 $3.99 US/$4.99 CAN

#8: _The Trackers_. In the blazing Arizona desert, a wanted man can end up as food for the buzzards. But since Clay Taggart doesn't live like a coward, he and his band of renegade Indians spend many a day feeding ruthless bushwhackers to the wolves. Then a bloodthirsty trio comes after the White Apache and his gang. But try as they might to run Taggart to the ground, he will never let anyone kill him like a dog.

__3830-7 $3.99 US/$4.99 CAN

Dorchester Publishing Co., Inc.
65 Commerce Road
Stamford, CT 06902

Please add $1.75 for shipping and handling for the first book and $.50 for each book thereafter. NY, NYC, PA and CT residents, please add appropriate sales tax. No cash, stamps, or C.O.D.s. All orders shipped within 6 weeks via postal service book rate. Canadian orders require $2.00 extra postage and must be paid in U.S. dollars through a U.S. banking facility.

Name _____

Address _____

City _____ State _____ Zip _____

I have enclosed $_____ in payment for the checked book(s).

Payment <u>must</u> accompany all orders. ☐ Please send a free catalog.

WHITE APACHE

Jake McMasters

Follow the action-packed adventures of Clay Taggart, as he fights for revenge against soldiers, settlers, and savages.

#9: Desert Fury. From the canyons of the Arizona Territory to the deserts of Mexico, Clay Taggart and a motley crew of Apaches blaze a trail of death and vengeance. But for every bounty hunter they shoot down, another is riding hell for leather to collect the prize on their heads. And when the territorial governor offers Taggart a chance to clear his name, the deadliest tracker in the West sets his sights on the White Apache—and prepares to blast him to hell.

_3871-4 $3.99 US/$4.99 CAN

#10: Hanged! Although Clay Taggart has been strung up and left to rot under the burning desert sun, he isn't about to play dead. After a desperate band of Indians rescues Taggart, he heads into the Arizona wilderness and plots his revenge. One by one, Taggart hunts down his enemies, and with the help of renegade Apaches, he acts as judge, jury, and executioner. But when Taggart sets his sights on a corrupt marshal, he finds that the long arm of the law might just have more muscle than he expects.

_3899-4 $3.99 US/$4.99 CAN

Dorchester Publishing Co., Inc.
65 Commerce Road
Stamford, CT 06902

Please add $1.75 for shipping and handling for the first book and $.50 for each book thereafter. NY, NYC, PA and CT residents, please add appropriate sales tax. No cash, stamps, or C.O.D.s. All orders shipped within 6 weeks via postal service book rate. Canadian orders require $2.00 extra postage and must be paid in U.S. dollars through a U.S. banking facility.

Name _____

Address _____

City _____ State _____ Zip _____

I have enclosed $_____ in payment for the checked book(s).
Payment <u>must</u> accompany all orders. ☐ Please send a free catalog.